MAR 1 2 2013

# NOSE

# NOSE

## James Conaway

THOMAS DUNNE BOOKS
ST. MARTIN'S PRESS
New York

This is a work of fiction. All of the characters, organizations, and events portrayed in this novel are either products of the author's imagination or are used fictitiously.

THOMAS DUNNE BOOKS.
An imprint of St. Martin's Press.

NOSE. Copyright © 2013 by James Conaway. All rights reserved. Printed in the United States of America. For information, address St. Martin's Press, 175 Fifth Avenue, New York, N.Y. 10010.

www.thomasdunnebooks.com
www.stmartins.com

Design by Steven Seighman

Library of Congress Cataloging-in-Publication Data

Conaway, James.
    Nose : a novel / James Conaway. — First Edition.
        p. cm.
    ISBN 978-1-250-00684-4 (hardcover)
    ISBN 978-1-250-02263-9 (e-book)
  1. Wine writers—Fiction.    2. Wine and winemaking—Fiction.
3. Wine industry—California—Fiction.    I. Title.
    PS3553.O486N67 2013
    813'.54—dc23

                                                2012042084

St. Martin's Press books may be purchased for educational, business, or promotional use. For information on bulk purchases, please contact Macmillan Corporate and Premium Sales Department at 1-800-221-7945, extension 5442, or write specialmarkets@macmillan.com.

First Edition: March 2013

10  9  8  7  6  5  4  3  2  1

For Ralph Dennis and Wallace Stegner
*In memoriam*

*The sense of smell explores.*
 —Brillat-Savarin

# CHAPTER ONE

---

## *Black Bottle*

# 1

"HIGHER."

So Clyde Craven-Jones gripped that magnificent stomach of his and hauled it farther in the direction of his multilayered chin, the two masses of rendered haut cuisine and the very best wine momentarily married in a vast floodplain of undulating flesh, exposing a bit more of what there was of him down there, enough apparently because there she went, transformed into something feral, angular, beyond his control, her shifting hips as if on rails, the lovable little gap between her front teeth exposed, making that melodious sound Claire claimed she wasn't aware of but that reminded him of mermaids singing in an unintelligible language of a place he had never seen.

Fog seemed to muffle the vineyard on the far slope. She, better mounted, speeded up their Thursday morning ritual, mindful not to kill him in the process. What determination his wife had: up at dawn for copulation, a third his weight, riding the vestiges of his pelvis until she collapsed, sometimes allowing him to go back to sleep for another hour, though not today, and waking him again for a simulation of breakfast.

At these moments she smelled a bit vinegary—seaweed?—from all the effort, the sharp aroma of bacteria overwhelmed by the ranker olfactory engine of sexual intercourse. He could pull all sorts of associations out of this basic act if he wanted, but Claire made more distracting noises. She was a gift, named for light but dimly outlined against the natural redwood ceiling of their Spanish colonial bungalow on the edge of a beautiful expanse of some of the most valuable agricultural land on earth: vines, olive trees, live oaks, and that dangerous scrubby stuff up there on the slopes just dying to catch flame and consume all that was good in Northern California.

Her sounds bordered upon desperation now. He envied her and at the same time was a little afraid: such passion. Clyde Craven-Jones was a prisoner of two sensualities—hers, and his just as relentless but involving no climaxes, whereas she rode raptly on, past the finish line and out onto the postorgasmic plain. There she sighed, succumbing to gravity, sliding from his girth and rolling onto the comforter, sides heaving, staring dazedly up at the reclaimed beams from a historic winery that after a century still smelled of fermentation.

Claire rose on one elbow, exhaled, and said with a smile, "Well, BTDT," a jocularity intended to make her husband feel better about his, well, supine performance.

True, he had been there, but he hadn't done that. No matter; the day beckoned.

"Anything special in the lineup?"

"Yes, you're going to be challenged today, CJ. By this valley's own. Nine Cabernets in the up bunch," which meant costing at least $130 a bottle.

"Why not ten Cabernets?" It was the usual arrangement of American *grands crus*.

"Well, the tenth one's a mystery. No label, nothing. I want to include it because it seems special and has been around for a bit. Arrived in a lovely cedar box, wrapped in a pashmina shawl."

Those things meant nothing. Vintners spend small fortunes encapsulating mediocre wine in a way that makes it seem of a higher order, the same logic used for building their expensive houses and wineries. Packaging, like labels, was deception. One of his duties as a premier wine critic—*the* premier wine critic, he liked to think—was to out deception in *Craven-Jones on Wine,* with its pass-along readership of, he often insisted, more than a million. "How did it get here?"

"By hand, that's all we know."

Why hadn't the dog alerted them? Clyde Craven-Jones didn't allow wine to be left on his doorstep; only the most audacious—or stupid—would attempt it. But he was curious, and any worthy critic welcomes the random chance to test his mettle. Besides, Claire had gone to the trouble of including it. "Let's begin."

Solemnly launching himself into a roll, the massive, custom-made bed protesting feebly, his wife nimbly getting out of the way. She went into the bathroom and he heard water filling a tub designed for corpulence beyond the American standard, with special handles for easing himself in and out. He thought he caught a trace of something floral—tansy? Camellia? His policy was no manufactured fragrances of any sort in the house, perfume being the worst, an assault fraught with plant renderings and mysterious chemical compounds that gave him an immediate migraine and affected his ability to taste. He demanded plain soap for his morning immersion, baking soda for his toothbrush, an electric razor for the graying scrim of beard accenting copious signature jowls.

# 2

IN TEAM VELOUR SWEATS—a gift from a wine distributor, unsolicited but comfy—and rope-soled espadrilles, Clyde Craven-Jones moves with deliberation from his boudoir to a hallway lined with cheaply framed photographs of himself with every personage in the wine world who matters, among them two of his late countrymen, noble, modest scholars of the grape and fine practitioners of the English language, both dead now.

He's the last of the ranking Brits and long ago succumbed to the allure of the New World, with its lack of ceremony, its unblinkered heat that even in the straw-hued mirage of summer he finds preferable to the damp determinism of his native land.

And, of course, the California wines themselves: heavily extracted, endowed with strangely scented variants that his English colleagues found perverse but he has come to admire for their richness and power. He's responsible for much of that intensity, favoring in his reviews those Cabernets and Pinot Noirs with some flesh on their bones, much to the disgust of the French who have been made to compete with California and what's sometimes called the Craven-Jones style, lest they languish on shelves absorbing light and drying out like old men abandoned in a sauna.

He pushes open the door. The organ that matters most to him, that distinctive protuberance bigger than other men's, more sensitive, gifted, in fact, beyond the bounds of ordinary human perceptiveness—his nose—has guts of its own. Also the ability to raise its lucky owner to the top of his profession and into the company of some of the wealthiest, most talented, sometimes most reprehensible people on earth, an appendage so remarkable that it has appeared in the pages of a leading newsweekly: slightly hooked, increasingly veiny, near infallible.

The former dining room is heavily draped, temperature controlled, with overhead track lighting, racks of Riedel glasses in every imaginable contortion for concentrating aromas, open cartons of wine, unlined writing pads, 3B drawing pencils—no pens!—a sterling spit bucket with splash guard, and, on the white tablecloth, ten bottles neatly wrapped in brown paper by his obliging wife and numbered by her current assistant, the perpetually distracted James. One of a procession of helpers in love with wine, soon disabused of the notion that caddying for the critic is a spiritual pastime, he has removed the foils and poured an equal amount of wine from each bottle into a stemmed glass elegantly constricted at the rim.

CJ pauses, slightly elevating his nostrils, priming them with a barely perceptible twitch, angling in the direction of the sideboard. He has detected an alien odor among the familiar ones. Ah, the felt pen, left behind with the top off, the acrid smell emanating from evaporating ink. "Ja-*hames!*"

The door swings open and in steps the ingratiating amanuensis. In Bordeaux he would be wearing, at the very least, a buttoned-up shirt, but in California it's open-necked rugby-style, with jeans: the uniform. Fuzz on the chin, smiling—everyone in California smiles—the young man's big brown eyes denoting apprehension. "What's up, CJ?"

"The Magic Marker's *up*, James."

"Shit. Sorry about that."

James scoops it up, smacks the cap in place, and goes back through the revolving door. A handsome lad, maybe a tad too handsome, chastened but overdue for remaindering; has Claire found something of value in James beyond his ability to heft wine cartons, open bottles, and run the dishwasher? (No detergent!) But now Craven-Jones is distracted by the right smells: Cabernet Sauvignon's infinity of masked components, its glorious potential enhanced by caresses of Cabernet Franc, Petit Verdot, Merlot, even Malbec, as well as oak and the panoply of botanical associations that push all else from his mind and bring to his palate an anticipatory wetness.

Almost daintily he takes his chair and eyes the delectable prey. The tease before the main event, the vinous equivalent of a naked woman walking around a boxing

ring holding aloft a placard with a number on it. Where
are the muscles and firm flesh, where the flab? Who will
have the up-front power and fruit, who the longest finish
in this matchup of potential champions? Sports refer-
ences are absolutely necessary for communication in
this, his chosen country, but CJ knows little of sport
beyond the terrible memories of rugby in the damp des-
olation of his Midlands preparatory school. Metaphor-
ically, he favors sumo wrestling: enormous combatants
pushing at each other, stately, powerful.

At his elbow sits a cut-glass bowl full of air-popped
corn, sans butter and salt, the perfect palate cleanser:
weightless mopper-up of all vestiges of sampled wine. The
popcorn's smell reminds CJ of his gnawing hunger, to be
put off until lunch, which today will commence with
wafer-thin sole fillets over which scalding French butter
has been poured, no other cooking required, comple-
mented by a slightly chilled Puligny-Montrachet.

He's getting ahead of himself; dining follows due labor, the reigning Craven-Jones maxim. Meanwhile, no
flaw shall pass this nose, these lips, this palate without
detection, no shortcoming shall go unannounced in what
Claire calls his doomsday book—dooming as many as it
raises up, more actually—*Craven-Jones on Wine*, printed
on actual paper, with a paid circulation of 120,000 and
a pass-along influence of, yes, a million. *Craven-Jones
on Wine* often breaks, as well as makes, reputations, vintages, business deals, marriages, even lives. Such is his
power and, of course, his burden.

Ready now, nasal chambers cleared with a mild saline solution, his copiousness fondly settled into the custom-made reinforced rolling chair set high enough to prevent his having to bend his knees, he passes flared nostrils over the glasses first, guessing the species of oak from which the barrels were made that until recently held these gems. Limoges? Allier. My God, Arkansas! He will soon know exactly who made the wines and how long the fruit hung on the vines, the blend, the barrel regimen, the fining agent, and how well they sell on the futures market depends upon his evaluation.

He picks up a glass by the stem and angles it, examining the color against the white tablecloth. Deeply mauve, Cabernet's own depthless version of purple, concentrated to the rim. Ah, these New World hues. His fellow Brits reeled in their presence, but CJ came to love them as a deliverer from the anonymous life of bottle drudge in the chilly cellars of Lily & Sons, Ltd., City of London, scribbling reviews for the firm's newssheet.

Compressing now one nostril with a forefinger and passing the glass under the other, he inhales deeply. The olfactory equivalent of matins in a village chapel go off in a brain inculcated with associations: black cherries, currants, brambles, lanolin, tobacco, cedar, chocolate. But also flaws: blatant woodiness—it's well known that Clyde Craven-Jones disapproves of harsh tannins—and a good but hardly spectacular finish.

He ejects a purple stream into the bowl, scribbles "gobs of fruit . . . too-rapid falling-off on the middle palate . . . predictable," and moves on to the next bottle.

An hour and twenty minutes later he leans back in his
wheeled throne and sighs. Nine bottles down and not a
clear winner. He thinks he knows who made half of them
and can come close to guessing the rest. Two hover in the
mid- to upper teens of his twenty-point ranking system,
which will make their investors moderately happy, but
no ecstasy in this tasting. If the mystery wine's among
them, then it's merely good.

The brown wrapping paper disguises the last bottle,
emblazoned with the number 10, the poured wine in the
Riedel deeply hued. He pulls the glass to him, picks it up
by the stem, and quickly, deftly twists his wrist, driving
the wine high up the sides. Its concentrated fragrance
reaches him even from that distance. He dips his nose
directly into the invisible pool of inspiration and inhales.
He's impressed by the wine's power, and annoyed: surely
this is not the mystery bottle, which means he failed
to detect the interloper among the previous nine. He
scribbles "barely ripe black fruit . . . toasty . . . a lean,
shimmering nimbus of cassis."

He takes a mouthful and holds it for a moment, lips
parted, drawing air in over the wine, then closes his
mouth and, without swallowing, exhales through the
nose, pushing the sacred "ether of harvest and extracted
oak," as he often puts it in his lectures, back out through
his nostrils, with a surprising result. He'll describe it as
"reverberating Cabernet bells." St. Paul's? Too grandiose.
A chapel? Too parochial. *This wine tolls on the nose with*

*all the power and precision of Christopher Wren's gem,
the Church of St. Mary-le-Bow. . . . If you can fully appreciate that complex melody, you're not Cockney, you're
enchanted!*

He swallows, the cascading flavors identifiable, married in an onslaught of what he thinks of as the essence
of Bordeaux, not California—elegant, balanced, with a
long trail on the palate that dwindles into *the soothing
convergence of light and shadow in a distant clearing. . . .*
Yes, that will do nicely. The wine might well be one of
Bordeaux's best, from a first-growth estate, introduced
as a joke. Detectable tannins but overall so silky as to be
forgiven. Less heat around the gums, meaning relatively
low alcohol.

It could represent the glory of France, but the initial,
decisive burst of fruit and lingering ripeness has the
power of California. Has someone finally managed to
make a wine in the valley with the contradictory merits
of France and America, or is this a con? If so, it's near
the top of the chart and worth a great deal of money.

He takes a fistful of popcorn and crams it into his
mouth, snowing all over his sweats. Now for the sober-
ing second swallow, the true test. He tears the wrapper
off the bottle and is confronted by a column of dark liquid in generic glass; that he has no idea whose this wine
is or where it came from is humiliating. A wine critic
without self-confidence is—how did he put it at the
Friends of Wine lecture in San Francisco the week
before?—*in the evening of his being.*

In the frenzy of stripping No. 10 he has upset No. 6,

spilling inky Cabernet over the white tablecloth. He attempts to mop it up with the wrapping paper, without success. More tearing to expose the other bottles, an array of family and fanciful names—Eagle Ridge, Block 69, Trifecta, Copernicus. He knows them all and he knows their makers; No. 10 is indeed the interloper.

CJ confronts the wreckage of his tasting, takes another swallow. Ah, is there anything better than a glass of fine red wine of an afternoon? Well, of a morning, actually. He can feel the alcohol now, not just No. 10's but the collective onslaught of the wines he has absorbed despite spitting, a hazard of his profession.

He peruses his notes. Numbers 2 and 5—Block 69 and Trifecta—are clearly the standouts, after No. 10. What comes next is tricky. He stands and pads to the hallway door, opens it a crack, softly whistles. Then, "Missy."

A scrabble of claws on heartwood Douglas fir, a blur of brindle hair ejecting from the bedroom, smiling if a mastiff can be said to smile, her soft brown eyes full of anticipation. He reaches down and digs his fingertips into her wiry coat, but the dog brushes past him.

CJ eases the door shut and returns to the disarray of the tasting. Bracing himself with one hand, he slowly kneels, groaning, and places the two winners on the floor while Missy watches, a timeless scene: dog, master, quarry. Older than history.

"Go!"

Missy creeps forward and tentatively smells each glass in turn. She settles on Trifecta.

"Back!"

She obeys, still eying the glasses as if they might take flight, and waits while he crawls forward, carefully blocking her view. He replaces Block 69 with No. 10. If Missy picks the mystery wine, this will complement his olfactory abilities since she's infallible, and very close to his own palate.

He crawls out of the way, sweeping aside wine-soaked wrapping paper and dropped pencils. Spilled wine drips through the crack between the leaves in the table; popcorn litters the carpet.

"Go!"

Used to the drill, Missy sniffs at Trifecta, then at the interloper, hesitates, and stays with the nameless wine. "Ah," says CJ proudly, since it's his choice too. He has to remind himself—down on all fours—that this colleague is, after all, just an animal.

# 3

"I THINK I'VE FOUND IT."

"What?" Claire sat resolutely at the desk in the living room, the valley spread before her a constant distraction from proofreading the galleys for the next *Craven-Jones on Wine*, which must be shipped this morning to the printer. He said, "A perfect score for a California Cabernet, if that's what the mystery wine proves to be. A very long shot, I grant you."

She turned, more perturbed than pleased. "Really? How do you know it's California?"

"I don't. Could be a Bordeaux, a Mouton, possibly. But I think it's local. Big nose, briary, just enough forward fruit. Fine tannins. Deucedly annoying, I must say, slipping that bottle in here. How dare they?"

"Twenty points for a California Cab would be a big deal, CJ."

"Oh, yes, and defensible in this case. If it is a California. My God, the length of the finish . . ."

"Readers would be enthralled," said Claire, biting reflexively on her 3B. "But how would we possibly find out whose it is?"

"Haven't the vaguest. We might . . . perhaps announce the conundrum in this issue and ask the culprit to step forward. Something along those lines."

The notion would once have been too preposterous to consider, but now *Craven-Jones on Wine* and its hemorrhaging circulation, if truth be told, needed a boost. CJ blamed the slump in his readership on the blogs, but he had other problems as well. For one thing, ranking wines by numbers had begun to lose its luster, and without that simple alternative to describing a very complex substance, he was in trouble, being no prose stylist.

"Half the valley would get in line," said Claire.

"Yes, and then we'd deal with it."

He meant *she* would deal with it, although he would help, of course. CJ's was the most prestigious list of secretive collectors on the West Coast; one of them might have heard of the elaborate charade of secretly submitting a wine. Part of CJ's burden was to chase it down, or see that it was chased down. "I'm considering writing a paragraph about this and inserting it in this issue today: 'Extraordinary discovery, if legitimate. Readers deserve to know, et cetera.' Add that it will take time to track down the owner and authenticate his wine. But in the next issue we will pull the veil. I say, shall we bump lunch up a bit?"

The sole was excellent, the Montrachet catching the light in a particularly mouthwatering way. Something about cold white Burgundy at midday, a lean, buttery complement to ever-so-slightly browned butter now in dabs on the ravaged surface of his plate. CJ toyed with the crust of a baguette. Should he do the dirty deed and eat that too, or leave it as a symbol of forbearance? He ate it.

"I've been thinking," Claire said. "What with our circulation problem, this really might help. If the unidentified wine is California, we might make something more of this."

"Absolutely. Get some . . . what is it?"

"Buzz."

"Just so. I'll check my contacts," most of whom were devoid of the sort of gossip required in this inquiry, but you never knew. He would start calling right after his nap, taken on a couch where he had to fight for space with layabout magnums of wine hoping to be reviewed. "And you check yours, Claire. Obliquely, of course. As in, 'By the way, any idea who might have done this incredible and absolutely verboten thing?' Like that. Add that I've found what I think is a twenty and, if it's legitimate, I want to share the good news with the faithful.

"The more I think about it, the more certain I become that this is a wise move. The wine's deeply impressive. If it turns out to be a fraudulent substitution, then we'll just say so and take credit for exposing it. More 'buzz,' more readers. 'Once again *Craven-Jones on Wine* proves a stanchion of taste and integrity.' QED. I assume we're having coffee."

CJ was in his other role now: navigator of the airwaves clamped into headphones, little stemmed microphone at the lips, pad at the ready, and hands free to scribble news and evaluations garnered from a host of obsessive people in whose lives wine has become dominant. Claire had gone off on errands—including procurement of a soy milk–fed piglet from a producer in the next county—leaving CJ free to act: Captain Nemo of the vinous depths, alert to any change of flora, fauna, or terrain at one hundred leagues beneath the surface, pulling information into his virtual submarine, thwarting subversions of taste, saving the world—his, anyway—the phone ringing far out in the Nevada desert. . . .

The ringing stopped, followed by silence. "Pud," said CJ, "Craven-Jones here." More silence. "I have a question about scents. How might one categorically distinguish between two barely similar Cabernets if all he had to go on—"

"Smell triggers its own kind of energy." Slight twang, more bronco buster than enophile. This notorious collector, one Pud Larsen, never away from his Las Vegas redoubt, was very knowledgeable, generous in donations of big vintages to charities, clad always in pointy-toed boots. And quite mad.

"As we know, tiny receptors on the tongue are responsible for all smell detection. Ten million of them live on a patch of lingual real estate no bigger than a dime. There are hundreds of different types. Some people have a lot of one type of receptor, others a lot of another. A lot of diversity. A lucky few with the right mix can smell cassis across a room before they can see it. You're one of them, CJ."

"Yes, but—"

"Odor detection makes up maybe three percent of every human's genome, but it can be a real advantage in the right mix, particularly if you have a good memory. Coordination among those wiggly little bastards is the important part."

"Pud, I'm wondering how one might make a convincing, if not statistical, argument that two wines are from the same place, even if one's much better than the other, and—"

"Can't be done."

"—and how one might prove—strongly suggest, at any rate—a wine's identity without, ah, you know, actually knowing."

"What's this all about?"

CJ told him about the anonymous black bottle. "The wine reminds me ever so slightly of Copernicus," he admitted, "but is much better."

"That's about the craziest thing I ever heard of. Got to be a joke, but I want to taste it." And Pud Larsen hung up.

Sighing, CJ made another call, this one to Larry Carradine, his erstwhile correspondent just across the valley who occasionally sat in for CJ at unimportant tastings, collecting tidbits for *Craven-Jones on Wine*. In a quavering voice Larry said, "Hello," and CJ was reminded that it was afternoon.

"It's CJ. Any idea who might have dropped off a bottle of Cabernet here anonymously?"

"Say what?"

"You're pissed, Larry."

"Am not."

"The wine's very good is the point of my call."

"How good?"

"A twenty."

"Jesus."

"Yes, so naturally I want to know who made it. Keep your ears open."

"Ears always open, CJ."

# 4

THE FIRST COPIES of the new *Craven-Jones on Wine* landed on Claire's doorstep a week later, and she tore open the packet with the aid of garden shears and took out a single issue. Usually she read it carefully, but not today. She had a mission, one best accomplished while CJ was away in San Francisco, this time to speak to state preservationists about Thomas Jefferson's introduction of wine to America, a subject he knew little about. CJ considered the third president guilty of a kind of regicide by proxy, so Claire had researched the subject for him and sent him off with notes and some prosciutto on a thinly sliced baguette in a paper bag.

She drove into town and parked down by the river, with a view of a scruffy little bar with the name Glass Act ostentatiously stenciled into faux antique glass. She had never been inside but knew of it by reputation, a commercial underbelly of the wine trade where intriguing and some rare vintages could be had and talked about, not by respectable people who made or evaluated them but by a subterranean clientele without clear objectives. Also a floating, clandestine market for contraband: wines left over from divorces and broken estates, sold under the counter to avoid federal taxation, and bottles purloined from tasting rooms and wine cellars.

CJ wouldn't dream of going into Glass Act, and neither would she but for the circumstances. Over the dozen years she and CJ had been married, Claire had assumed responsibilities never envisioned when she met him, at the Little Rock Marriott. She had grown up in a place called Hardy, Arkansas, determined someday to get away from cousins who kept possums in cages and a stepfather who operated grower houses for a poultry magnate. Claire had clawed her way into the office of the Marriott's events coordinator, and there she would have stayed if she hadn't been told to help a visiting wine critic set up a wine tasting.

Claire hadn't known what Bordeaux was in those days. But she knew what it—and CJ—represented: deliverance. He was an older man with an exotic accent, attractive enough if already getting heavy, and nice to her. Gradually she had come to love many things about him and to learn more about the world than she had ever thought possible. Claire was grateful and over the years had shown it repeatedly, but sometimes the duties were overwhelming.

With the copy of *Craven-Jones on Wine* under one arm, she pushed through the glass door and into a dim interior ringing with the recorded voice of Eddie Vedder.

Barstools faced a daunting array of bottles behind the
bar, many reachable only with the help of an old library
ladder on a brass track. A wall of wine crate butt ends
was punctuated by the horned heads of wild animals.
The smell of fermentation, not young wine in a barrel
but the spilled sort, wafted about a room mercifully
empty except for the ponytailed bartender.

He came forward, a towel over his shoulder, and asked
pleasantly, "What can I do you for?"

"Well, I'm not entirely sure."

"Today's specials are up there." He indicated the chalkboard, one corner broken off like a bitten cookie. "You
visiting our fair valley for the first time?"

"Lord no, I live here. I'm Claire Craven-Jones," and
she offered her hand.

He took it in a broad calloused paw, a leather thong
about the wrist. "I'm Ben. Of course I know the name, he
must be your husband?"

"That's right."

"I read him religiously, everyone who comes in here
does. Great man, great publication."

"Why, thank you. I brought you the new issue, in case
you haven't seen it." She knew he hadn't. "There's been
an interesting development, unprecedented, actually. I
don't know but thought you, or maybe a customer here,
might know something about this." She took a breath and
spread the issue on the bar, pointing to the black-lined
box at the bottom of the first page.

Ben dutifully read the paragraph. "Oh, yeah," he said,
"I heard about that."

"You've already heard about it?"

"There's not much that happens in the valley that doesn't pass through here, *tout de suite*. A lot of it's bullshit . . . sorry, unreliable. But this has people talking."

"And have you heard anything?"

"Nothing useful. To tell you the truth, Mrs. Craven-Jones, I think you've got yourselves a little problem."

Claire's heart sank. "Oh, God. What?"

"Just my opinion, mind you. But I don't think anybody's gonna come forward."

"Why?"

"The pretenders will be afraid of being caught out. If they are, your husband will never rank their wines again. And the guy who brought it off will be afraid his wine won't stand up in a second tasting, and then there'll be no way he can prove the mystery wine's his. So he'll be . . ."

"Screwed," she said.

"I was going to say toast." He slid a glass across the lacquered slab of wood and, despite her raised hand, poured into it something cold, golden, no doubt sweet. "There could be a way out of this," he added, "if you could find out who this guy—or gal—is, on your own. Then you could taste another bottle of his wine on your own, and if you got a match, you'd have your scoop."

It all sounded a bit grubby. "That's a lot of ifs," she said.

"Yeah, but not impossible. A good private investigator might be able to help you."

"Oh, please." She tasted the wine. "Lovely. Beaumes-de-Venise?"

"Very impressive. Could yours be the palate behind the great man?"

"No. And a private eye is out of the question. It's tacky. My husband wouldn't like that."

"Nothing wrong with using PIs, legit people do it all the time. What you need is someone who's personable, reliable, and, you know, cleans up real well."

"Thank you, Ben, I appreciate the suggestion. But I'm sure someone will come forward soon. And thank you for the taste of that lovely wine."

She walked to the door, eager to get beyond the place and the idea she had brought into it. Claire now regretted agreeing to open her husband's editorial castle keep to a callous world. CJ had never given readers even a glimpse of the inner workings of the *Craven-Jones on Wine* operational machine, and to have done so in a time of growing competition from blogs and declining subscriptions had been a mistake.

"Mrs. CJ."

The bartender followed her, and in his eyes Claire thought she detected genuine sympathy. "Give me your card," he said, "and I can get in touch if I hear anything."

While she was searching for it, he added, "And here's my friend's. He recently lost his job, through no fault of his own. He knows something about the wine business."

He offered that card, and she glanced at it. The words *The Valley Press* had been scratched out with a ballpoint pen, leaving only a name—Les Breeden—and a profession. Oh, no, she thought, a journalist's even worse than a private detective.

# CHAPTER TWO

*Into Enotopia*

# 1

WHEN LES BREEDEN was a second-semester junior at UC Davis, his lifelong sweetheart stepped out of his life as nimbly and as finally as she had stepped into it during high school trigonometry class in Chico. She was Jewish, one of the few he knew. Her name was Paula, and she had elongated eyes he would one day hear described as lozenge shaped, dark lashes and hair, and pale skin with an exotic, almost bluish cast particularly striking when she took off her clothes in afternoon light angling between the blinds in her otherwise deserted house.

Her mother worked in the state agricultural extension office downtown, so Les and Paula started making love in the fierce afternoon heat of early summer, the air conditioner off because it was not supposed to be on when Paula wasn't home and she was supposed to be at the library, not naked with what she affectionately called a goy, both of them slick with sweat and besotted with each other. Afterward, they would take chaste, separate showers and go off to their utterly insignificant other lives, later to talk themselves to sleep on cell phones because they used the same carrier and it was free.

All he cared about was Paula and her skin and low-slung, beautiful breasts with dark nipples that got hard even when they talked in the hallway in the happy days of their senior year, and then she had to cross her arms and step back and forth like she was dancing. He was fair-haired, with a physique shaped by hard work in the out-of-doors and what Paula called an all-American chin. Les had not been her first, but he had gotten over that. She was his first, and he assumed all sex an irrational, irresistible, sometimes violent conjunction repeated over and over again, entered into as enthusiastically by the girl, sometimes more so.

One afternoon in bed, Paula whispered, "Les is more," and he, flattered, assumed it would go on like this forever.

Fortunately he lived just inside the city limits and in the same school district as Paula. But weekends and summers, Les was out on the family acreage, working with his father, leathery and lean from years under a sun that had reduced him to essentials. Les was going to be a farmer too, and he bought an old Toyota pickup with 175,000 miles on it, one of those early indestructible models, and did all the servicing himself, even painting the undercarriage with the used crankcase oil.

He chose UC Davis for its powerful agricultural component and to get away for a while, since Paula was going to Sarah Lawrence in far-off Bronxville, New York, on scholarship. While he studied things like botany and rotation grazing, she read Coleridge and Wordsworth and, later, French novelists, and after that somebody named Derrida. Les had never heard of him or the others who followed, although he was a reader too, mostly of science fiction. Kid stuff, he knew, but he pursued it, working backward from Herbert and Heinlein though Clarke, Asimov, Bradbury to H. G. Wells and Jules Verne, then into the really weird modern stuff. These books lifted him temporarily out of a community headed into a time warp of its own, from dependence upon graze and soybean fields to low-rent commercial lots, with heavy equipment and car lots and tilt-up warehouses.

Many of his friends moved away, their houses filling up with Hispanics who would work for next to nothing. "It's over," his father kept saying, without stipulating exactly what "it" was. Then in Les's last year at home, he saw guys and girls his age with bony arms and bad teeth wandering the streets like aliens, and pretty soon people were locking their windows and doors and the sheriff was discovering meth factories in old houses.

Les had bucked hay with bare hands, walking along behind the farm truck and muscling up the bales as had been done forever, work that filled out his shoulders and built biceps like softballs. The sun had permanently bleached his hair and given him little premature wrinkles at the edges of eyes that Paula said were sexy. Few people harvested hay like that anymore. Now it was all big equipment and big debt, government subsidies you couldn't live on, his father said, the beef and grain markets "going up and down like bare asses in a Reno whorehouse."

But agriculture in some form had to endure, everybody said. People have to eat. "But don't think you're gonna make it farming on your own," his father told him, "and your mother and I are getting what we can out of this place. I'm sorry, but you couldn't fight the corporations anyway. Get into genetics or something and hire on with Monsanto or one of the other outlaws."

At UC Davis he lived cheaply in a dorm, eating out of cans heated in water on the electric coil until right before they exploded. He hung out with other ag majors, who were surprisingly heavy drinkers, but saved himself for Paula. They corresponded now more by e-mail than cell phone, Les using the school's computers, and saw each other on vacation and holidays. They didn't have as much to talk about now, with Paula distracted except when they were in bed.

Then, right after Christmas his junior year, she wrote him a long letter instead of an e-mail and told him that no, they wouldn't marry when they were out of college because she was going on to eventually get a PhD in comparative literature and was not leaving the East Coast. The California they had known was dead to her, and the fact that she had grown up studying about people like Junipero Serra embarrassing. What she didn't say, but Les knew to be true, was that she found him embarrassing too.

So began a succession of girls, starting with the barmaid at Gloria's. There was a string of group housemates with privileges, and then online partiers, all of them inspiring horny remorse. He discovered that most women were something less than the orgasmic Gatling gun Paula had been. His drinking increased, with the occasional stimulant thrown in to get him through exams and papers, and he switched his major from ag to journalism, not much of an academic interest at Davis, but writing came more easily to him than chemistry.

This put off graduation another year. Agriculture in general was clearly going the way of the Sacramento River—down. He joined the ad hoc boxing team to get back in shape, pounding a dent in the heavy bag and trading body blows with misplaced farm boys like himself. His parents had moved to Ventura by then, and he mastered the classic inverted news pyramid instead of legume genomes and organic growth compounds. He got into graduate school but then dropped out to take a job as a starting reporter at *The Sacramento Bee*.

Les wrote obits and bounced around the rubber-chicken circuit, eating for free while listening to politicians in shiny cowboy boots give speeches to Rotarians and other worthies about water theft by the feds and weirdos living in San Francisco and L.A. One day, sitting hungover in a taqueria with friends and an ice-cold Bud, he heard a mention of an online ad by *The Press*, a daily published not fifty miles from where he sat, in

what was known as the valley but not to be confused
with the Central Valley and another world altogether, its
fame resting on the twin pillars of premium wine and
wealth. Les didn't drink wine but thought it would be an
adventure to go check out this other valley.

Winemaking and viticulture had been big at Davis.
Those studying it strutted around like religious converts
instead of celebrity-struck wannabes, working guys
seeking to improve their social or economic standing,
business majors wanting to serve one of the big corporations buying up choice properties, and sons and daugh-
ters of established winery owners preparing to take over
when their parents moved on. Les didn't belong to any of
these groups and so kept a skeptical distance, although
everyone at Davis imbibed some knowledge of wine by
osmosis, rootstock and vine parasites and hoary tradi-
tions imported from Europe always in the air.

Two days after answering the ad, he was hired via
e-mail and summoned by a publisher interested in Les's
experience at *The Bee* and in his knowledge of agriculture, much of it already forgotten.

# 2

HIS FIRST VIEW of the valley was so striking that he had to pull over and get out of the pickup. This was not what he had expected. Vineyards conformed to rugged contours of a green crease between little mountains, the breeze lifting in from the unseen Pacific over a range named for dead Indians, shadows lying in the low places and swallowing a river barely worthy of the name. Old wineries and houses looked regal in the distance, with meandering roads that reminded him of daguerreotypes he had seen of nineteenth-century rural California that, then as now, must have smelled of Douglas fir and dust hot in the sun.

Feeling an odd nostalgia for something he had never known, he drove on through a landscape carefully maintained but still natural. He didn't have to know a lot about vines to recognize their opulent accommodation, the rows alternating with carpets of wild mustard. The vineyards ran right up to the edge of the little town of

Caterina, its Main Street lined with restored Victorian façades in pastels. The hardware store, running a special on pruning shears, was right next to an art gallery with a painting of a giant peach in the window. Bunches of plastic grapes hung on the gas pumps.

The county seat at the bottom of the valley had a courthouse like a brick fortress, a police compound across Main just like the Sacramento lockup, and, nearby, his new employer's one-story stucco compound. THE VALLEY PRESS, the sign said, A NEWSPAPER WITH COMMUNITY VALUES.

The man with whom he had spoken, Richard—"never *Dick*"—was from Minnesota and wore a sleeveless argyle sweater with big diamonds on it. A tie constricted his narrow neck, he wore shiny tie shoes, and he stated the obvious: "Well, Lester, here you are."

Then Richard praised local merchants, up-valley socialites, big corporations that had "brought a new spirit of accomplishment and entrepreneurialism to this valley," and Les felt the optimism running out of him like sand. "So, Les, you're our new guy for police, the courts— mostly petty theft and drunk Mexicans—and agriculture. Use your own car, keep track of your mileage, file two stories a day. Minimum."

"I thought I was general assignments."

"Those are general assignments, Les."

"I don't have a car. It's an old pickup."

"Okay, you can use the company Taurus, parked behind the building. Get reimbursed for gas and never use it for pleasure or take it home. We'll see you bright and early."

No offer of lunch, no drink, no enthusing about Les's experience in the capital. And no introductions to the handful of people standing idly around or staring into the pale gray fog of their computer screens.

Later, sitting in his pickup, Les wondered if *The Bee* would have him back. But the national economy was tanking, and there were too many J-school graduates looking for too few jobs. He was stuck.

The apartment he had found online, in a working-class neighborhood near the highway, turned out to be a converted garage belonging to a retired geology professor. His powdery wife said, "Dr. Billings will be with us shortly," and then he came in drinking a Sierra Nevada. "No pets and no drugs," pronouncing it *droogs*, "and keep the windows closed because of the goddamned cats."

The apartment had a steel-frame bed with a soft mattress and a two-burner stove, and smelled of mineral dust left over from the old man's geologic specimens cut on the electric bench saw now rusting in the sun. "This whole valley's sitting on unstable ash and mud that washed out of the Sierra in the Pleistocene," he told Les. "The San Andreas fault runs more or less under your toilet."

Les moved in his stuff and went back downtown. It was early, and the first bar he went into had more tourists than locals and a towering wall of wine bottles. He ordered a Bud Light, and the couple seated nearby looked at him with pity.

He left and walked along the river, watching the tide go out. The little park was deserted except for two deeply suntanned men with bundles of clothes under their butts, contemplating mudflats. Les found his way blocked by what he thought was a fast-food shack until he saw half a dozen stools on a sawdust floor, seemingly at odds with the name stenciled on the door: GLASS ACT.

Two shiny couches, what looked like walls of unfinished timber, and not a single customer. He went in and sat at the scuffed, darkly lacquered bar with no beer taps. Those walls were really the ass ends of wine crates, branded with family names. A heavyset man in a leather jerkin and gray ponytail was climbing down from a ladder used to reach bottles stored in what looked like old feed bins. He asked, "What's your varietal, cowboy?"

"My what?"

"You're not from around here, are you?"

"I just got hired by *The Press*. I want a beer."

"That's not a sin. *The Press*, huh? Well, you have my sympathies."

He was Ben Something-or-other, Slavic-like, extending a sandpapery hand at the end of a stout, hairy forearm wrapped with a sweat-stained leather bracelet.

"I'm Les Breeden. From Chico."

"Well, Les from Chico, don't you think you might like some familiarity with the valley's main product? To adequately serve that great metropolitan daily?"

Not waiting for an answer, Ben held up a black bottle with an elaborate silver device in the neck and poured two fingers of red wine into a big stemmed glass. Les wished he had just walked out, but it was too late. Then he noticed the price chalked on the board behind the bar. "Seven dollars? No way."

"Indulge me. The first glass for a visiting fireman in hard times is free. Taste a Pinot Noir from the Central Coast to launch you on a voyage that, if you're like the rest of us, will be long and eventful. Stick your nose into the glass, inhale, and tell me what it smells like."

Les went along with it. "Grapes?"

"Not specific enough. Think fruit."

"Strawberries?"

"Better. Now drink, but"—Ben already had a mouthful of wine—"*don' schwallow. Shuck som' air. Then closh lips and blow out da nose. . . .*"

Les tried. A surprisingly potent, fragrant liquid went up the wrong way and came painfully out his nostrils and all over the bar. Ben clawed the towel from his shoulder and wiped down his jerkin first. "That wasn't auspicious," he said. "Let's try again."

"Don't think so, but thanks for the introduction."

"Wait, you've got to try the Syrah, for contrast. Don't aerate this one, and you don't have to spit." A web of smile lines transformed Ben's otherwise scary face. "Okay, Syrah's called Shiraz in Australia and in Persia where it came from. Got that? This one's made right here. Ancient grape, modern renditions."

This wine was darker than the first. Les could smell it

from two feet away and feel it coating his teeth like little furry sweaters. Ben was sloshing his wine around in his mouth, so Les tried that too. The Syrah was delicious. "Hot around the gums," he said, taking a chance. "No resemblance to the stuff in jugs or the wine coolers we used to drink at Davis."

"We're making progress. The heat comes from high alcohol, our big problem in California. And a paradox: if sun's good for grapes, how can it be bad for wine? Because it drives up the sugars."

"What are sugars?"

"Don't get hung up on the lingo, Chico. Words like 'sugars,' 'varietal,' they make some people sound smart so they're here to stay. The important thing is, sugar makes wines pop, with the help of microbes. Basically the little buggers eat the sweet juice and excrete alcohol. The more sugar there is to eat, the more alcohol's produced, the more powerful the wine."

"So we get high on bacteria shit?"

"Basically. Alcohol also masks a wine's defects, so winemakers love it. And big alcohol gets people thirsting for that initial blast of fruit, but it also makes them drunk."

"What's 'Californicated'?"

"Too much oak—splinters in the gums from too much time in new barrels."

They drank again. Ben placed a basket of crackers on the bar. "Cleans the palate," he explained and turned and climbed back on the ladder, the treads worn by the passage of many feet. Ben looked up and down the bins, fingered a bottle, and brought it down. "Now for the coup de grâce, Cabernet Sauvignon, the valley's triumph. Don't let anybody tell you differently. The best ain't Pinot, it ain't Syrah, it ain't Sangiovese. Merlot, Chardonnay, Sauvignon Blanc—they all fall beneath the jackboots of Almighty Cab. The fuel under the fire, the sex in the enological equation."

With a stroke of a mounted contraption looking like a bronze bicycle pump, he delivered the cork right through the metal foil. "Ideally the wine should breathe, but life's short."

Then he reached down and produced two fresh glasses that might have held goldfish at the county fair and generously poured. Les's mouth was watering as he watched the wine rise in his glass, the smell differing from the others. He said, "Dusty."

"That's tannin. What else?"

"Some kind of berry?"

"Good. And?"

"Sawdust?"

"Pencil shavings?"

"Yeah."

"Spot on, Les."

The door opened and a couple came in, he in a white shirt and jeans, his long, dark hair in ringlets, she looking Asian but wearing a safari suit and wide-brimmed felt hat. "Hey, Benny," the young man said.

"Hey, Train. Kiki."

They sat down and Ben dragged the bottle of Cab over to them, covering the label with the soiled towel.

"This gentleman and I were just sampling a very excellent expression of mountain vines on a southwest-facing slope. What say?"

"Sure," said Train.

Les noticed the Ferrari parked at the curb outside and was glad he had left his truck up the street. A clear plastic shield covered the outsized engine, which was painted red. "Testarossa," said Train, noticing his interest. "Eats BMWs for lunch. Who're you?"

"This is Les," said Ben. "A reporter, and a damned good one."

"I'm Train, this is Kiki. And this is . . ." Train smelled, tasted, sighed. "This is an '02 . . ."

Les didn't catch the name, not that it mattered. Ben whipped off the towel. "*Mi complimenti!*"

"*Grazie.*"

Then somehow the bottle was empty. Kiki text messaging, Train and Ben talking, Les looking up contentedly at the wall of famous wineries with proper names, some of them famous, but also those of mountains, ridges, creeks, valleys, trees, flowers, fish, mammals, birds, women, even pickups. The variety was mesmerizing.

"I'm feeling the need of a flatlander," said Train, and Kiki squealed with delight and pushed aside her cell phone. Ben moved crabwise toward his ladder, saying in passing, "You're on your own now, Chico."

# 3

THE DREAM WAS MAUVE, smelling of some violent
earthly upheaval. Darkness filled with faces, all wom-
en's; each time he reached, they receded. Then he was
drifting on an incoming tide that flooded the flats, un-
burdened except for the pain behind his eyes, something
unspeakable gaining on him, the tide turning, carrying
him backward. . . .

Thin morning light lay in neatly scissored strips on
the concrete floor of Les's apartment. His cell phone
alarm had used up the remaining battery power, and
Les still wore his trousers and socks. A scrub jay sitting
on the landlord's rock-sawing bench outside the window
reminded him that it was a new day, but he couldn't let
go of the faces of the night before. New ones had appeared at the bar, indistinct now, but not the feeling of
bonhomie, everyone happy, knowledgeable, privileged,
including Les.

He showered and put on clean clothes and drove

downtown, parking outside a still-darkened Glass Act and walking to *The Press*. The little newsroom barely merited the name, with Richard in his box like a foreman noting people's tardy arrivals. He popped out to state the obvious—"You made it"—and to introduce Les to any staff handy: Alice Principio, a pleasant woman in pleated slacks straight out of J-school, covered county government and the "social round"; Lance Stouffer, wine editor, had a peevish look, maybe because the rubber-chicken circuit was also in his "capable" hands; and the two men on the coffee-stained horseshoe "take care of us all" but seemed to be worshipping at their computer terminals.

"Les is handling agriculture for us," Richard concluded. "Also schools, courts, and cops. Which reminds me, Les, we do a weekly crime wrap-up, everybody starts that way. We call it the Perp Burp. Okay, we have a newspaper to put out."

The scabrous building Les had noticed across from the courthouse received him with the same slightly sour air he remembered from the Sacramento police station, another humiliation he had not foreseen. What had he been thinking? That they would offer him a column and a secretary? Why couldn't he see these things coming? A woman with brightly studded glasses secured by a velvet cord handed him a computer printout, and he stepped back out into the street convinced that he had made the biggest mistake of his short life.

Noon, and the square vividly etched into his still uneasy brain. What had Ben said? "If I don't have one before eleven, I must have eleven before one." The words had been attributed to a Spanish sherry producer, touched each day with a yearning for artisanal alcohol. Les could see Glass Act from where he stood, open now, a crummy old Volkswagen parked out front and the river beyond under a full tide, as in his dream.

He walked across to the wine bar, printout in hand. It was cool in the depths of Glass Act, the door hanging open to the view of willows on the far side, in the lee of half-finished construction out of another century. Ben was up on the ladder—lived there, it seemed—sleeves rolled, a case of something balanced dangerously on his head. Shirttail out, heels fleshy nubs at the back of clogs. "Yo, Chico," he called. "Have a seat."

Les spread the printout on the bar. *The suspect was observed attempting to open the kitchen window with a garden trowel....* Ben dismounted and plunged a hand into the cooler; he lifted a dripping golden bottle like some miracle from a blessed fount, the fancy rubber stopper coming out with a *whishhh*. The bottle advanced on two narrow glasses.

"No," said Les.

"Don't tell a soul, but this is French. It's also the best fucking Muscat on earth."

Pouring now, the exotic smell swimming through the intervening air like something alive, the glass absorbing all available light. "Beaumes-de-Venise." Ben was grinning, for, yes, it was the best thing Les had ever tasted.

For a time he couldn't speak, gulls calling as if from a great distance, car doors slamming, classical music Les couldn't identify seeping from dusty speakers in the dark corners of the ceiling. "Albinoni's Adagio," said Ben. "We should settle up."

"Settle up what?"

"Your bill."

"I didn't know I had one."

Ben placed the itemized receipt on the bar, Les's initials scrawled at the bottom but the items listed above it all too legible. "*Two hundred and seventy-three dollars?*"

"You bought a Ridge Zin, then insisted on buying into Train's super-duper Tuscan. I thought that one was a bad choice, but you guys wouldn't listen. Then . . ."

"It's the biggest bar bill in history."

"Welcome to Enotopia, Chico."

He didn't have the $273, and before he knew it he owed $341 and change. What little cash he had scraped together had gone into the rent and paying down his credit card. What little there was in his pathetic retirement plan at *The Bee* was worth half what it had been; cashing that out wasn't worth the penalty. When Ben finally asked for something down, Les said, "I don't get paid for another week."

"Okay. But I have to put the cork back in the bottle until then."

It was another noon and Les couldn't stop staring at the basket of sandwiches behind the bar, each with a white card on which was written, in lovely red script, things like *baguette with frisée and country pâté* and *creamy St. André.*

He gazed out at Ben's ancient Volkswagen in the street, the trunk open to accommodate an ill-fitting load of wine cartons collected on his weekly cellar run, held down with a spidery clot of bungee. "You need a pickup," said Les.

"Trucks cost money."

"Not an old one. What you need is something fashionably run-down. Good mileage, retro classy. Maybe painted to look more, you know, agricultural. Earth tones, 'Glass Act' stenciled on the side. Splattered with green, but discreetly."

Ben looked at him, then outside, at Les's truck sitting pathetically in the sun. "That thing belong to you?"

"What you need, Ben, is an old Toyota made between '86 and '94. You know, with that discontinued but super-efficient engine. A pickup with character. With a mere two hundred and seventy-three thousand miles. Don't make them like that anymore."

Resplendent new steel occupied all the other slots on the street, many of their owners crowding into Fantasia Pizza. The gulls reeled; it was getting hot. "How much?" asked Ben.

"Two grand."

"No way."

"Okay, sixteen hundred."

"What would you do for wheels? Everybody has a car in California."

"I have a bike, old but okay."

"Tell you what, I'll swap you the Volkswagen for the Toyota, more suitable for a reporter, anyway."

Now it was Les looking out at Ben's dilapidated propulsion device. "Maybe, but you have to eat my bar bill and give me a fifty-dollar cushion."

"You must be desperate."

Les ignored that. "Now I think I'll have that Monterey Jack and serrano on the sourdough baguette."


In the evenings, wisdom bobbed like miniature hot-air balloons trapped beneath Ben's old pressed-tin ceiling: *Matanzas Creek's a go, likewise Sky. . . . Beringer may have good vineyards, but they didn't get into this bottle. . . . Never put birds on a wine label, particularly seagulls. . . . Never have salad dressing when tasting the good stuff. . . . Never have salad dressing, period. . . .*

If Les sat alone at the bar, or in the sticky embrace of one of Ben's stressed couches, he methodically read the canon: Johnson et al., *Craven-Jones on Wine*, the lesser stars like *The Wine Taster*, trade journals full of articles on rootstock, leaf mold, the glassy-winged sharpshooter that attached its lethal snout to unsuspecting vines, even marketing and investment meditations by investors and trendies.

*If sweaty saddle was once an attribute, why isn't it today? . . . Because Davis turned everybody into wine snobs. . . . Because branchiomyces smells like shit. . . .*

*Because it means spoilage . . . In the nose of the be-holder . . . In the mind of the fool. . . .*

He drove home through the mostly empty city streets, words reverberating in his overstimulated brain while he marveled at the quality of his high: no bloat, no back-of-the-eyes ache now, just a free-floating appreciation of things he never saw by day. Some nights he left the VW and Train drove him home in the Ferrari, Kiki jostling on Les's lap, the engine moaning, its vibrations so har-monious, the wind raking his face with the fragrances of fall, or fog off the Bay, the pressure of Kiki's soft little butt disturbing.

Les would have invited them in, but he had nothing to offer and was ashamed of his room. So much in this world was new, even though he had been born not a hundred miles from here, this valley another country, certainly, where the natives spoke of gods he was only beginning to recognize.

# 4

"YOU'VE GOT THE SICKNESS."

Ben rested his arms on the bar and studied Les. It was ten o'clock Sunday morning, cleanup done, Les helping. He had put the empty bottles out in containers, allowing the rare labels to show so passers-by would know what treasures had been consumed the night before and want to get in on the action; the place was ready-o for day-trippers from that shining city across the Bay.

Ben held a can of Pepsi while Les sipped his triple-shot latte from Kiss My Cookies up the street.

"The interesting thing," Ben continued, "is that the sickness seems perfectly normal to those who have it. Right now, for instance, you're asking yourself, 'How could anybody *not* want to talk about wine?' No real cure for early wine obsession, I'm afraid. Just more wine and more talk about it. Best to recognize this and go to the beach or find a girl. Maybe it's time you met Esme."

Her eyes looked as hard as polished lapis, but her smile was all for Les. No Pacific Heights orthodontia there, just healthy enamel behind plump lips a little too bright and well tended for Northern California. Black hair in a kind of duenna's tortoiseshell comb—"to hail with that endangered species stuff"—and clothes curiously formal. She was short and thick, but the proportions were most definitely all right. She said "ahm" for arm and "balled" for boiled, and when served an inferior wine, "Thi-us jus' idn't doin' it," sliding the glass away with one finger.

Esme Desmour was married to an Amarillo takeover artist but seemed to know California intimately. After being introduced, Les politely asked, "So you live in Amarillo?" and she said, "Lester, no one *lives* in Amarillo."

He tried again. "Does your husband like wine?"

"My husband likes Coors Light"—*lie-ut*—"on the rocks. At least he did the last time I saw him."

Esme was, according to Ben, a custom marketer who scoped out select wines and vintages for friends from Santa Barbara to Ukiah and sold them to other friends. She and Ben dickered over costly bottles that Ben was able to find when no one else, it seemed, could. It was these surprises that brought the varied clientele and added a bit of adventure to wine appreciation, but it was clear that Esme was the better trader, moving effortlessly between treacly charm and scorn. When her cell phone squealed on the bar, she would punch it, say, "I'm in a meeting," and punch it again.

They haggled over bottles of wine they intended to sell later, like the Bordeaux standing regally on the bar, one Les had never heard of, from a case she was trying to sell Ben. That negotiation went on so long that the three of them ended up drinking it.

When she had left, Ben told him, "She has a genetic ability to consume vast amounts of alcohol. In New Orleans, whence she comes, this is an evolutionary trait, still in early stages of development, maybe, but already altering the species. So, Les, never try to outdrink her. And never, ever try to get into her panties."

"Why did you want me to meet her?"

"She goes to tastings all over the valley and lots of dinner parties. Occasionally she requires an escort. And she likes them decent looking, neither gay nor married, harder to find than you might think."

The next day she invited him into her immaculate little Lexus and they drove to a "ranch" just north of town, where they milled with hopeful lesser winemakers and vintners, tasting from barrels, an event put together by a publicist who hoped that an unusual under-the-radar gathering would bring critics. It didn't, and Esme whispered to him, "You're a reporter. Why don't you take some notes? It'll make them all feel better."

He did, and then she drove him back to town, her cell phone bleating. "I'm in a meeting. . . . In a meeting . . ." Outside Les's apartment, she pulled to the curb and, instead of letting him out, said, "I want to see where you live."

"There's nothing to see."

"Don't be rude."

She was already out, teeth illuminated by the street-light, arms swinging like an equatorial explorer's as she strode ahead of him into the yard, past chunks of lava, a pile of quartz from Tahoe, God knew what in the ever-accumulating primal rock garden. Les unlocked the door.

"My," said Esme, looking around.

"I told you."

"Where's the closet?"

"There's not one."

"Where in the world do you hang your clothes?"

"Behind the bathroom door."

The only chair was draped in cycling gear, so Esme sat on the bed. "Do you have a jacket?"

"Yes."

She wanted him to model it, so he did. "Brown cordu-roy with the worn elbow patches might be good enough for Davis and Sacramento, but not for this valley, Lester. You need a dark jacket, double-breasted, with *tasteful* gold buttons. Do you have black shoes?"

"No."

"Do you have dark trousers, a silk tie?"

"Same answer."

She took his hand and pulled him down beside her, the mattress rising at the corners, threatening to enfold them. He breathed deeply of her perfume and, to his surprise, Esme stretched upward and kissed him in a tight, tongueless acknowledgment of something. He put a hand on her breast, and she sighed. "Les, I have HSDD."

"You do?"

"Yes."

"I'm sorry. What is it?"

"Hypoactive sexual desire disorder."

That sounded promising, but she added, "In old-fashioned parlance, frigidity. Think iced tea on a hot day in Orleans Parish," and he felt his confidence stutter like the bulb in his one functional reading lamp. "It comes from a combination of factors, my therapist says, including a strong daddy." She patted his thigh.

The windows of his apartment framed a dark sky matted with black trees, against the silhouette of his bike hanging upside down from the hook he had screwed into the ceiling. Esme was saying, "I'm not looking to hook up. Frigidity has its benefits, you know."

He couldn't think of any.

"No distraction, for one thing. And it's a surefire way to find out how much somebody really cares for you. Now, Les, are you hungry?"

# 5

THE NEXT DAY HE WROTE a three-graph story about the tasting that was free of any wine evaluation, the idea of seeing "cedary," "buttery," or "berry-ish" on the screen of his desktop outlandish. Richard read it and said, "You've been bitten by the wine bug. Happens to everybody sooner or later. We'll run it, but you'll have to make your peace with Lance."

Lance Stouffer covered the wine scene in his pale pink, too-tight blazer and disciplined beard rendered something other than gray by copious applications of Just For Men. Lance was a sycophant, but Les envied his access to people who mattered. "Why do we care about these losers?" Lance asked, of the wineries Les had mentioned, his feet resting on the rim of the wastebasket.

"Because they're in the valley. Because they deserve some coverage. Because a couple of the wines were pretty good."

Lance snorted. "You can write about them if you want

to, but don't try it with the big boys. You'll be a laughing-stock. And you'll mess up my arrangements."

Driving home in the Volkswagen that smelled of spilled wine and french fries, Les wondered what those arrangements might be. He had the next two days off and, exhausted, went straight to sleep, hugging the pillow, the open window containing, the next time he saw it, three inquisitive feline faces and another beautiful day in paradise.

On impulse he showered; put on his cycling shorts with a worn crotch pad; made a sandwich and wrapped it up with what was left of the ramen in the refrigerator; stuffed the package, a half gallon of water, and his old rip-stop Patagonia one-man tent into the pannier; and headed west on a county road. Rush hour was mostly over, the road rising and emptying completely as it entered what his landlord said was a commingling of Franciscan and other soils supposedly unsuited to vineyards, although plenty of them lay like a green chop on the otherwise arid earth.

Sweating, exulting in the briny smell from the Bay, he felt better, passed by the odd flatbed truck loaded with pallets of fertilizer or steel rebar, buffeting him with dust. He passed under the interstate and entered the canyons leading to the ocean—sharp two-lane curves and no driver wanting the legal hassle of running down a biker in California. He dismounted in front of the general store at the crossroads, bought a Coke, and ate half his sandwich sitting on the barrier in the parking lot. He had forgotten the unburdening that came with pumping a spindle, leaning into the wind, the sun on his neck, and he rode on westward, his other life falling away.

Hours later, he stood astride the bike overlooking a long line of confused and dangerous surf, the breeze off the vast cobalt sea drying his sweat and forcing smells of salt air and chaparral up his nostrils: pleasant, provocative. Tiny figures hiked the headlands below, their cars clustered in the parking lot like stalled metallic lemmings. The weekend was not yet in full swing, and he found a place for his tent in the campground; no view, but who needed it? This was a new beginning; he didn't have the wine sickness, after all, and he would stop going into debt and would find a girl. Maybe one day they would climb Mount Tamalpais together.

He ate the rest of his sandwich, the ramen, a slab of dark chocolate, and an orange he had bought at the general store. He pulled the bike into the tent with him, rolled himself in one of the blankets from the apartment, and slept contented through the thin, rhythmic streams from two different eras, Beyoncé and Paul Simon, seeping from nearby vans.

He didn't get back until after dark the next day and, famished, devoured a bacon cheeseburger and a chocolate shake while sitting at a plastic table in the valley's one McDonald's. Then he pedaled slowly home, showered, pulled on sweats and, instead of going to Glass

Act, opened a novel about reversed time that carried a protagonist backward from the distant future through successive reigns of terror to a promising present.

Sunday morning: same room, same cats' faces in the window, same sun. He drove downtown for coffee before work, and on impulse, sucking scalding latte past the plastic lid, strolled down to Glass Act, surprised to see the door open and a man and a woman sitting at the bar.

Ben called out, "Where you been?"

"Point Reyes."

"Esme missed you."

"She doesn't like my wardrobe."

"And you missed the big news."

"What's that?"

"Clyde Craven-Jones found a California Cab he thinks rates his top score. Problem is, he doesn't know who made it. I want to talk to you about that later, but right now meet Kevin and Marilee. This is Les Breeden, also known as Chico, of *The Press*."

Les knew their names—Nomonity and Tavestani—but these two minor celebrities gazed at him without interest. Kevin Nomonity's mustache and unhappy eyes looked considerably more weather-beaten than in his photograph in *The Wine Taster;* Marilee Tavestani was very thin, but pretty, her intertwined legs appliquéd with faded denim. So he sat down the bar from them, nursing his coffee, then abruptly left.

# 6

"LES, GOT A MINUTE?"

Monday morning, and Richard in his glass box, offering Les a chair. The publisher had undergone a change: raccoon eyes, messed hair, and a casually knotted tie. While talking, Richard shaped things unseen with his hands, as if what he was trying to say could be fashioned out of nonexistent Play-Doh. His desk reminded Les of a salesman's, little on it but letters neatly stacked, an award from Sons of the Golden West, encased in a clear plastic cube ( . . . *for outstanding contributions to the furtherance of Manifest Destiny in our fair land* . . . ), folders with tabs in bright colors.

Richard picked up a particularly thin one. "This isn't going to be easy for either one of us. Now we've got a problem—not with you, Les, hell of a job, but with the economy. Every newspaper in the country's feeling it. The industry's going through . . . I don't know what it's going through. Who would have thought two years ago

that a well-run newspaper in a prosperous community
with lots to write about in a positive way would end up
with an incredible shrinking ad base and a bunch of
skittish investors?"

He pretended to mold something small and repel-
lent. The newspaper was privately held but the drift
clear: not enough merchants wanting their logos in that
puce-colored business section, not enough response to
the mattress ads.

"I'm sorry, Les. I know it hasn't turned out the way
you wanted. Some of the things I thought might happen
didn't. No breaks at all. You have initiative, but you were
the last hire."

Back in the newsroom, Les gazed out over the diminished collection of clerks and reporters straggling in.
The word "buyout" hadn't been in the air long when faces
had begun to disappear, unmourned. Alice Principio,
standing next to her desk, looked at Les in a sisterly way.
She had turned down the first buyout offer only to have
it reduced by half the following week.

"I'm not sure exactly what happened in there," he
said, and she said, "Les, I think you were just laid off."


Ben said, "Seniority doomed you. It was unavoidable,
tragic. End of story. Have a taste of this Calera '06 pinot
from the sun-blasted boonies of middle Enotopia."

Glass Act at 10:35 A.M. and the fog finally moving
out. A lot of sniffly hot-air balloonists would be sitting in
up-valley hotel hot tubs. Les suffered from wine-induced

altered lucidity, as did Ben, apparently. Gazing into the proprietor's eyes, Les thought he glimpsed a future Wolfman-ish version of himself. His memory of the night before was truncated: two gorgeous women on the arms of dot-com start-up beneficiaries who had driven up from Menlo Park; a drifting cast of locals; immaculate Esme ("I'm in a meeting. . . ."); Train and Tiki until the bitter end. A glass of the '98 Screaming Eagle that Les prayed to God he wasn't helping to pay for; and Ben taking from beneath the bar, very late, a pearl-handle pistol and shooting a mounted head across the room. *Pop* went the little .25-caliber automatic, *thwump* went the bullet, the old stuffed mule deer exhaling a cloud of century-old dust.

Les said, "I'm thirty-two years old. I have no girlfriend and no job. I live in an abandoned fossil factory, and I drive a dangerous clownmobile. I owe you and Visa money. My head hurts."

The appraisal left a long and silent wake. Finally Ben said, "You can work here for a while."

"Thanks, but no." He feared internment in Glass Act. "I need a makeover, totally."

A herd of tourists passed by on the street, bound for the farmers' market in the municipal parking lot. Ben said, "Why not try PI-ing?"

"What's that?"

"Private investigator. Kidnap rich runaways from cult camps, photograph husbands screwing in backseats, follow the money in divorce cases. Lots of those."

"You're kidding."

"I'm not. You can do it. You know something about the cops, you know how to ask questions. You're clean-cut, well-spoken, college-educated. Why not?"

"Because I wouldn't know where to start. How do you know about this stuff, anyway?"

"Because at some point I've tried it all." Ben turned over yesterday's specials menu and took out his pen, about to start another of his lists. "Now, how should we word this for craigslist?"

Discreet inquiries, north San Fran Bay, the Valley, and adjoining counties. Any legitimate personal, family, or business assignment considered. Professional investigator with impeccable record. Absolute confidentiality assured. Satisfaction guaranteed. Rates reasonable, negotiable . . .

Within forty-five minutes, Les got the first call and knew immediately this scheme wasn't going to work: "How much to go over and smear mayonnaise all over my girlfriend's car door handles and then throw the mayo jar up onto the condo balcony, where it'll break?"

"Mayonnaise?"

"She's violently allergic to it. And I know for a fact she and that shit head'll be Texas two-stepping in Vallejo until midnight."

Then a young woman in Santa Rosa called late to say she wanted her mother's cat kidnapped "but taken to the SPCA shelter, naturally. Hey, I know it sounds weird, but she loves that cat, and I hate it. Mom would kill me if she found out. So what would you charge?"

He renewed the ad anyway, and a guy in Solano County called in search of an "adaptable" CPA, and that, Les thought, was that.

Days later, pedaling near the Bay, he looked out over un-dulant waves of tule grass and felt drawn by the wet-land's isolation. He too could exist removed from a world in continuous motion, with limitless demands, the fetid smell of low tide reminding him that even the basest organisms were duking it out, down there, surviving, no peace even at ground level.

Why not smear mayonnaise on a stranger's car or stuff a clueless cat into a bag? All part of the greater plan. Because he couldn't. Meanwhile, his cell phone was vibrating in his fanny pack, and he pulled up just in time to catch the call: a woman with a tired, pleasant voice asked, "Is this . . ." and was drowned out by a semi loaded with pallets of vegetables.

"That was a truck," Les said. "I'm biking. Who is this?"

"I don't think of private detectives as riding around on bicycles." Pause. "Don't suppose there's any reason why they shouldn't. Well, I need someone to make some inquiries. The bartender at Glass Act gave me your number, but frankly I'm not sure this is a good idea."

"Mrs. . . . ?"

"Jones."

"I think we should meet, Mrs. Jones. Cell phones aren't secure." He didn't know that this was true, but it sounded good.

"You sound very young, Mr. Breeden."

"I'm not too young. We could meet."

"All right, but someplace other than Glass Act, if you don't mind."


Kiss My Cookies was full of tourists tearing into pastries and drinking lattes and cyclists in synthetics drinking colored liquids from plastic bottles. He perched at one of the elevated tables, and the time came and went with no Mrs. Jones. Les felt like any local forced to watch outsiders eat the things he wants and can't afford. Then a woman in Bermudas came in who lacked the tourist's telltale aimlessness, clearly looking for someone. Older than the voice on the phone, good legs, energy in the bounce. Blond on the way to being something else. She gazed past Les, maybe expecting a guy with a gut and a Bogey hat. It had to be her. "Mrs. Jones?"

She tried to hide her misgivings, and suddenly he wasn't up for the interview, the unnatural string of questions, something that had bothered him in journalism class. He had learned abruptness the way some people master a language, to get others to say things that maybe they shouldn't. But Mrs. Jones would be asking most of the questions today.

Without a word she offered a small, hard hand. Skin the uniform color of butterscotch; the gap between her front teeth at odds with the image of the immaculate, sun-burnished deck bunny. "Mr. Breeden, exactly how long have you been doing this?"

"Shouldn't we order something first?"

"Okay, I'll have a cappuccino."

She settled onto a stool and let him go for it. He would immediately be ten dollars in the hole and couldn't resist a biscotti for another buck fifty. Of course he then had to buy two. Mrs. Jones took the cup and asked, "So, how long?"

"I've been in the information collection business"— Ben's brilliant circumlocution—"for more than five years."

"So you're basically a reporter."

"Maybe you should just tell me what you need, Mrs. Jones. I'll tell you whether or not I think I can help you."

"What I need, Mr. Breeden, is someone to look into the identity of a bottle of wine. I know that sounds odd but, you see, my husband's in that business and needs to know where this wine came from. I'm afraid there's not much to go on."

"So you're Craven-Jones's wife."

"Yes. And your newspaper, by the way, if it was *The Press,* makes CJ sound like some kind of freak instead of the determined, disciplined, incorruptible person he is. Some publications don't like that, and they didn't like his influence."

"It's not my newspaper." But Lance Stouffer did dwell on stars like Jerome Hutt rather than on the quality of their overhyped wines; *The Wine Taster* ran pieces by Nomonity full of anesthetizing prose about various fruit bombs, with an occasional unflattering aside about Craven-Jones, his competitor—a *mixed if energetic record* was the phrase Les remembered. Marilee Tavestani was immune to the stars, or so Les had heard, and had recognized Craven-Jones's enormous impact on the wine business.

"Look," Les said, "I'd like to be in on this. I can't promise results, but I can follow a lead if you give me one." Beguiled by this woman, the problem, and the aroma of fine-grind Arabic and Colombian under steamed foam dusted with cocoa, he scalded his lip. "*Shit!* . . . Sorry, but I do this all the time. Now I'll get a blister and people will think I have a cold sore."

She took a little tin out of her shoulder bag, popped the lid with a blunt thumbnail, and dragged the edge of a paper napkin through salve smelling of pine sap. "Here. The sooner you put something on it, the quicker it'll get better. Of course you have to trust that I don't have anything contagious, either."

Was this a test, and how desperate was he? Yes, he thought, pretty much, so he wiped the stuff on his lip. Now his cappuccino had a turpentine finish. "Where did the wine come from?" he asked.

"We don't know. Someone just dropped it off, without a card or anything. It looks like any other Cabernet, but my husband thinks it's very good and could possibly be some kind of phenomenon." Resting sharp elbows on the table, she gazed out into the parking lot. "Frankly, I'm surprised I'm even talking about this."

Smearing mayonnaise on someone's car door handles

was preferable to taking advantage of her. He said, "Maybe you need somebody with more experience than I have, Mrs. Jones."

"Claire."

"I got laid off, Claire, and thought I could upgrade, you know. Shouldn't be hard to move up from writing about ag and purse snatchings."

Her throaty laughter drew the attention of the pod of cyclists. She touched that little gap with the tip of a very pink tongue, ignoring the string on her halter that had slipped from a shoulder. She picked up his biscotti, looked at it reflectively, broke off half, and pulverized it. Attractive overbite.

"Lester, you might just fit the ticket. You can legitimately claim to be a journalist, nobody will have to know you work for me unless you tell. What's your day rate?"

Prepped for this too, he quoted a figure. It sounded preposterous, but she asked, "What about expenses? A private dick on a bike I guess can't charge for mileage, unless . . ." This struck her as particularly funny. "Unless you use a pedo . . . a pe*dometer*! Sorry, I lost it. Let's talk in my car."

It was a lavender hybrid with mud all over the flanks. People in the valley don't drive dirty cars, but she seemed too busy and distracted to notice. He plucked a pile of papers and a sunglasses case from the front seat and held them in his lap while she settled. She took them from him and tossed them into a backseat already crowded with manila folders and three bottles of red wine speeding toward an early grave on direct rays of the sun. Her upholstery smelled of chewing gum (mango-orange). The Post-it on the dashboard advised: *This is the first day of the rest of your life.*

Les asked, "Do you still have the wine, Claire?"

"Yes, CJ put nitrogen in the bottle to preserve it. I want you to find out what's being rumored about this, who thinks who might have done it. Stuff like that. Who's considered gutsy enough to bring a bottle in a cedar box to my husband's doorstep, knowing that's not allowed. Go see a man named Larry Carradine who helps CJ with gossipy stuff now and then—make sure you get there in the morning because by afternoon he's generally blotto. How *do* you plan to get around, Lester?"

"I have a car."

She reached into the backseat, located the leather strap of her purse, dragged it forward. "You're going to need some—what do they call it?—walking-around money."

Les walked straight to Glass Act, in the early stages of awakening. "My good man," he said to Ben, "the bill, if you please."

Ben stared, then brought up the past-due accounts on his screen and turned the computer so Les could see. "Read it and weep."

Les extracted his wallet from the pocket of jeans going in the seams and took out two hundred-dollar bills, part of the advance, remembering the tendons in Claire Craven-Jones's lovely neck. He spread the bills on cracked,

damp varnish that had long ago ceased to protect wood
of no discernible species.

Ben stared at the money as if at an incubating virus.
"Will you look at this?" he said.

# CHAPTER THREE

*Home*

# 1

THE LITTLE GIRL'S ARM was weightless, soft as down. Sara Hutt Beale held it gently, smiling as she brought the syringe forward, wishing this patient would listen to her mother and look away. But outsized, liquid brown eyes held her, as if Sara possessed something more valuable by far than smallpox vaccine. "What a brave little girl," she said, withdrawing the needle and pressing a cotton ball against the exposed shoulder. Still Esmeralda smiled: this was an adventure, not just a visit to the clinic. She wasn't to be distracted even by pain and watched intently as Sara dropped the lot into the wastebasket and picked up the white index card on the desk.

"*Gracias, señora.*" Esmeralda's summery dress had been ironed for the visit; she wore dark pumps more suitable for church. "*No mas?*"

"*No, todo está buen'.*"

Sara touched the girl's shoulder again. "It may be sore," she added in her just-serviceable Spanish. Everyone working at the Doc Shop was supposed to be fluent, still a problem for Sara. She dipped into the canister of low-dose aspirin tablets in the bag in the lower right-hand drawer. "No more than three a day," she told the girl's mother. "*Comprende?*"

"*Sí. Muchas gracias.*"

"*De nada. Adiós, Esmeralda.*"

These people had such grace. Sara had dealt with Mexicans all her life and still could not explain how they maintained it in the face of so much uncertainty—work, medical care, commuting between this valley and the shadowy laborer-generating matrix south of the border.

"*Adiós,*" whispered the girl. "*Adiós,* doc-tor," trailing her mother, leaning back so her little face, framed by the circular white collar, was the last thing to exit, still expecting not a cure but a revelation: how had the señora ended up in a white tunic?

Sara's cell phone came alive. She glanced at the number but didn't answer. Instead, she sat and watched a big yellow gondola full of grapes trundle up Caterina's Main Street. The crush was on, the most stressful season, when the grapes were ready but not yet harvested, a year's efforts and expenditures hanging in the balance, made worse this year by the shortage of pickers and wine buyers. The prospect of financial reversal went right up the valley's social spine, the anxiety palpable in everyone from migrants sleeping under the bridges to the blue-jeaned proprietress of the secondhand bookstore across the street.

Hot wind from the desert had dried out the grapes

and further unhinged people. The ocean's moisture that usually seeped into the Bay at night and worked its way up the river had been repelled by the wind's turning east, a vast, atmospheric blowout from the much vaster Central Valley. Evil, sweat-soaked days were temporary reminders that where Sara lived would be a desert but for the proximity of the Pacific. Without its cool, constant antidote to drought and biological anarchy, the entire view would be of chaparral, not Cabernet Sauvignon.

The publicist at her father's winery, Tina Schupe, kept calling: the annual Hutt Family Estates harvest party and latest Copernicus vintage release were in the making, and would Sara attend this year? Maybe. Sara had a job already: physician's assistant, taken in large part to avoid such beseeching and responsibility. Of course she could still be made to feel guilty about this, and when the day came would no doubt drop herself like a dollop of beurre manié into the hot cauldron of winery politics and promotion. But Tina Schupe's call sounded too urgent for mere party planning.

Sara had passed up lunch so she could leave early. She worked only four days a week and was trying to command the lingo, which meant studying. She took off the white coat, an old-fashioned touch but a reassuring one to many who came to the clinic, particularly the men. When they called her "Doctor," she had at first corrected them, but explaining the difference between an assistant and a medical technician was difficult.

The most serious maladies resulted from neglected

pregnancies and wounds, usually involving heavy ma-
chinery. Throw in the odd toxic shock and snakebite
from the valley's unique subspecies of rattler that lay up
in the vines in the early days of harvest, and you had the
routine of the part-time *médica* giving authorized polio,
rubella, and chickenpox vaccinations and wondering
why she'd come back to the valley when she could have
gone to Oregon, or Bangladesh.

Sara hung the coat behind the door and caught sight
of herself in the mirror: bobbed hair the color of ma-
hogany that hid her face when she leaned over a patient.
So much for the utility of butch cuts. High forehead
without her father's overshadowing brow, thank God,
and dark lashes trending laterally to the edges of what
were her late mother's eyes. Gray was how Sara described
them, of a hue that in the right light was liquid marble.
She liked having her mother's eyes but had never admitted this to anyone, not even her now-estranged husband.

The anteroom was empty except for a large woman in
black stretch pants asleep on the bench, her cane propped
against one dimply thigh, waiting for Dr. Gomez. On the
immaculate sand-colored wall above her were the words
MAMÁS Y BEBÉS SANOS and a bright print in the style of
Diego Rivera: blocky men and women laboring in distant fields not unlike those outside, where the September sun spread an awful clarity and rising thermals made
the trees along the river dance.

Squinting behind big wraparound shades, she hur-
ried to her car, opened the door, and stepped back from
the blast of hot air. She powered the windows down and

listened to the air conditioner howl in the depths of her
aging Honda. A haze rose behind it for which she felt
guilty, again. "You will get the oil changed," she told herself, one more glance in the mirror to check her pale pink
lip gloss, then out onto the highway between a pickup
and a stretch limo.

She picked up coffee at the bakery, dense with crois-
sants and gorgeous inventions in flour smelling of almond and glazed sugar, left over from morning rush.
Customers were fewer than in times past: tourists in
Bermudas and baseball caps, two locals in straw hats and
khaki shirts, one of them calling, "Yo, Sara."

She drove on through town, past shops with sales on
outsized glass globes and designer clothes, counters of
satellite showrooms of the best-known wineries, the
racks empty. No one was admitting it, but sales of Cabernet Sauvignon, what the valley was all about, were
down thirty percent, the official figure. Fifty was more
like it. Big corporations were circling costly start-ups
that could be had for a fraction of an investment in new
tanks, hospitality rooms, and acres of bright steel cables
holding up the vines.


Turning into the Hutt Family Estates, she found herself
gently time-machined from the twenty-first to the nineteenth century: manicured gravel drive; big, dappling
live oaks obscuring the electronic surveillance cameras;
a heavy-gauge steel gate matching the white wooden
fence; and vines trellised in the old manner, with red

and white roses planted at the row ends. Beyond stood her father's prized walnut trees, another living tribute to the past, the trunks painted a correct historic white, and a prune grove deep in shadow. A dozen rows of wheat stood beyond that, a demonstration plot for wine enthusiasts enamored of the authenticity of diverse agriculture. Schoolchildren brought up regularly from the city could see what the valley had looked like when recent European immigrants lived here and nourished their crops with the natural bounty of roaming livestock.

As if summoned by these expectations, sheep waded belly-deep in native bluestem grass, bright as sunlit cumulus. A signboard built by a cabinetmaker had been erected next to the driveway, stating in tasteful gold leaf: THE HUTT FAMILY SEEKS TO PRESERVE WHAT IS BEST AND MOST LASTING IN THE VALLEY, AND TO KEEP IT FREE OF THE DISCORD OF OUR MODERN WORLD. OUR UNCOMPROMISING GOAL IS TO PRODUCE HARMONY IN A SPECIAL PLACE, AND A WINE—COPERNICUS—OF SUCH EXCEPTIONAL QUALITY THAT IT WILL LIVE AND NOURISH GENERATIONS TO COME.

Not mentioned was the fact that the place had been a calf-and-cow operation of great squalor when Sara's father purchased it. The rancher had filled the streambed with trash and grease-stained, axle-sprung tractors; threatened tourists trying to turn around in his rutted road; and had to be evicted by the sheriff after firing a bullet through the side of his own pickup. The original house had been demolished and replaced with the beautiful confection now coming into view, a perfect if greatly outsized replica of a Victorian farmstead, with period siding, a long porch behind rampant rosemary, and guest quarters cleverly disguised as a California water tower. The handsome weathered barn, with its big hay boom and unsullied horse stalls, cleverly designed, massively built, fronted a thoroughly modern winery set into the hill.

Looking at that weather vane imported from Vermont, Sara felt the force of the dream that had set all this in motion, and the weight of the unforeseen, unhappy, possibly calamitous present. The winery was in trouble, the family dysfunctional, and Sara's own prospects as bleak as they had ever been. The speed with which this had all come about stunned and saddened her.

She parked in the lot, known as the Grove, and went in through the tasting room. The pourer on duty waved cheerily as Sara passed the display racks of wine paraphernalia and monogrammed polo shirts she detested. In the lab, Michael Phane sat with elbows propped on either side of an equipment catalog. She said, "Hi, Michael."

He had arrived more than a decade before with a confidence so assured as to be comical, the lean-beaked, handsome wunderkind. He had made his bones at Vin-Monde and, at an even bigger salary, was hired to turn Copernicus into a powerhouse. Michael's unyielding nature had been shaped in the hallowed halls of UC Davis, to make his own version of rocket juice and so transform the dross of a mere family operation into a *premier cru*. Nowadays, however, he was mostly silent.

"Where's Jerome?" she asked.

"Haven't seen him."

Never easy, she thought, working for my father. The tension showed in Michael's shallow breathing and flared nostrils, seemingly carved from tallow. Declining sales had proved the big oversight in Michael's otherwise carefully orchestrated career.

She left the lab and went back outside. The heat of the sun radiated from the crush pad, the winepress silent, a big mauve drape molded to its expensive contours. The Italians could make even a tarp look good. Meanwhile other machines crooned, and front-end loaders shuttled in and out of deep shadow. How had little Hutt Family Estates become an industrial complex, Sara wondered, corporate values taking over their little clan so utterly?

Coming out of the office, a figure in black, like a lovely exclamation point: Tina Schupe, without her sculpted sunglasses. She resembled a figure in a hard-edged Dalí landscape, beaten by imaginary winds and her stature magnified by those rising thermals. She had seen Jerome through prostate surgery, hip replacement, and shoulder reconstruction, helped him deal with his wife before she died, and coddled his ego-stricken architects and forever-adolescent friends. Now she walked up to Sara and said, "There's something you should know."

But the cell phone in her fist was mewing. Ignoring it, Tina added, "Jerome's in L.A. He needs you to do something. He needs you to talk to Eduardo."

Sara understood: Alyssa, her stepmother, wanted to

sell Hutt Family Estates and no one else did. She held
forty-nine shares of the winery's one hundred, Sara held
twenty-five, and her father twenty-one, the minimum
required to be managing partner. That left five shares.
Sara had always assumed those were assigned to Tina,
who deserved them, but now saw that they had gone to
Eduardo Cardinal instead, the original vineyard manager who had turned a barren, cow-stricken wasteland
into prized vineyards. So old Eduardo was, ironically, in
control.

"Alyssa's already been to see him, so Jerome wants
you to sort this out. He has absolute faith in Eduardo,
that's the tack."

Sara nodded, dutiful to the end. "Okay. We have absolute faith in Eduardo. Bottom line."

# 2

THE VALLEY HAD LOST all evidence of the morning's moisture under the hot sky, except the deeply green corrugation of vines and the long, sinuous hardwood canopy above the unseen river. Sara drove into Browntown, part of a large subdivision of middle-income Anglos in redwood ranchers, with views of sunrise and sunset over different mountain ranges, lap pools, and names and credos on mailboxes. But turn left at the oleanders and another world unfolds: old clapboard bungalows with deep porches, densely planted gardens, lawn furniture, and pickups and outboards on trailers sharing the narrow streets with tawny kids and the occasional storage pod doubling as a soccer goal.

Sara had first come here at sixteen, to the Cardinals' Cinco de Mayo party. During those early years, she had regularly found herself on the porch, under hanging gourds trailing blossoms, talking to Eduardo about soil and vines and everything related to the business of what in those days really was a family winery. Noisy children wobbled past on trainer bikes and older ones inspected their cars. Sara was one day to take over the vineyard operation, maybe even the winemaking—that was the tacit understanding, or so she thought. But as things turned out, it wasn't even close.

She walked from car to front steps, glimpsing Pia in the picture window, smiling but fearful, Sara knew, of some breach of decorum. Eduardo had the door open before she could touch it. *"Hola!"*

Creased jeans, snap-button shirt, leather sandals with dark socks: that was Eduardo. His old face, creased at intervals like an otherwise perfect melon, was set with dark eyes, one of them hazy. A cataract lifted from the other, but laser technology had come too late to save this one. "Sara," he said, taking her hand in two of his, warmly, but no embrace unless she initiated it, "you come in here and sit. It has been a long time. Now, Pia, what can we give this beautiful young woman? You're too skinny, if I can say that to a . . ." searching for a word, one that would surely not offend, *"médica."*

She put her arms around him, then around Pia; it was like hugging the same warm person twice. "So nice to see you," she said. "Please, nothing to eat, thank you."

But there must be something—coffee, sopaipillas with powdered sugar. Did this wonderful person ever stop cooking? Sara knew the drill well: sit on the couch with the tartan plaid, watch the Fiesta saucer arrive on the low table with *National Geographic*s stacked under glass.

Eduardo winced as he settled into his lounger. By the

time the fancy new winery had been built, Eduardo was already history, Hutt Family Estates' *former* major-domo. "So," he said, "how are thing's going?"

"Not so well, Eduardo." She wanted to ask outright what he had done with his shares, but one didn't put questions directly to Eduardo Cardinal. The more insistent the query, the more elusive the subject, his head resting against the spotless antimacassar. She heard sounds from the kitchen and knew she would drink the coffee even though her caffeine tolerance had already been exceeded. "This is a bad time," she added. "Talk of selling has gotten serious. The family's trying to deal with it, and you're part of that."

"Yes?"

"Of course. I know about your shares. If Alyssa tenders hers, there could be a vote."

Outside, children at some game, the sound hopeful, as heedless as hopscotch. Then she was thinking not of financial squabbling but of making love to her husband-to-be the first time, on Potrero Hill in south San Francisco, and listening to similar sounds of schoolchildren playing outside. Maybe if, right after he became her husband, he had joined the Copernicus team, things would have worked out. But over time Jerome decided that Fred Covington Beale, transplanted East Coast graduate of the Wharton School, had a bothersome sense of the absurd and lacked drive. The truth was that Jerome was unable to turn anything over to anyone else, including Sara. Jerome been playing her, and probably Eduardo, all along.

"The shares your father gave to me," said Eduardo softly. "I never asked. They weren't worth much in those days."

"They might not be worth much today, either. It's a bad time to sell, but Alyssa's set on it."

"I don't have anything to do with that now. Paco's in charge of such things. Pia, where's that coffee?"

"I guess I need to talk to Paco."

"Not today. My son's at the cockfights at the compound, and"—the old man's cackle surprised her—"you don' go there, Sarita."

Workers' access to the sprawling Abruzzini vineyards was an ungated dirt road far from the winery complex, a living compound that had survived intact for 150 years. For more than half of those, it had been in the grip of the Abruzzinis, as Sara, like anyone long in the valley, well knew. This same road passed beneath elms that had managed to survive close to the mountain's moisture dump, then snaked around to the north and down toward a random collection of clapboard shacks, with big sheds for heavy equipment in the shade of creek-watered oaks.

For all their sins, the Abruzzinis had the foresight to build worker housing long before that became an unavoidable political issue, since even the worst land now was valuable beyond anyone's earlier dreams. The frightening decrease in wine sales and the simultaneous upward trajectory of bankruptcies did little to ease the autumnal demand for men and women with bandannas tied around their heads and collars buttoned against the dawn cold and insects. Not tending to the vines would have been a vintner's admission of apocalypse, but the lack of vineyard expansion had significantly cut into the ranks of labor. Sara could see it in the large numbers of immigrants outside the gourmet market in Caterina every morning, hoping for work.

Evening was already on the base of the western range. Cars parked at random angles under the trees had open windows and some raised hoods, men in shirtsleeves delving into the mechanics. From inside the old redwood barn, trailing bits of lathe in the weeds, came an indecipherable clamor. The man sitting inside the entranceway watched her. He wore an old-fashioned white cotton dress shirt, free hanging, the pocket crowded with cell phone and a pack of Marlboros, an ax handle propped against the wall beside him. She said, "*Con permiso.*"

"You want to go in, señora?"

"*Sí.*" He couldn't refuse her, but she had complicated his life. "I won't stay," she promised.

"They pay five dollar."

The only woman in the enormous, shadowy hall, she held back from the crowd. The cigarette smoke, the shadows, and the dust conspired to limit her visibility. Three dozen men, mostly young, stood on pallets, absorbed in the negotiations under a single dangling bulb above bare earth. Two tattooed figures in tank tops held roosters under their arms, the gorgeous russet tail plumage extending behind them, the birds' beaks, inches apart, outthrust, their round, uncomprehending eyes murderous.

The birds' owners leaned over another man, with a chamois on his upraised palm. Arrayed there was what looked like jewelry: hooked blades, the light glinting from honed steel. Maybe coming here wasn't such a hot idea. First one spectator and then another turned to face the crowd, holding up folded bills, deft fingers panto-miming the ever-changing odds.

No sight of Paco, or any face she knew. Most old-line Hispanic families wouldn't touch this ritual that be-longed to another time and different class, these all transients willing to risk arrest and, for some, deporta-tion. The handlers were lashing blades to the roosters' legs with leather thongs and sucking on their bloodred combs to further enrage them, the combatants coming alive in their hands. Sara saw the tattoo of a spiderweb around the elbow of one handler and a bright Mexican flag unfurling down the arm of the other that rippled with his flexing triceps. They set the birds on the dirt a few feet apart, still pinning their wings, and thrust their beaks together.

At a signal from the referee, the birds were released and instantly at each other, leaping, their strikes so quick Sara couldn't tell which, if any, struck. In the me-lee of feet and feathers, the handlers rushed forward to separate the birds, stood them off, released them again. One of the roosters stood stupidly, as if having second thoughts, and this time Sara glimpsed the thrust—so quick, seemingly inconsequential—and saw the other bird's svelte length of plumage stretch out as if to sleep, eyelids in spasm, a dark stain creeping onto the hardpan.

Everyone was shouting. A dozen men pressed close to the handlers, some laughing, others angry. The owner of the vanquished stood over his contender and spat. He shouted, *"Chinga su madre!"*

Something had gone wrong in that brief, furious pageant, leaving the loser and a bookie inches apart, the men around them taking sides. And then Paco Cardinal, in a plaid shirt with rhinestone snaps, was there, almost casually shoving his way into the middle of the arena. He grasped the loser's shoulders and hurled the man aside, herding him toward the far end of the shed. The crowd followed, including Sara, passing a boy squatting next to the dead rooster and plucking it in a vengeful storm of russet feathers.

Outside again, Sara stood in the deep shadow of the trees. Someone turned on headlights; in the sudden glare, the loser took the litany of abuse while Paco, off to one side, slipped on yellow calfskin gloves, fitting each finger and tugging at the bottoms. He stepped into the middle of the harangue and backhanded the loser, and the man instinctively raised his fists. Even Sara knew that was a mistake. Her desire to resolve family business right here was, she realized, inappropriate and self-indulgent. This was present reality, and watching Paco knock the guy around heightened her awareness of the vulnerability of human beings' soft tissue.

Paco's victim walked unsteadily away, trying to maintain some dignity. When he turned to spit, she saw that his mouth was full of blood and she might have been of some assistance. But to approach now would doubly humiliate him, so she fled into the assembling darkness and the sound of revving engines. Her car was parked up the road and she stepped aside to avoid a lowrider passing in a clamorous cloud of mariachi and laughter, lavender and pink neon emanating from beneath restored running boards of an old '70s muscle car, wondering who among these laborers could afford such a fancy rig. Then she saw that it was the one who had rented out the honed killing spurs and she caught the smell of pot. What exactly was Paco Cardinal doing in this crowd?

She was about to get into her car when she heard the sonorous rattle of a big diesel behind her and turned to see the pickup on oversized tires, silver hubs, pale blue supercab. In the light of the dash, Paco smiled, as if he and Sara were meeting by chance on a country lane. His window smoothly descended, and he said, "Hello, Doctor. What brings you down to the native quarter?"

"You beat the crap out of that guy, Paco."

"He deserved it. Bet against himself, then slipped aspirin up the bird's ass. If I hadn't done something, one of these guys would have cut him."

"How comforting."

Cars lined up behind him, the drivers content to wait and watch. Paco pulled ahead and parked and cut the engine. He climbed down and walked back. She said, "Eduardo told me you were here."

"I figured."

"I know you and your father have a small interest in the winery. That's what I wanted to talk about."

"Eduardo's out of that now."

"Okay, then you have the interest. I also know that you've had a discussion with Alyssa."

"Let's talk in the vineyard. People live on this road, you know."

Without waiting for her to respond, he crossed to the trellised rows of flatland Cabernet, a dark mass against the faint orange glow of a rising moon. Sara hesitated, alive to the danger. How had she—how had everyone— ended up here? "Paco, please don't go along with Alyssa. If you tender your shares with hers, the winery, everything, will go on the block."

"Our bit doesn't amount to jack squat."

"It's enough. Alyssa wouldn't have gone to Eduardo if there was any other way, believe me. But it's not in your family's interests to cash out now. From what I understand, the winery's debt is enormous, and you and Alyssa, all of us, won't have anything left after selling into this market."

"The shares were supposed to be Eduardo's reward for all the cut-rate work he did for Jerome." His laughter was dry as the September night. "I already told Alyssa I'd meet with her."

"Talk to Jerome first, please. You owe him that."

"I don't owe him a thing," Paco said and put a hand on her shoulder. He stepped closer. The smell of his aftershave took her back to that other vineyard and an earlier time that Paco had apparently never left.

"But promise me you'll talk to Jerome before you make a decision," she said, little space between them now.

"On one condition."

"Paco, don't say something you'll regret."

"I never do."

His hand was still on her shoulder. She remembered the short, straight blow that same hand had delivered and the way the man's head had snapped back as if he had no vertebrae. Paco said, "Put your arms around me."

"Don't be stupid."

"Are you afraid of me, Sara?"

"No."

"Do you trust me?" His lips were close to her ear.

"Not entirely."

"Well, it's no big thing, anyway."

He had a yoke of muscle across the shoulders; everything about him, sternum to knees, was solid. She wouldn't get out of this grip if he decided otherwise, his ever-so-bristly cheek against hers, irrepressible lungs crushing her chest. Many may want to make love to this guy, but no way you're going to.

"Say, 'We're from such different places.'"

"Paco . . ."

"Say it."

"'We're from such different places.'"

"Say, 'Someday, maybe, but not now.'"

Had she really been that irresponsible and cruel, so many years ago? Sara had completely forgotten the words she now dutifully repeated, wondering at their effect, more enduring than all hers and Paco's dreams. Neither spoke for a while. He might have pushed it, given the old, mindless provocation, but he released her. "I'll speak to Jerome," he said, "but beyond that, no promises."

# 3

SARA WENT HOME, to the bungalow on the far edge of
Hutt Family Estates, a few independent acres far removed from the Copernicus phenomenon. She put the
teakettle on the celery-green Viking range, the kitchen's
only extravagance, and pulled open the deck doors, feeling the hot breath of late afternoon as if a seal had been
broken. The smell of things growing traveled on some
ambient moisture, almost tangible, all of it from the little overgrown vineyard next door, as different from her
father's enterprise as day from night.

Her house, built in a long-ago California, had been
the only truly historic structure on the Hutts' newly ac-
quired property, an abandoned school full of wasps and
once a scorpion, where she had played as a kid. She discovered ruler lines on one wall where students once stood
to be measured, and names recorded with a blunt pencil
like runic notations from another world. Then she was
grown, and the wall painted over, supporting a bookshelf

in which her eclectic library, brought from the city after she and Fred split up, was massed. But those children still lived behind the shelves and under the expensive lemony latex from Restoration Hardware, giving her a strange but pleasant sense of community.

One bedroom, shower outside—watch for rattlers in the lavender—kitchen *without* an island, original Douglas fir floors, sash windows with wavy panes, and a little deck under spreading, messy eucalyptus the Copernicus vineyard manager would dearly love to cut. The vines were all downwind of her place and so were the chemicals dispensed by Copernicus's masked, white-suited specters riding mechanical sprayers.

Shortly before she was married, some men had showed up in a shiny Land Rover with surveying equipment, maps, shovels, GPS gadgets, and cameras and taken off for the far reaches of the Hutt Family Estates. They replotted, dug around rock piles, took photos of ancient redwood grape stakes left in the brush by early Italian settlers, and at the end of the process presented plans for lot-line adjustments and old house sites "authenticated" with the help of accountants, lawyers, and a couple of compliant academics.

Densely argued applications were then presented to the county for exceptions to zoning laws, sanctioned by a bureaucrat and—presto—the Hutts had many new, valuable real estate lots. But Jerome bequeathed the land to the local land trust, with much ceremony, claiming to have protected the valley from further development, receiving huge tax deductions in the process.

One specific beneficiary was, of course, Sara. Jerome gave her the old schoolhouse on three acres strung narrowly along the western property line like an old isolate principality, with a little covered reservoir up the mountain where purified winery wastewater was stored. The house, a fixer-upper if there ever was one, had been a prewedding present that Fred, after he and Sara were married, rarely visited, even this proximity to Jerome being more than he could bear.

She never forgot her disappointment at Fred's first reaction—not aversion but indifference. She had wanted him to love the house as she did, but all he could think of was in-laws just over the hill. Even hiking the mountain was no relief, since the view contained the winery and the rest of it. Driving up together from San Francisco on weekends became rarer, and then it was Sara driving alone, wondering how her husband and his friends from the brokerage firm were faring of a Saturday in front of a television set or at Candlestick Park or wherever.

Meanwhile she went back to school and earned a nursing degree. The idea was to return to the valley and do something valuable, unrelated to wine, and be content with a new self-chosen, truncated life. To sit—alone, it turned out—on the deck and look not at Copernicus but in the other direction, as she did now, tea mug in hand, feeling a stray eucalyptus button under one bare foot, at her other scruffy little neighbor, Puddle-jump.

Grass grew lushly between those rows of vines, studded with opportunistic white daisies, a former stock pond overhung with sedge and wild gooseberry, and dimpled

by rising bass. Mismatched trellising, no plastic irrigation tubing—cult farming, people said. Cow horns filled
with manure and buried for the winter, planting by
phases of the moon.

It was Puddle-jump's frogs Sara heard on spring evenings, Puddle-jump's flowers she smelled in the prevail-
ing westerly breeze, a real historic barn she overlooked:
sere gray boards lit by the rising sun, a swaybacked shed
covering a laughable little hybrid tractor that the owner,
Cotton Harrell—aka Calamity Harrell—plugged into an
electric feed every evening and that often stalled in the
vineyard the next morning. Cotton would then just sit
under the solar panel that also served as a sunblock, as if
waiting for the cavalry.

Rarely did Cotton use the old wicker rockers on the
porch of a paint-needy house not much bigger than hers.
When he did, he held an unopened book in his lap. Sara
liked Cotton, had known him since she was a teenager,
when he was getting his vineyard started, although he
was already one of Jerome's professional casualties. Sara
had heard all about Cotton's river conservation, had
watched Cotton and his girlfriend living there and even
felt oddly, weirdly jealous, and then her own life had
sharply intervened and the next time she looked, the girlfriend was gone and so was Fred.

The details of Cotton's relationship with her father
were ugly. Sara knew them all. Often she watched Cotton cross her meadow, rangy, determined, his walk un-
mistakable. No outsider was allowed on the Hutt Family

Estates, but Cotton Harrell came anyway and often turned on her that angular face, eyes in shadow, teeth bright in a smile she knew well by now, his hand lifted in a hail or a farewell, she was never sure which.

# 4

HE HAD CAUGHT AND RELEASED brook trout in the steep streams of the Blue Ridge since he was old enough to handle a four-weight fly rod. Cotton Harrell would remember for all time the first dusky gold, indigo-flecked creature that fought valiantly and emerged wet and glistening as if from an alternate reality, its wondrous lubricity and the way it looked up at him through the luminous lens of a beautiful and unblinking eye.

He had wanted to be a stream ecologist since he was ten, before he ever heard the term and long before it had moved into the common realm. So he was spared the agonies of choosing a profession that his friends underwent at the University of Virginia, passing through all phases of natural science with ease and planning to move directly into a doctoral program in the land of his dreams. But Stanford didn't see it that way. Berkeley did find a spot for the promising son of an information specialist working for the U.S. Department of the Interior who wished he had done something else with his life, and one muggy August dawn the two of them—father and son—struck out from Washington, D.C.'s, thriving urbs on the banks of the Potomac.

They fly-fished their way west, notably the Yellowstone and the Gallatin rivers, the Henry's Fork, the Snake, the Boise, and in little streams rising on both slopes of the Sierra Nevada. In all that time they ate exactly one trout, a clueless cutthroat (*Oncorhynchus clarkii*) hooked in the eye by mistake outside Jackson Hole. It wouldn't have survived anyway, and Cotton was unsentimental about how the natural world functioned, but even the loss of a single fish bothered him.

By the end of the trip, he had read *The Structure of Scientific Revolutions* by Thomas Kuhn, begun outside Lincoln, Nebraska, while his father drove, and started *Personal Knowledge: Towards a Post-Critical Philosophy* by Michael Polanyi, a chemist. Those two books destroyed everything he thought he knew about science, and he told his father, "I'm switching to philosophy."

"You never left it."

Later, his father gripped the back of Cotton's neck, said, "It's your life," and boarded a plane back to Washington, D.C.

Cotton drove down to the university by the Bay, where the dean didn't think much of his conversion. The elaborate funding apparatus set up for doctoral students would collapse the following Monday, so he randomly drove around while deciding and, in the valley, tasted an amazingly good red wine on the banks of an insignificant little river, behind the town of Caterina.

In the vineyards, Mexicans, Anglos, men and women, worked without the assistance of large machines, except for some with propellers on towers like alien craft long since assimilated. He decided to take a year off and meanwhile to work, as it turned out, in the famous Abruzzini Winery, scraping liver-colored tendrils of rubbery mold off the bottoms of massive redwood casks. His knowledge of riverine biology got him promoted to hose hauler, washing down the insides of fermentation tanks and plastic bins recently brimming with blue-black grapes. His entomological fluency got him promoted from there to collecting insects in the vineyard, on the lookout for glassy-winged sharpshooters and imprisoning them in jars.

His basic experience doing research led to a series of apprenticeships around the valley and to a knowledge of wine from the bottom up. In his spare time he walked the river, rented a canoe when the water was high enough, talked to the odd fisherman although there were few of those, trout being practically nonexistent and migrating salmon and steelhead elusive shadows panicking in the skinny autumn riffles. He met Mexicans who slept under the bridges and bathed while grape gondolas and tour buses passed overhead, and everywhere he saw evidence of erosion and a falling water table in exposed tree roots and sloughing gravels.

———

One year became two, and he weaned himself from the corporate wineries and went with the independents, all obsessed with capturing the essence of the grape, where Cotton's knowledge of chemistry and his uncanny ability to associate various tastes with their components proved an asset. Then an odd thing began to happen: his interest in water and the critters in it lessened, while his interest in wine and the compounds in it increased.

He took crash courses at Davis, sometimes careening up the winding road toward the university before dawn and back again at night, his trunk full of winemaking and other paraphernalia that spoke to him in the curves. He found himself thrown in with the polyglot assemblage of enthusiasts who had, like Cotton, abandoned more respectable careers for one both tenuous and consuming. They formed a diverse itinerant priesthood of sorts, pursuing something as infinite, inspiring, and elusive as any god he knew of.

He agreed to make wine according to a computer-generated formula for a Silicon Valley consultant who drove up on weekends and liked to get his fingers purple and operate the front-end loader as a kind of therapy. This consultant let Cotton use his facilities to make his own wine too, from Cabernet Sauvignon grapes Cotton tended himself, picked according to his notion of ripeness, and paid the consultant for. He slipped a bottle of this to a fat English wine critic on one of his passes through subsistence-level winemaking in the valley, and to Cotton's amazed delight got a mention in Craven-Jones's sidebar, "Ramblings Roundup" ( ... *intense red berry* . . . ). The wine Cotton was paid to make didn't get a mention, and he got fired.

"What do you need?" his father had asked over the phone, sounding very far away.

"Three hundred and seventy-five thousand dollars," said Cotton. "Thirty-seven thousand in cash, with a loan guarantee and you cosigning."

Seven acres, a bit of vineyard, a little frame house separating from its porch, swaybacked barn unsuitable for much, head-pruned Petite Syrah vines, and a concrete fermentation tank for making home wine from excess dropped fruit, dark with age and that grape's dense pigmentation. Classic story, a fluke, really: man dies, wife wants out of a decade-long feud with a calf-and-cow operation next door.

He just happened to hear about it after following a stream up from the river, a hobby now, collecting caddis larvae, and seeing the woman hanging out her dead husband's clothes that she planned to donate to charity. The place, not yet on the market, was run-down and had a crazy neighbor. The rarely surprised real estate mavens in the valley were near apoplectic when Cotton bought it for less—a lot less—than what it was worth and moved in, sleeping in the living room and cooking on his Coleman camp stove, listening to wood rats in the walls.

He knew what was required in the vineyard but had never done the actual work. As if evoked by his need, two Mexicans showed up who had worked harvests for the former owner and offered to do the same for Cotton. They were from Michoacán and knew the place as if it were their own, showing him how to prune in winter, the three of them warming their hands at flames leaping from stacked vine cuttings, the smoke acrid and quite wonderful, roiling the cold February air under conifer-green mountains.

The Michoacanos showed him how to pick in the fall, then disappeared, only to reappear like deft, calloused butterflies at ease in the natural world. It seemed that a year passed before he looked again in the hall mirror and saw a skinnier version going gray at the verges, behind him stacked cases of his own wine, some made in that old concrete tank and the rest at a custom crush outfit out on the highway. Wine crates filled every room, the weight of them threatening to bring the house down before he crawled underneath with a hydraulic jack and cinder blocks.

So much wine made dating a problem, the women put off by a house with a single narrow corridor between cartons leading directly from front door to bedroom. Only one found it amusing, Jill: compact, with physical ease that comes from doing things outdoors—surfing in frigid waters off the Marin headlands—and not blond. Jill had worked at Abruzzini when Cotton was there, and then they ran into each other at the bakery. Jill had her own little public relations firm on a back street in Caterina, and Cotton was a vintner barely worthy of the title, each touched by the other's independence.

Jill moved in on what she called a provisional basis.

He told her, sitting on the front porch—no chairs—"I won't ask you to push my wine if you won't ask me to help your clients. We'll meet in the middle, between our professions," and she said, "Deal."

His parents came out to meet her, and Jill's—she called them Marin-iacs—drove over from Bolinas. Cotton called her Scout because she took care of everybody; she called him Calamity because he talked too much about ecological consequences of human activity. They were an unlikely couple, everyone agreed, she outgoing and bemused by his taciturnity, he captivated by her resilience and desperately in love.

5

COTTON'S WINE BECAME KNOWN for an intensity attributable to old-fashioned, risky methods, and also depended on the happy accidents of good slope. His was one of the few reputed "white man" vineyards in the valley, mostly put in by him though with indispensable cohorts. Cotton named it Puddle-jump, after the pond, and gave whimsical names to his lesser blends: Tadpole (Cabernet Franc), Dragonfly (triaged Cab Sauvignon, Cab Franc, and Merlot). Puddle-jump, his estate wine, was all dark and delicious Cabernet Sauvignon, in need of some aging, and he sold it all from the winery and pocketed money that might have gone to middlemen.

The critic for the *San Francisco Chronicle* liked Puddle-jump, which helped a lot, and he got another mention, this one in a long list of California comers in *The New York Times*, which pleased his father. But the journals were something else again. A pompous ass called from *The Wine Taster* and told Cotton that the names of his wines were trivial and his approach too pants' seat. "You have to get serious," one Kevin Nomonity intoned, and Cotton said, "I am serious, you jerk," and hung up.

Only later did he learn of the caller's influence, and that he, Cotton Harrell, had made a serious mistake, one that dismayed Jill while at the same time sending her into fits of hilarity.

Clyde Craven-Jones proved to be a problem of a different sort. He showed up one day, sweating in a panama hat and open-collar shirt thin as toilet paper, holding a black notebook secured with a rubber band. Almost too big to fit into the renovated tool shop, Craven-Jones tasted from barrels and tasted from bottles, spraying purple wine indiscriminately, panting and scribbling. "The wines are good," he said, "but too tannic. Why mask the marvelous fruit California offers?"

"It just needs time to develop."

"Mr. Harrell, people don't have time these days. And harvest more sunshine, let the alcohol hold sway." And the famous critic was gone.

Cotton heard that the cattle-spawning dust-and-mud province next door had been bought by a wealthy real estate developer from L.A. named Hutt. He had grand plans for a vineyard, house, and winery, no expense spared, and almost anything would be an improvement, Cotton thought. At the property line, he noticed a black SUV full of expectant faces and a man wearing cowboy boots, a new plaid shirt, and a baseball cap—the uniform of new arrivals—getting out. He and Cotton shook hands across the fence. "I'm going to be the best neighbor you ever had," said Jerome Hutt, "and this is going to be the valley's showcase, with wine to match."

"If I can help you, let me know."

"I've heard you're a wonderful human being."

"A what?" asked Jill later.

"I've been telling you that all along," said Cotton, and they both had a good laugh.

Within a week, a new post appeared near the lower corner of Cotton's property, and when he walked down he saw another, and two caballeros putting in a third. He told them to stop, and in their long regard he plainly read—or liked to think he had—all the problems that lay before him.

That night the best neighbor he ever had called from Ventura. "Instead of pulling the new fence posts," Hutt said, "why don't I just buy your place? I'll give you twice what you paid for it, plus some equity in Hutt Family Estates. I'll hire you as winemaker. We can all be part of the new Margaux, the new Mouton in the valley," and Cotton said, "Puddle-jump's not for sale."

The posts were moved, though not quite enough. Cotton let it pass, not wanting to inspire Hutt to undergo a lot-line adjustment, the rich guy's way to harass his neighbors and steal some of their land. Nothing more was said about Cotton making Hutt's wine, either. Then he heard about Hutt's winery plans: tunnels, a cave of mythic proportions requiring huge machines used to cut mine shafts in Wales, and the greatest threat of all, the disruption of aquifers, trashed streams, gray water that would find its way to the river.

Cotton gave silent thanks that his property was slightly higher than Hutt's and upwind of the chemical storm soon engulfing the new vineyard. He joined other neighbors and a colorful assortment of enviros and slow-growthers to oppose the winery permit, and so began another demanding transition. His testimony proved crucial in hearings before the county's planning department and board of supervisors, and his proximity to the project meant his constant vigilance and less time at home.

Jill never objected but did point out that he was acquiring a reputation he might not want, that of zealot rather than ace winemaker, which could complicate Puddle-jump's toehold in the boutique wine market. "And the outcome of the battle," she predicted, "will be stalemate. Hutt has the best lawyers, the backing of pro-growth supervisors from the county's ass end, testimony from soil and hydrology 'experts,' and lots of money for injecting into charities and fund-raisers that help keep people muted and on the fence."

Then she came home early one afternoon and said, "Pour me a glass of Tadpole, Cotton, and give me a kiss."

She dragged him to the couch, an arm around his neck. "Okay, Jerome came into the office today and asked me to build a premier brand for him. He wants me to come up with a strategy and a campaign, the works."

"I hope you told him no."

"I didn't."

"Scout . . ."

She held up a finger. "Let me talk, please. In this business you don't wait, you don't question. Things happen fast with start-ups, much at stake. That winemaking slot just went to a star from VinMonde instead of to you. Now, to counter public outcry over the size and grandeur of his winery, Hutt's going to need more than money. He needs distinction."

"And you're going to provide it for him. You're edgy, adorable, and you know everybody. I have to give it to Hutt. Not only would he be getting talent in you, he'd be showing himself above the fray, niftily neutralizing ill will from his outsized project by hiring my girlfriend."

"Cotton, this is the opportunity I've been waiting for. Good product, money no object, a chance to make a real splash. I know Jerome's an ass, maybe a dangerous one, but I can deal with that. If it gets too bad, I'll bail. But if he's willing to make the concessions you and others want, why not give it a try? He's going to get his winery whatever you do. At least this way you can help make it better."

Cotton began to watch as if from the wrong end of a telescope as Jill's involvement with his neighbor deepened, her hours at work grew longer, demands slopping over into weekends and holidays. Her ad hoc style got less so, and more expensive: darker clothes, less of them and closer to the body, long dark hair cut low across her forehead. Lipstick, dark, and something around the eyes making them shine. That natural ease in her own physical realm added to her natural appeal. What lover could object?

Hutt came up with a name for his premier wine. "Copernicus," Jill said. "You should like that. Copernicus was a scientist."

"It's grandiose and idiotic. But otherwise just dandy."

"I've roped in one of the best label designers. He's charging Jerome a mere two hundred thousand dollars for a rendition of the sun on some kind of reflective paper."

"I designed my label on a legal pad and ran the initial batch off at Office Depot for three hundred bucks."

# 6

ONE NIGHT ON THE PORCH—rockers now, pillows—Jill said, "Cotton, I'm shutting down the agency and going to work full time for Copernicus. I'm getting a piece of the action, and the money down the line's incredible."

He was speechless.

"Jerome's committed"—it had been Jerome for what now seemed a very long time—"to having the best."

"Can we handle this?"

"Yes. Remember that, because there's more."

He should have seen it clearly then—a change of manner, a hint of resignation—but he didn't. He felt betrayed but told himself: stay rational. She would of course be the one chosen by Hutt to bring the proposal to him, and it was sophisticated, expensive, compelling: capture wastewater from the winery, purify and release it into an existing stream. Intriguing to any scientist and conceivably a standard that could be applied to every new winery in California. And if Hutt was willing to pay, who was Cotton Harrell and his merry band to oppose?

Gradually the knot of opposition began to come undone, but not until Cotton agreed to vet the new process and get mired in the details, insisting upon the best, costing Jerome Hutt a lot of money and assuming he would eventually back off. He didn't. So Cotton founded Friends of the Flow as a kind of penance for facilitating the birth of Copernicus and launched a clean-up of the river, raising money to riprap eroding river banks and observe aquatic life in situ. He collected water samples for measuring the future health of the river, learned to scuba dive to gather specimens, applied for grants, proselytized in public about bugs and salmon, even among schoolchildren, who looked at him as if he had stepped out of a spaceship. All the while he knew something precious had been lost and that it had more to do with Jill than with any endangered species of fish.

Something had begun to happen within the structure of Hutt Family Estates that Cotton heard of only indirectly and Jill wasn't privy to. She had been promised some of the action, not real estate but "brand equity," which she had created out of nothing. "Jerome wants me to release him from the early agreement," she told Cotton. "The one that promised me a percentage if the brand popped."

"Which it did."

"Right. But now percentages are somehow unwieldy, according to his lawyers. And inaccurate in view of the product's current worth. So I'm supposed to sign a waiver."

"Don't."

But she did. And life went on, more salary, trips, wine still flowed to them. Jill inquired, casually at first, about how much of the action was still hers and received no response. She wrote Jerome a note in longhand, sitting at the table on the porch, a scene that in retrospect nearly broke Cotton's heart: lovely script, pale blue ink reflecting, he imagined, the broad Pacific of Jill's childhood, the clean wind of trust and optimism blowing over her. *Do the right thing,* she wrote, and later repeated in the shower. Cotton would hear it above the rush of water and call out, "Hey, Scout, who you talking to in there?"

But it wasn't a joke. Jill was forgetting things, misplacing stuff. Cotton had to assume that this was noticed at work too. Tina Schupe, a seemingly loyal if ambitious assistant, would cover for Jill, but Jerome Hutt had radar just shy of paranoia and wasn't going to be fooled for long. One of Cotton's great regrets was that he hadn't insisted then that Jill quit and sue over the ownership issue, claim her fair market share, create a stink, pay the legal fees. But she still believed in redemption.

*Follow your decent impulses, Jerome. I know you have some. Do the right thing.*

She called Cotton from the doctor's office and said matter-of-factly, "Glioblastoma. Funny name, glee followed by an explosion."

He Googled it while waiting for her to get home: *tumor of different types of cancer cells...difficult to treat...deadly...* He began calling people then, and the responses were unrelievedly dire: do something, do it now. What followed was a farrago of consultants, the hardest to take the oncologist in his suite of costly furniture, showing that the sicker you are, the more you pay. The prospect of surgery terrified them, but there wasn't time to think about it. He longed for something encouraging to say but could only come up with, "I love you and I know it's going to be okay."

At first it looked like it might. The tumor was removed, chemo launched; Jill lost hair wholesale but in the process acquiring a new beauty, wrapped in turbans and shawls, fronted by a depthless smile. They slept entwined, grateful shipwreck survivors. Then two months into remission Jill was fired, not by Jerome or anyone at Hutt Family Estates but by a lawyer calling from Los Angeles.

Cotton was grateful in a way: at last she was free. But outrage prevailed after Jerome refused her calls, and his, and Cotton went out and climbed the fence and walked to the winery through Copernicus's vineyard, wishing he had brought along a machete to take down the Cabernet slaves along the way.

"May I help you?" asked the pourer behind the bar.

"May I *help* you?" asked the receptionist.

He got to Hutt's outer office before Paco Cardinal came up behind him and without a word pinned his arms. The two of them danced, struggling and grunting, back down the hall, through the tasting room, and out under the wisteria where Cotton was released like some exotic strain of lepidoptera that might injure itself.

A week later, Hutt Family Estates canceled Jill's health insurance, making her a ward of the state. Cotton's carrier wouldn't take her. *Don't worry, Scout. Puddle-jump's profitable, we're going to be just fine.* In a way, this offense of Hutt's transcended the original diagnosis of cancer in its awfulness, providing another, deeper peek into the void of depravity. He watched Jill drift involuntarily away, aware that her neurological problem went far back, perhaps as far back as her decision to make Hutt's brand for him, and now she was a kite on an infinite, uncoiling string over blue and unbridgeable water.

Tina Schupe came, to see not Jill, who was asleep, but Cotton. Recently promoted to Jill's job, she sat in Puddle-jump's little farm office in an expensive outfit and told him how sorry she was, then placed on his desk an envelope.

"What's this?"

"An offer, from Jerome. For Puddle-jump. He's willing to pay top dollar. . . . Wait, Cotton. He's willing to settle and pay all medical expenses from this point on."

"If I sell?"

"Yes."

Tina took his scrutiny as smoothly as the pleating in her trousers. "What's happened to you?" he asked, but he already knew: young woman moves from outer office to inner sanctum, which includes a bed; lingering fidelity to Jill detectable, if barely.

"Nothing's happened, Cotton. Life goes on."

"How old are you? Thirty, twenty-nine?"

"Age has nothing to do with it. It's a different world from the time you arrived, and this is a one-time opportunity."

Was she talking about Cotton, or herself? He said, "Take your envelope."

"You aren't even going to open it? You don't even want to know how much?"

This time he didn't even bother to respond.

She grabbed the envelope and tossed it into the wastebasket. He retrieved it and followed her outside and flicked the envelope into her new Lexus before she could get the door closed.

He didn't tell Jill about the offer. Copernicus, a ragged emotional escarpment jutting into their lives like the broken edge of a tectonic plate, had simply fallen away. Jill said, "No more calamities," holding his hand in hers, a tight bundle of veins, tendons, and mottled skin, surprisingly strong. "I don't want you to stop trying to save the world, Cotton. But I don't want you to expect to save it, either."

The day she died, he went home from the hospital and without a word to anyone loaded his diving gear into the pickup. He drove down to the river, fitted out, and dropped straight off the cut bank into a deep spot he knew well. The water still quite cold in May, he sinking through shadows until his feet touched gravel and loamy runoff from the surrounding vineyards. Drowned, gnarled tree roots, a pebbly wall of mud, and sunken branches. No collecting bag, no gloves. He tore at the bank, abrading his hands, while frightened little salmonids fled and the current carried off clouds of mud and debris, his oxygen going, the light failing, Cotton still looking.

After that, he tried to hold on to the things that made living in the valley worthwhile. That included the bearded figure who had showed up at the end of his road one morning in a straw hat with a busted crown: Cousin Pete, vineyard consultant from the Sierra foothills, passing in his pickup. This had been the beginning of what people called Cotton's weirdness: planting and harvesting by the moon, packing cow horns with excrement, burying them in the vineyard, letting livestock wander to naturally replenish the soil. His visitor pointed out that Cotton was already conforming in most ways to the tenets of "biodynamism" and with fine tuning could be made whole. Cotton paid him to bring a little herd of sheep to fertilize Puddle-jump, still more scientist than follower of nineteenth-century agrarian visionaries, or so he told himself. He had never irrigated because plastic piping was expensive. Dry farming might be risky, but it concentrated flavor.

Cousin Pete began to show up in that rattle-trap Chevy loaded with unidentifiable detritus from Luddite farming elsewhere, pushing "the next phase," the Johnny Appleseed of the closed system. Most difficult to accept was the chart of planetary phases and the notion of homeopathy. Cotton could almost hear his old professors chortling, yet he felt oddly at ease with this, even opening up to a truckload of cow horns. He had covered the first pile with a tarp, to conceal them as much from himself as from customers. He had mixed the residue of what he dug in the spring with well water, in the old tank inherited from the former owner, and sprayed it on the vines, mindful of homeopathy's creed.

On one of his visits, Pete took from a carton behind his front seat a copy of the *Tao Te Ching* and handed it to Cotton without a word. That evening, alone on his porch, Cotton opened the stiff new paperback at random and read, *The more you know, the less you understand.* And, *See the world as yourself.*

He read the last one again, aloud, and saw that his life had become a constricted tunnel from which he couldn't escape, at the end of it the lone figure of Jerome Hutt. In between lay a reeking, slippery slope. Jill's lawsuit against Hutt over her compensation, defunct since her death, had been only the beginning. Cotton's involvement in things Copernican had lengthened as he examined from every angle whether or not Hutt's winery was being run according to the requirements that he—Cotton—had helped put in place.

He had come to know more about Hutt than he would ever have thought possible: his past, his land use squabbles in the valley and in SoCal, the way Hutt manipulated his wife and child as shareholders, his evasion of massive debt. Cotton became a source for outside investigators, journalists, lawyers, people with bones of their own to pick with Hutt, and pretenders from Hutt's own camp who inadvertently provided Cotton with additional information by the very questions they posed.

Meanwhile, he felt his own soul wizening, the joys of earth and water he had lived for seemingly silly and self-deceptive. When he looked in the mirror, he saw one of those shrunken heads from remote islands in the South Pacific reduced to an agonized intensity. Once he had envisioned a humane ecology in which people prospered along with creatures, but he had witnessed the perversion of this concept all around. His cherished vision from his first visit to the valley had dwindled while the corporate model had risen, damaging both the place and—paradoxically—the product upon which it depended.

Sara knew most of it and suspected the rest. By now Cotton Harrell was a bona fide valley personage, more character than celebrity. She admired the way he held on to an issue long after others had fallen away, wished they were real friends, and knew it would never be.

# CHAPTER FOUR

*Nose*

# 1

LES BREEDEN'S FIRST ASSIGNMENT as a PI lacked, he thought, opportunity for finesse. Its object, Larry Carradine, Craven-Jones's gofer, had been asking around about the origin of the mystery Cabernet but, according to Claire Craven-Jones, had now gone to ground. The only way to contact him, she said, was to visit an old stone cellar converted to walk-up apartments, next to the railroad tracks.

Les parked the VW and entered a hulk that looked like it might collapse the next time a train passed. He had seen others like it in the valley, used during Prohibition to produce bulk sacramental wine that was then shipped across the Bay by rail by the Abruzzinis and other families, supposedly bound for the bishop of San Francisco but sold instead, in large quantities and at a huge profit, to a thirsty and thereby a lawless public.

Deep grooves had been worn in the floor by the

passage of massive iron wheels; the faint smell of fermentation would live in the tufa until the building did come down. Meanwhile the upstairs provided sanctuary for the likes of Carradine, down on their luck, and Les hauled himself up the stairs and stood looking out the window at the end of the hall at creosoted railway ties, cheerful in the noonday sun, laid long ago by the Chinese.

He knocked; someone shouted, "Who?"

Les leaned into the scarred doorjamb. "Lester Breeden, Claire Craven-Jones sent me."

"What do you want?"

"To talk."

The door moved and Les was presented with a sliver of salmon-colored face and a pendant cigarette. Carradine opened the door wider, but there wasn't much of him to add to the picture: baggy sweats, suede slippers. Les recognized the complexion of the committed taster-swallower, who asked, "Why are you working for Claire?"

"She asked me. Mind if I come in?"

Carradine backed into the anarchic domesticity of wine journalism: piles of paper, dirty glasses, stacks of stylish wine publications, technical and viticultural journals, bottles. A well-worn Victoria's Secret catalog had its own place of honor on the couch, next to a sculpture made of wire cages from discarded Champagne bottles. "What do you want?"

"What you've learned, Larry, about the anonymous Cabernet."

"Nothing. That's the problem."

"As in . . . ?"

"As in lots of people talking about CJ's possible twenty but nobody with a clue. That means it's either a fake, or the person who made it's far out of the mainstream, as in unplugged. Why am I telling you this? Tell Claire to call."

"She has, I'm the message. That all you know?"

Larry scowled, his cigarette now dark dregs in the bottom of a stemmed glass. He located the sole armchair by feeling behind him, but instead of offering it to his visitor sank into its lumpy embrace and murmured, "Please."

Les got it then. He crossed a carpet covered with loose change, as if Carradine had sown dimes and quarters in the collective grunge, and went into the kitchen. He opened the refrigerator, confronting a thicket of bottles with protruding corks like pale spring shoots exposed to the glare, the reds darkly tumescent, the oxidized whites the color of his host's eyes. Les took out an Australian dessert wine and poured some into the cleanest glass he saw.

Carradine took it, making a deeply felt sound, and drank. He two-handed the glass to the armrest and held it there as if it might escape. "I've heard some stuff that's sort of related. A savvy collector I called in Vegas suspects that the wine's Jerome Hutt's, though he wouldn't say why. Thinks it's similar to Copernicus but a lot better, made in small quantities and slipped into the tasting as a ringer. This guy wants a heads-up if and when the wine's identified, which I wouldn't give him even if I knew."

So that's how it's done, Les thought. Learn about a

high score even an hour early, make a killing buying a chunk of the vintage before the price spikes. He said, "Then why doesn't Hutt claim victory?"

"Don't know. Hutt Family Estates is in trouble, I know that. Something about Jerome's debts. That wife of his wants to sell, his daughter doesn't, big-time sparks. If some stealth project got a twenty rating from CJ, that winery's value would be boosted. It could turn around a place like Copernicus and keep it in family hands." He drank. "Now if you don't mind, I have *important* work to do."

Having already seen the backseat of Claire Craven-Jones's car, Les expected to encounter the same disarray in her house, a mission-style split-level with a barricaded vault where the garage should have been. She opened the door not in jogging shorts or a swimsuit but a kind of smock. She didn't seem to recognize him, then said, "Oh, hi, Lester," and led him into a living room with a cathedral ceiling and glass wall facing west, a utilitarian metal table set up in front of a priceless view.

Reams of papers were being spat out of the high-speed printer. In the middle of the room a rug had been pulled aside and a trapdoor raised to reveal a broad staircase leading down into darkness.

"CJ's idea," she said, following his gaze. "He likes the idea of a hidden cellar. Not really hidden, since everything's delivered downstairs. Showing this to guests is very dramatic, though. The baroness de Rothschild loved it."

The cellar's existence explained the bolted, metal-lathed garage doors Les had seen outside. He could feel its gravitational tug, a dim netherworld brimming with rare vintages and impossible-to-get bottles.

"Is your husband here?"

"No, he's in New York, talking to some investor group. People who know little about wine but want to sound like they know a lot. Why don't you sit . . . there."

She pointed to a deep circular chair with armrests too far apart for comfort, probably his chair. The sofa was already occupied by wine bottles, forcing Claire to perch on a lofty desk chair with rollers. Les wondered if the plush feel of everything sit-on-able in Craven-Jones's living room had been his choice, the decorating equiva-lent of the critic's love of big, moderately soft, "approach-able" wines. "What are you working on?" he asked.

"The next issue. It never ends."

"Why don't you put it online?"

She laughed, an easy, genuine sound. The idea had obviously never occurred to her. "Getting CJ to carry a cell phone was a major accomplishment. Computers are the enemy, we represent the old-fashioned approach. You know, pencils, last-minute telephone fixes. Crazy, I know, and expensive. Paper alone's twenty grand a year."

The idea that she was Les's employer and he indi-rectly dependent upon an enophilic bimonthly dinosaur added to his unease. "I talked to Larry," he said.

"Do tell."

"He hasn't heard much. Some people seem to think Hutt Family Estates is behind the submission. How exactly did the bottle get into the tasting, by the way?"

"Left on the doorstep. Samples are supposed to be shipped, always. There are a lot, and it's my job to keep them straight. With the help of an assistant I no longer have. People shipping wine check with us first, then send two bottles in Styrofoam, one for later reference."

"Maybe this guy didn't know how to submit."

"Maybe, but why no card? He knew, all right. Anyway, we're still leading the next issue with that tasting, even if no one comes forward."

The two landline connections on the telephone console blinked on and off. Les found it easy to imagine the scene here when production ramped up: last-minute pleas, prevaricators waiting in the ether, trying to get through to Craven-Jones. "Why do you have a trapdoor, instead of, you know, regular stairs?"

"CJ's uncle had one. In Shropshire. CJ likes the psychological effect—all that wine under you, in the dark. Bottled subconscious, he calls it. And he likes the dramatic effect of throwing back the rug and hitting the switch, watching the trapdoor come up and the staircase descend, the railing popping up, inviting you to descend. Would you like to see the cellar?"

As he stood, Les noticed a small brindle dog standing in the hallway, watching him. Without provocation, it gave a single, sharp bark. Claire said, "Missy. Go in," and the dog disappeared. "My protector."

Les followed her down the steps, her pale, streaked hair darkening as the light receded. He felt the cool, constant fifty-odd degrees Fahrenheit, ideal for storage. It climbed past ankles, thighs, chest, until he was immersed in atmospheric perfection, a prickliness about the back of his neck. This wasn't just the lair of the famous Clyde Craven-Jones, it was the graveyard of all sorts of duplicates salted away for whatever, forever: future testing, ceremonies, donations, also oblivion. He said, "Amazing."

"Impressive, I know. But it can be a burden too."

The shelves were all metal, each aisle distinguished by a dark pine board on which had been scrawled, in chalk, the inhabitants of rank upon rank of bottles: Bordeaux, Burgundy, Champagne, Loire. Les didn't know enough to recognize them, but he knew what they represented: *petits* chateaux and grand, pocket beauties from Baja to the Willamette Valley, monsters from Barolo to Barossa, all incubating away with platoons of port, sherry, Madeira, Tokay. They passed single malts and weird Dutch gins and misshapen orbs containing bourbon from the wilder recesses of Appalachia. Cognac and Calvados and alembic brandies from Spokane to the Transvaal.

"CJ doesn't like spirits," said Claire. "He thinks they're common. But he does sometimes drink eau de vie, or very old Armagnac, on Christmas Eve."

The California wines began to assemble now in great variety. Les glimpsed some going back to Prohibition, auction lots with quaint yellowing labels from this valley's early days, names that had helped define the place, right up to the present: bright, imaginative, edgy labels, all trying to breathe in the present oxygen-starved market, their pleading almost audible: *Please, CJ, open and smell me. Taste me!* A mention by the master was a major triumph, Craven-Jones's silence a sentence of obscurity and heartbreak.

Claire raised her chin in the direction of the assembled Styrofoam cartons, dense with shippers' stickers, crowding the long potting table against one wall. "The delivery guys leave it outside the big double doors, under a trellis CJ had built for shade. There's a sealed space inside, so hot air can't get into the cellar. All that wine has to be moved inside, then the iron doors closed, and the cellar door unlocked. Then all the cartons have to be opened."

They had reached the far end of the table, and Claire switched on the low-hanging fluorescent lamp. Dozens of black bottles leaped out at them. She hefted one with a cork protruding from the neck and no label.

"Can't taste like much," said Les. "Been open too long."

"I put nitrogen into the neck, right after CJ evaluated it. Seals off the air absolutely, so it should have some oomph left." She handed the bottle to him. "Keep it upright."

"What am I supposed to do with it?"

"I wish I knew."

# 2

"A BLOG."

"Who's gonna read it?"

Glass Act after one in the morning became a theater of objects, Les noticed, the stuffed heads seeming to inch forward, daring Ben to shoot them. The bottles all closed ranks against further encroachment by eternally thirsty human beings. This room had stumbled into existence on Ben's obsession and borrowed money, and was a bit out of his control. The up-valley scions who arrived by the Beemer load to display their vinous bona fides and girls from the city thrilled by authentic squalor had all gone home, exhausted by too many short pours and the requisite commentary.

So were the workers and groupies from winery tasting rooms in the valley, happy to see someone else pour and to pick up new descriptors and wine babble: *Is garageist getting to be a put-down? . . . Is Tavestani better than Nomonity? . . . Is Craven-Jones better than No-monity? . . . Is . . .*

Les said, "Everybody will read it. Because it'll be different."

"Who's gonna write it?"

"Me. Us."

This elicited a collective, decidedly noncommittal, "Hmmm." Then Kiki said, "That's a good idea. And I can set it up."

"You can?"

"Didn't you know I was in IT at LucasArts, in the Presidio?"

He didn't, but then he knew little of the others beyond what they let slip from time to time. Ben and Esme seemed oddly untethered to past or present, and Train just nodded, his ringlets touching the starched collar of a white shirt left over, Les suspected, from board meetings down in Menlo Park. He had been named for John Coltrane, Les learned, and took his multimillionaire status in stride, never commenting on that other valley to the south that had once supported blooming orchards and was now laminated in silicon.

Les said, "Great."

"We could do some swaps online," Esme said, getting interested. "Sub rosa, natch. What else'll be in it?"

"Anything hot. News, rumors—good ones, like this stuff about Copernicus."

"I have plenty of those," said Esme.

Les finished his wine and stood. Inspired, he said,

"Somebody's got to put it all together, though, and that's gonna be me. But everybody's got to contribute."

Ben was already writing something on a legal pad; Les wanted to get away before being required to read it. "I'll need copy," he said over his shoulder. "Anything . . ."

"Aspirational," said Train.

"Wait!"

Ben mounted the ladder and grasped an open bottle of Cask 23. He held it up to the light. "Two fingers left, not even a fifty-dollar pour," and up-ended this dreggy prize over the bar. They all watched dark, redolent Cabernet spread like a costly Rorschach across the boards, rivulets following the grain. Ben dipped a blunt forefinger into the wine and drew an X on his forehead, and without a word the rest of them did too.


In his apartment, after coffee and three bananas, Les sat at the board under the window and turned on his computer. He keyed in a list of suggestions his coconspirators had made for the blog and saved it. For a time he watched the dark silhouettes of cats cross the driveway, night stalkers of infinite grace and ferocity. He had had enough to drink to free him but not enough to befuddle, and without thinking too much about it began to write:

Could that be the collective stench of a thousand wine opinion mongers and publicists and wannabe sommeliers pouring with sweat as they turn out a collective magnum opus of bullshit so prodigious that it threatens to destabilize the globe and send it out of orbit?

It could. And while, Dear Reader, you're searching for what's left of your emasculated skepticism, the load has gotten heavier. Seismologists are warning—LISTEN!—of a reactivation of the San Andreas fault and the tipping of millions of gallons of *Vitis vinifera* into the bowels of the earth.

You might as well watch, having nothing to lose but your subscription to that brothel towel, *The Wine Taster,* and its lame imitators. You don't need them. You're tired of being bloviated about which wine to buy but not who's doing what to whom in which cellar (is that wine thief going into a cask of aging Cabernet or into the proprietor's spouse?), of lifestyle vintner *amuses* and celebrity auction addicts buying matched sets of jeroboams of old Dripping Creek Cabernet.

All passé. Forget numerical ratings and the latest two-buck fuck, forget medals. What you need is an unsanitized morning-after whiff of the infinitely varied, often tight-assed *infiniti di vini* on America's western edge, where they're staging the last agrarian act in that amazing, transformative, longest-running, sputtering musical, *Manifest Destiny.* And now you've got one! Right here!! Nose!!!

So just log on, and kick back. Sniff, sniff . . .

———

He went to bed feeling alive for the first time in weeks, remembering that night in the tent at Point Reyes, seemingly auspicious. Then, as sleep enfolded him, he saw standing on the back of the toilet the black bottle Claire Craven-Jones had given him, looking vaguely disapproving in the thin electric glow of the streetlight.

# 3

IT WAS CLYDE CRAVEN-JONES'S AFTERNOON for perambulating about the valley—figuratively speaking. He emerged from his house in a houndstooth hacking jacket a tad too warm for California in the fall, carrying his signature notebook bound by a heavy rubber band, and walked to his car as jauntily as a fat man can, spectacles swinging from the chain around his neck as he hummed a Puccini aria.

He drove straight to VinMonde, maker of a number of wines, the foremost being Trifecta, prime competitor in his recent, increasingly controversial tasting. That Trifecta was made by a foreign-based multinational meant that a whole cadre of people were devoted to collecting intelligence of one sort or another in what the corporation's principals still considered a wilderness—California—and that if anything of moment took place in the state, these savvy Frenchmen would quickly be aware of it.

CJ was expected, met at the door by the glycerin-smooth Benoit Guillaume, his head back to show new teeth that had replaced those stained by Gauloises gitanes CJ remembered from their first meeting, years before. *"Cee-jeh!"*

"Hello, Benoit."

They shook hands, and CJ was ushered into the tasting room, noting the spacious chairs and the wide doorway to the cellar, designed to accommodate his bulk, though no one spoke of this. A row of gleaming glasses had been partially filled with dark wine, and although CJ had not asked for a tasting to be set up, and had no desire to conduct one, he would avoid giving offense. Benoit and those like him knew the value of their marks in CJ's tatty notebooks and automatically assumed that the critic would perform and his runic musings end up in print.

CJ went through the flight of VinMonde products with speed and efficiency, spitting most but not all of the wine into the silver bucket instead of into a wooden wine box filled with sawdust, as in the old days, when hitting such a target provided a welcome diversion, and the illusion that this was a more basic, agrarian exercise. Included in the tasting was the current release of Trifecta, and CJ recognized the nose and slightly truncated finish. He wrote a few words, said, "Lovely," and rubber-banded his precious ink-blotted trove of complex, invaluable, sometimes damning jottings.

"So, would you like a little repast, CJ? Perhaps a bit of foie gras . . ."

"I've had lunch, thank you. So, Benoit, what news?"

Now, this was tricky. CJ would never be told anything not to the advantage of VinMonde, but neither could Benoit have nothing to say to Clyde Craven-Jones when the critic was in a rare receptive mode. Whatever Benoit might say must not offend his visitor, or enhance a competitor, or reveal a weakness in the parent company, or be without some real interest. All these calculations swam in the chief executive officer's crinkly edged eyes and enduring smile, until finally he chose one, like a raffle ticket, and blurted out, "Of course we've heard that you are on the lookout for the maker of a particularly interesting wine. No?"

"That's right."

"And I have a thought about this. It seems entirely possible to me, perhaps probable, that someone removed the label and recorked a bottle of Trifecta, and somehow—despicably, of course—introduced it anonymously into your wonderful tasting."

"I don't think so, Benoit. Sampling Trifecta today reaffirms my belief that it's not the mystery Cabernet."

Benoit's smile collapsed. "Are you sure, CJ? Perhaps . . ."

"I'm sure. Although," CJ quickly added, "Trifecta's showing well, very well. I had hoped you might have heard something else."

"Well, I have read that you detected a similarity in the unnamed wine to Copernicus, of all things. Although the latter wine is of course far, far inferior."

"Where did you read that?"

"Ah, in a blog, CJ, I don't remember the name. There are so many, you know, what's one to do?"

CJ had never read a blog but knew well enough what they were: electronic drivel laid down by uninformed people for the titillation of other uninformed people with nothing better to do than to read that swill. "How does this person know that?" The only one CJ had told, other than Claire, was a wealthy recluse in the desert.

"CJ, no one takes this material seriously, I assure you."

"What is this blog? Where can I find it?"

A touch of panic in Benoit's eyes. "I can bring it up for you, certainly."

"I don't read things on computer screens, Benoit." And CJ didn't deal with that abomination, e-mail, either. Already the day was turning out to be less than he had hoped.

"I will have it printed for you instantly," said Benoit, who was out the door, shouting in French to an office staff that would have to deal with a disconsolate boss for the remainder of the afternoon. In three minutes he was back, unhappily holding aloft a leaf of foolscap. CJ took and folded the paper without reading it and slipped it into his jacket. "Thank you. As I said, Benoit, the wines are lovely, lovely," and he left.

In the car, CJ unfolded and propped the sheet of paper on the steering wheel.

Nose has heard, in the beating of tomtoms in that precious den of rare yet affordable wine and savvy

confab known as Glass Act, a shocker. The famous wine critic Clyde Craven-Jones, currently
searching for the identity of a California Cabernet
that has been given a perfect score of 20 points,
detects a similarity between it and Copernicus.
But only a similarity. Because Copernicus is only
knee-high in structure and complexity, according
to Nose's impeccable sources, when compared
to a real champ. . . .

CJ looked up at passing traffic beyond the burnished
silver gates of VinMonde, feeling that something had
been stolen from him, brazenly and hurtfully. This kind
of leak was insidious and quite possibly disastrous. Who
other than CJ could have talked to Pud Larsen, unlikely
to repeat CJ's words to nobodies on the vast, ragged
edge of wine bloggery? Or whatever they called it. He
read on:

Speaking of Copernicus, Nose has further heard
that the winery might be for sale. Apparently the
family's split, Jerome Hutt's wife wanting to unload,
he determined to hang in, the friction between
them considerable, the stakes sky-high. There's
lots more intriguing info to be heard from a perch
at the bar at Glass Act, including rumors about
ole Copernicus, natch. Like a mountain of debt,
but that particular story will have to wait for Nose's
nosing.
	So, stay logged, sniff, sniff. . . .

Intolerable, absolutely. No other word for it—no by-line, no attribution, nothing but, well, facts. All of them unfortunately true. That didn't mean that this person, these people, had the right to indulge in such anarchy, whoever they were, putting this stuff out, the anonymity of it enough to drive a man mad. CJ intended to nip this in the bud, whatever that took.

# 4

HE DIDN'T CARE for the county seat, that polyglot little city of some historical charm but with a scruffy outer ring of commerce that interfered with CJ's vision of rural perfection. CJ parked near the old vaudeville house, now transformed into a cinema, and across the street from the den in question, Glass Act, looking to him like a perfect place for shanghaiing innocent wine lovers. He had never been inside and didn't relish it now, detecting two round-shouldered silhouettes lurking under overhanging antlers, but he gripped his notebook and hauled himself out of the Prius.

Inside, he was struck by the unrepentant air of bohemia. This was no pretentious wine bar, more rotgut wormwood than hundred-dollar Cabernet Sauvignon, but then he got a look at the labels behind the bar. He sat carefully on a stool, fearing as always the pain and embarrassment of its collapsing, and obliquely faced the young couple bent over some calculation on a yellow pad. She wore a black pantsuit with dramatic lapels, and her companion, the standard blond Californian, an open shirt and sneakers riding the rungs of his stool.

"My God," said the bartender, adding, "Literally."

CJ turned to face what must be a retired motorcyclist with ponytail and unshaven lantern jaw. This apparition continued, "Clyde Craven-Jones, as I live and breathe. You have been sorely missed, sir."

"Well . . ."

"Not a day passes that your name is not invoked here, Mr. Craven-Jones. Not an evening sky darkens that all eyes don't turn to the door, hoping that somehow, some way, you will cross our lowly threshold. And now, at long last, you have!"

"I say . . ."

The young woman swiveled. "You're Clyde Craven-Jones? I can't believe it. *Can't believe it!* I read every word you write, Clyde. I couldn't exist without you."

"Oh, come now."

But she was off the stool. "This is just *so* excitin'." Pretty if chunky, Southern accent similar to Claire's, fuller dark hair. Something to be said for a little flesh on a woman, hair done by a stylist, lipstick. Slipping onto a stool beside one, smiling. When was the last time that happened, someone who wasn't a vintner, a publicist, a wine-stained wretch from the fourth estate, and who wanted nothing in particular from Clyde Craven-Jones? He said, "You're very kind."

"I'm Esme. You know that '08 Meritage you gave a thirteen to? I absolutely agreed with you. Overoaked, testosteroned to the back of its teeth, perilously alcoholic. So glad you had the courage—the grace—to say, 'Wait a minute, folks. This is a cha*rade*. No more!'"

The bartender was pouring something. CJ raised a hand. "I won't," then saw it was sparkling water, no ice. He drank it all. "Actually," CJ said, "I just stopped by to . . ."

"What shall we open on this august occasion?" asked the bartender.

"No, no, please."

"How about a Château Chasse-Spleen?" asked the blond young man in sneakers.

"You must be joking," said CJ. "At three in the afternoon?"

But the biker had disappeared without a word. Esme said, "And have you discovered who made that wine you mentioned in the last issue, Clyde? So intriguin', that unidentified interloper. It must be a huge inconvenience for you, Clyde, a person doing such a thing."

"It's CJ, and yes, it is inconvenient. Very. Which is what brings me . . ."

The bartender reemerged with the Bordeaux *cru bourgeois* cradled for decanting. CJ recognized the label and felt the old rush of pleasure. This was the vintage that had helped make his reputation, and vice versa. The proven depth and reliability, after he "discovered" the vintage for Americans, had catapulted him to the upper echelon of wine criticism, the rest history. Now he watched with perverted fascination on a warm afternoon as an unkempt fellow lit a candle on the far side of the counter and, with skill and aplomb, inserted a long, old-fashioned corkscrew.

Slowly he began to extract the geriatric cork, watching the flame through the neck of the bottle; CJ edged forward, on the lookout too for the long, dark line of evil sediment. He could smell this powerful, luscious blend of Cabernet and Bordeaux's lesser grapes, despite the not totally disagreeable distraction of Esme's perfume.

"There!" cried CJ and the bartender together.

The bottle came up, and CJ laughed despite himself. All quite unorthodox, but merry; they could indulge themselves, he decided, while he learned what he needed to know and departed. But the bartender was slipping a bowl of palate cleansers under his nose, not popcorn but perfectly acceptable stone-ground wafers, and unconsciously CJ took one, watching the wine go from decanter into huge tight-lipped, tulip-shaped Riedels. He said feebly, "I couldn't," and the bartender said, "Now, Mr. Craven-Jones, you can smell it, at least."

They all did, and then drank, none saying a word because of the august presence among them. Feeling churlish, CJ took up his glass and thrust his nose into the ambient air above the wine, then drank and intoned, "Ripe black cherries."

"Oh, CJ," whispered Esme. "Now wasn't your nose once on the cover of *Time*?"

"*Newsweek*, actually. And inside, I'm afraid."

"I remember that article. It got me so excited. I decided right then that wine was the way to go."

His suspicion aroused, CJ asked, "And what do you do in wine?"

"Nothing really, just drink it." She laughed airily. "Please tell us, CJ, how you recognized your own talent."

"I assume you mean how I got interested in wine. Well, I did a long apprenticeship in the best wine shop in London. Something I recommend, by the way. It helped tremendously to have been introduced to wine by professionals and not by wine writers, I must say. Which brings me to this"—extracting the piece of paper—"blog. It mentions your establishment, bartender, as well as me. Any idea who wrote it?"

They all peered at the printout while CJ took another swallow. The bartender said, "Must be that guy who comes in here from time to time. Don't you think so, Les?"

The blond said, "Probably."

"Well," said CJ, "it's irresponsible and very unprofessional. How does he know I detected a slight similarity between the unidentified wine and Copernicus?"

The bartender poured more Chasse-Spleen. The problem with these big glasses, CJ thought, was that they made drinking too easy, and they disguised the amount one had consumed. He decided to press on. "What's this fellow's name, anyway? The blog's not signed."

They all looked at one another and shrugged. Esme placed a soft palm on his shoulder. "CJ, I just love your accent. Was wine a family affair, when you were a kid?"

"Oh, yes indeed. My uncle used to take me to Sauternes." He saw with utter clarity the cellar, smelled dank stone, heard Uncle Jones shrewdly buying vintage

Château d'Yquem. In a flash he was watching that same uncle, in Shropshire, lean over a bloody haunch of beef, a knife in one hand, a stemmed goblet of golden liquid in the other. *The sugar beautifully cuts the fat, little Clyde, but never, ever have a second helping.* Good advice, which CJ had subsequently ignored, to his expansive regret.

"The variables within wine are literally infinite," he continued, warming to the subject. "So it's important to get an early start. Man has always used the talents available to him in a dangerous world, including the powers of detection. Man must not just survive, he must prevail."

In a rush of sentiment, he saw himself as the rightful successor to noblemen of old, preserving that most august expression of culture against the onslaught of the vine louse and the wine blogger, throwing himself into what boiled down to a triumph of quality over numbing mediocrity. "Which is why we pursue the subject so carefully and relentlessly, that and the transcendental experience man has been searching for since the dawn of time."

The bartender said, "Here's one I'll bet not even the foremost wine critic in America has ever tasted."

The *cru bourgeois* already gone? CJ looked at a new bottle squatting on the bar, a string under the wax seal. The label said *Farallon 1962*. "Where did you get this?"

"We have our ways, CJ. This one's been sitting around for a year. Time to release it, don't you think?"

"What is it, anyway?"

But CJ was distracted by the plate of sliced serrano sliding across the bar, with bread crusts, a wedge of some strange cheese streaked with azure mold, and—my

God—shelled walnuts. Now this CJ couldn't resist, delicious with fortified wine, itself inky but more delicate than he expected, heavily infused with some homegrown brandy. "Very long on the palate," he murmured, "but not too sweet. An altogether original taste. Lovely."

He took another swallow, unable to identify the grape. No one seemed to care, and that was refreshing. He got so tired having to perform, and these simple folk didn't require it. "You have quite a nice place, here, Mr. . . ."

"Ben."

"And you're quite knowledgeable, Ben."

"Why, thank you. That's quite a compliment, coming from you, CJ. A tad more?"

The next time CJ looked, the sun had angled noticeably. Claire would be wondering. His reasons for coming here in the first place seemed remote and lacking in importance. "Let me contribute to this very interesting tasting, if you please, Ben."

"No way. It's our pleasure."

CJ stood with some difficulty, said, "Well, I'm touched. My lady, gentlemen, I thank you," and sat on the floor.

# 5

LES DROVE HIM HOME in CJ's car and waited in the
driveway for Claire to emerge and take him back. She
came out hurriedly, a little flustered, pulling on a wax
jacket, checking her handbag. When she was behind the
wheel, she said, "You're nice to drive him. Whatever possessed him to go into that place?"

"He read a blog and didn't like it." Les didn't mention
that he had written it.

"CJ's getting too old for this kind of thing."

"Have you told your husband I work for you?"

"No, I haven't. It would just make him uneasy, the PI
part. He and I agreed to look into this each in our own
way, so there's no subterfuge. Have you found out anything else?"

"I'm not much help to you, Claire."

"You're a journalist, follow your instincts. We have a
deal, remember? Find some likely suspects—I mean
wines—maybe somebody to analyze them. *Do* something,

Lester, besides sit around Glass Act." And left him speechless in the street, next to an ailing VW with mismatched fenders.


"Some weird German."

Ben was talking on his cell phone while sorting bottles, judging from the background noise, and Les still in his pajama bottoms. "If you want a wine broken down, I'm told he can do it," Ben added, "but I don't think it's going to tell you anything, Chico."

"Got a number?"

Les heard him set the phone on the bar and begin rummaging in the curtained-off under-the-stairs that served as Glass Act's office. Something tumbled; a command was issued to one of Glass Act's ever-revolving pour staff, and apparently ignored. Les had already talked to Claire this morning, who called to tell him two people contacted her anonymously to claim the twenty-point prize, but none could describe the box the mystery Cab arrived in, or the shawl so delicately woven it could pass through a wedding ring. And to tell him that Marilee Tavestani had written about the mystery Cab in the *Chronicle*.

Ben came back on the line. "Name's Wolken, Rudolf Wolken. Lives outside Rileysville, up north. Way up north. Claims he can reduce wines to crystals on blotting paper and then statistically compare them. Sounds like hocus-pocus to me. Oh, I just sent you my *Nose* contribution."

Les went to his e-mail and started reading Ben's offering.

Enotopia begins in dry, straggly Baja, with *Vitis vinifera* vines scorched by the sun and strewn with Chicano wind chimes (beer cans) and Chiclets wrappers. It skirts L.A., brush-kisses Santa Barbara, embraces Santa Cruz, engulfs Sonoma and Mendocino hanging over the Pacific, leaps extreme NoCal and lands in the woolly Willamette Valley of Oregon, finally spiking up into Vancouver for the other, sub-Arctic extreme. . . .

Dear Reader, the best place in all of Enotopia for appreciating its bounty is Glass Act, easily reached from the East Bay. And guess who recently dropped by? None other than the grand pooh-bah of wine evaluation, Clyde Craven-Jones! On his avid search for the maker of that elusive, oh-so-good orphan Cabernet Sauvignon currently being sought . . .

Today Les had a real objective—*Do something*—and he brought up a map of the valley's wineries on the computer screen and settled over it with a cup of coffee. Studying the stretch around Hutt Family Estates, he listed the prominent vineyards in addition to Copernicus—Clementine, Trifecta, an unpronounceable one belonging to a rich Cabernet-struck Iranian—and, to the north, one little home winery. All shared the same appellation, similar soils, night breezes funneling up from

the Golden Gate along the valley's constricting mountains.

He called Claire back, assuming her husband let her
answer the telephone, and said, "I need a bottle each of
Copernicus, Clementine, Trifecta, Lashoush or however
you say it, and something called Puddle-jump."

"We have them all except Puddle-jump. You'll have to
buy that one. Just send me the bill."

He found the bottles in a box on her doorstep. Passing
Hutt Family Estates, his gaze moved up to the point
where the Copernicus vineyard touched its neighbor's,
the former all military rows and bare ground, Puddle-
jump random, with knobby vines and riotous under-
growth. Les pulled into Puddle-jump's road and felt like
he was time-warping up to the house: rockers on the
porch, a spavined wagon that must have once been full
of manure. He parked next to a shredding tarp over dark,
mounded soil, held down by old tires.

Nearby sat a pile of moldy cow horns. Volunteers
bloomed in the vegetable garden; an abandoned bat-
winged mower completed the impression of time past.
He opened the car door and smelled decomposition, and
lots of stuff—wild mustard, grass—all requiring work.
As he stepped out, a rail-thin man came around the
house. "You lost?"

"I don't think so," said Les. "You must be Cotton Harrell."

"That's right."

"I'm Les Breeden." And he added, "Journalist." But Harrell didn't seem particularly interested, maybe not even listening. "I was wondering if I could taste your wine."

"Sure."

He led Les into what looked like a tack shop. Various awards hung on the winery walls, and a topo map of the Medoc; stacked bins stored the bottles that were for sale. Overturned wineglasses glinted on a slab of polished stone, and Harrell took down one, not two, and placed it in front of Les, then turned and reached for one of Puddle-jump's lesser cuvées.

"Excuse me," said Les, "but I'd like to taste the estate Cabernet."

"I don't pour that one, Mr. Breeden. My overhead's too high."

"Why don't you just charge for tastings like everybody else?"

"Because I don't want to."

"Well, I'll buy a bottle."

Harrell took one from the top bin and set it carefully on the counter. "That'll be sixty-eight dollars," he said, although a charge of any sort a wine journalist rarely encountered. Les took out his wallet and fingered his credit card, but Harrell smiled and shook his head. This place was straight out of the nineteenth century, Les thought, teetering between happy cinematic throwback to the family farm and *Wine Country Chainsaw Massacre*.

He didn't have the cash, so he wrote Harrell a check. "Would you open the bottle, so we can taste it together."

"Here?"

"Yeah."

Harrell got another glass and did as asked. They raised glasses of dark, translucent wine, and tasted. Harrell swallowed, so Les too ignored the dented spit bucket.

"Well?" Les asked Harrell.

"Well what?"

"What do you taste?"

Wine usually launched vintners into paeans of praise for their own blend, couched as explanation, words to make the mouth water and the wallet levitate. All many critics did was kick back and start recording, passing along the grace notes. But Harrell said simply, "It tastes real good. The right balance for Cabernet grown in hot country, without irrigation. About what you'd expect."

*About what you'd expect?* Jesus. "I saw cow horns outside. You're not biodynamic, by any chance?"

"As a matter of fact, I am."

"Certified?"

"No, getting certified's too expensive, and a racket. Endless inspections, thousands of dollars in fees. The idea of having to bring outsiders into a closed farming system, and then to have to pay them to say it's working, is silly."

The wine was very good, but biodynamic Cabernet Sauvignon? "I grew up on a farm and went to ag school," Les said. "I don't know how you justify biodynamic procedures that go against accepted scientific principles."

"I don't justify them. Do you have to know how something works, Mr. Breeden, to know that it does work?"

Unable to counter this, Les said, "So you fill the cow horns . . ."

"With shit, yes. From a dairy farm in Sonoma. Bury the horns, dig them up again, put what's inside into a crock insulated with peat moss. Mix a small portion in a water tank and spray it on the vines. Homeopathy, basically."

"The weaker the solution, the stronger the effect."

"Less is more."

Memories of barroom discussions of biodynamism at Davis came back to him. "Sounds like magic, you know, lunar currents."

Harrell laughed. "Don't forget, there are measurable effects of planetary movement."

"But statistically insignificant."

"You can't say there are no real cosmic influences, can you? Consider the sun. Plant metabolism's closely tied to it. Granted, the logistics of tending vines according to a planetary calendar are demanding. But *bio* simply means 'life,' *dynamic,* 'energy.' Just put them together."

This wine, tannic, powerful, was no fruit bomb. Give the man credit, Les thought. Besides, he liked him.

"Cow horns and the other stuff are just the sacraments," Harrell said. "Don't get hung up on those. The main idea is to take care of your land, control what comes onto it, what goes off. The closed system. Take care of things, do the best for your place, whatever limits that imposes. Including limits on profits."

"How can a big winery do this and still pay quarterly dividends?"

"It can't, which is why their wines aren't as good as mine. Wine's just the vehicle for the soil, Mr. Breeden, and vineyards like the one next door"—he meant Hutt Family Estates, maker of Copernicus—"are little more than underground nexuses of chemicals. They're always replacing vines over there, when they should be looking at the dirt vines sit in."

Harrell, looking out the window, seemed to have forgotten he had a visitor. "Our universities support that approach because the chemical manufacturers pay for their research, and so the university keeps their products in play. I didn't mean to preach, it's just hard not to talk about it. Remember what Einstein said about this kind of system: it's so elegantly efficient it must be true."

# 6

THE ROAD NORTH was sparsely traveled. Les ate his sandwich leisurely, the napkin tucked into his shirt, glad to be back in the twenty-first century, Puddle-jump's open estate Cabernet riding in the carton now with the others, for convenience, cork in place. All the bottles were very similar, so no clues there.

How would Cotton Harrell's compare with the big boys'? It had tasted anything but crude to Les, who found it almost astonishingly rich, but he was a novice. Why not taste them all, on the way to Rudolf Wolken's where they would be sacrificed to science anyway? Had anyone ever dared conduct a tasting of a thousand dollars–plus worth of premium wine while driving over a mountain? They had not. It would be an experiment, an adventure, only fair since the mystery wine had been open for weeks.

He pulled over, took a pressurized corkscrew from the glove compartment, plunged a needle into each cork, and watched them rise like something extruded from the earth. The car filled with the aroma of Cabernet, the corks lined up on the seat, a plastic cup in the latte holder. Les began to sip his way through the jiggling chorus of bottles.

An hour later he was still driving, in a fine mood but apparently lost. Dry country, few signs, no people to get directions from, lots of scrub stuff growing near the road. Cows, for God's sake. He caught a glimpse in the rearview mirror of his own bug eyes and a dark cavern of mouth encircled by wine-stained teeth. Tombstones in a bog. He had forgotten to take notes.

After finally finding Wolken's road, he passed his place and had to turn around and go back. You'd think Wolken would be considerate enough to open the gate wide enough to get in, so the VW wouldn't bang into it going through, as it did. Trailers were parked haphazardly on what had once been a heavy equipment depot, judging from the looks of it. A double-wide served as an office for this unidentifiable outpost, a chain-link monastery of arcane viticulture where he parked and lifted the wine carton from the seat.

Les banged on the side of the double-wide, and the door was flung open by a stolid-looking middle-aged man in overalls. Les had expected a felt coat and a Tyrolean hat with a feather in the band. "Don't make so much goddamn noise," said Wolken.

"Sorry."

He didn't acknowledge this, so Les followed him inside. Lots of charts and a chalkboard, a big grid on the wall covered with colored balls, photographs of conglomerations of metal tubing and hoses, one with wheels—a mobile lab? On the long metal table were laptops, milk crates full of indeterminate gizmos, screw-pulls, cartons of wine. Les's job would be at the end of the line.

A sign on the wall said THERE IS NO GOOD OR BAD, JUST MATTER AND ANTIMATTER. Les set his carton next to a report and glanced at it: ". . . furfural contributes a pleasant odor, sweet butterscotch, light almond. . . ." He asked, "Can you compare these five wines with this one," lifting out the labelless one. "We need a matchup."

"There will not be one." Strong accent, a certainty at odds with all the junk.

"How do you know?"

"Because eetz impossible to say categorically if one wine is same as another."

"We don't care about categorically," said Les, who hadn't thought this through. "I just want to know if there are strong similarities between the test wine and any of the others. I'm told you can do that." The idea that he might have driven all this way for nothing was depressing.

"We take alcohol from wine," said Wolken. "We fix the pH. We get rid of off-odors and alien elements. We don't do matches." He paused. "However, we can compare alcohol and sugars, other elements. Crystal formations are a possibility." He gazed out the window. "Goddamn it!"

Lunging to the filing cabinet, Wolken took from behind it a pump shotgun, levered a shell into the breech, and shouldered Les aside. Throwing open the door, he screamed, "*You goddamned sonsabitches!*"

Aiming, he fired, and the trailer shook with the reverberation. Les said, "What the hell?"

Wolken charged outside. Another blast. Les dropped to hands and knees, hearing the door bang against the metal siding and frantic footfalls in the gravel. Silence, no way out of this pod except the door, nothing inside to defend himself with but a fire extinguisher. He crawled to the window.

Out in the postindustrial wasteland he saw what looked like two teenagers—a boy and a girl—running into the chaparral, skinny limbs flailing, bodies seemingly in rebellion against the effort of escape. "Meth addicts," said Wolken, standing in the doorway, panting. He flung the shotgun onto the table. "I don't shoot them, just over their heads. Makes no difference, they don't run any faster."

He passed a hand over his face. "Pot production moved here from Mendocino, these kids steal anything to feed the habit—solar arrays, drip irrigation tubing—slaves to drug cartels in Mexico. They leach water and fertilizer off the vineyards, take what they can. Last week they stole the hood ornament from my old GMC. A hood ornament!"

Les wanted out, but he would have to cross the parking lot without Wolken as an escort. "Is this a complete waste of time?" he asked, wanting only coffee at the far end of the open road.

"Oh, we can give some kind of comparison," said

Wolken wearily. "Throw in a fungal test. Fungi facilitate mineral uptake from the soil; it's a way of tracing the origin of agricultural products."

"Okay, here's my number." He gave Wolken one of his business cards, left over from *The Press*, the newspaper's name scratched out with a ballpoint. But Wolken was watching the chaparral. "How did this happen to California?" Wolken asked. "How did it happen to America? If I had known I would never have come to this country."

# 7

LES DROVE BACK DOWN to the valley, his day only half
over. He was doing something, by God. On impulse he
turned into Hutt Family Estates and parked in the Grove.
He took from his wallet the list of phone numbers Claire
had scribbled the day they met, and it included Jerome
Hutt's. He thumbed open his phone and punched in the
number. Two distinct bells sounded, then a click and, to
his surprise, the assured, slightly annoyed voice of the
vintner: "And you are?"

"Lester Breeden, Mr. Hutt. You may know my name
from *The Press*. I've written about wine in the past and
I'd like to talk to you. I know this is unusual. . . ."

"How did you get this number?"

"To tell you the truth"—lying—"I'm not sure. It's just
that I'm here now."

"At the winery?"

"Yes."

A large engine in the background revved: Jerome

Hutt was speeding, wherever he was. "Tina Schupe handles our public affairs, Mr. Breeden. Unfortunately, she's unavailable right now. What is it you wanted to talk about?"

"Just your story." Go for it. "Your vision. You know, Copernicus, what's happening to the valley. I'm kind of new at this and talking to people."

Hutt downshifted, an expensive gear box meshing its teeth like Train's Ferrari, though shriller. Hutt murmured, "Fuck. Why do they let these goddamn boat trailers on county roads? If we had a decent highway in this valley a man could get somewhere. . . . Move over, asshole!" Full-throated internal combustion baritone now, followed by outraged honking. "Bite me! . . . Mr. Breeden, have you had lunch?"

"Actually, no."

"Sit tight."

But he got out and started walking, hoping Hutt wouldn't notice his multihued vintage VW. Before reaching the winery, he saw the owner overtaking him in a burnished piece of high-concept automotive art Les couldn't identify but knew would never be parked in the Copernicus lot, subjected to falling eucalyptus buttons. Hutt raised a hand through the open sunroof, and Les waved back, then realized that Hutt was signaling not to him but to someone in the front office. As if by magic, a hole opened in the mountainside and swallowed car and driver.

Les passed under the wisteria-draped colonnade or whatever it was called and in through big glass doors to the tasting room. He gawked at the towering ceiling, a hay boom in lustrous redwood, massive rafters, authentic-looking iron implements. A silver-maned woman in black behind the bar smiled tightly at this new prospect; it wasn't easy to be welcoming and exclusive at the same time.

Before either could speak, Hutt's voice rang throughout the long hallway, issuing commands. In a billowy white linen shirt, he strode across the polished limestone with his hand still in the air, wearing a straw hat with a preposterously wide brim. "Bliss, give us a bottle of the '05."

She lifted one down from the diamond-shaped bins while Hutt offered his hand. "Jerome Hutt."

"Les Breeden." And he was seized by Hutt's lean muscularity: precise calluses, manicured fingernails. Hutt said, "You mentioned vision. No one has asked about that for a long time. The valley's become too successful, jaded. But vision's what it was once about. Not sensation—vision."

Bliss smoothly violated the cork with the mounted bronze screwpull and replaced it in the bottle neck. Used to the drill, she slid bottle and two generous glasses across the bar, and Hutt swept them up. He headed for a side door. "It's the vision I want you to understand, appreciate, Mr. Breeden. Because without vision, none of this would exist. Sometimes it takes a young man like yourself, just getting started, I suspect, to feel the full weight of it. By the way, you're a wonderful reporter."

"Thank you."

Les started to ask what articles of his Hutt had read, then realized that he had of course read none. And was he forcing Les to drink Cabernet to get lunch, spitting not an option?

Less followed Hutt outside. The autumnal glare seemed to have intensified. A multiwheeled terrain crawler for upscale farmers murmured at curbside, where some factotum had left it, HUTT FAMILY ESTATES stenciled on the side. Hutt slid across the seat and handed Les a glass. He floored the accelerator, and the machine rocketed across the lot. Hutt drove through the vineyard at high speed and abruptly turned, depthless purple climbing the side of Les's glass and trickling over his fingers.

"Give it a minute to breathe," said Hutt, urging his all-wheel-drive steed on across the twenty-first-century hacienda whose campesinos had for the most part snuck out of sight. "Now try it. Powerful, right? The wow moment's up front, the way I've wanted it from the beginning. In that first pop lies the essence of Cabernet—rich black cherry, grace notes of cassis and cedar back in the shadows, doing the antiphonal bit. That's Copernicus, my friend. And here you're looking at its nursery, the most important part of any great wine."

The speed with which they traveled through this maternity ward was downright dangerous. Stripped vines and parched earth packed between rows by the wheels of tractors, stippled with light. Miles of plastic pipe with the drip valves, legions of bright metal trellising. "Know what it cost just to put in this vineyard, Les? I'll tell you. Forty thousand dollars per acre, that's what. On top of a quarter mil an acre to buy the land. Now multiply both those figures by fifty, Les, and you begin to get the picture. And that doesn't include upkeep, pest control, fertilizer, insurance, taxes. Always goddamn taxes."

Hutt wheeled to the right, more wine pouring over Les's hand. "Oh, yes, and science. We're on top of that too. Have to be. Without science we'd be at the mercy of every alien species on earth—glassy-winged sharpshooter, egg-laying moths, sap-sucking whatevers. Russian thistle, cheatgrass, you name it. Comes into the valley on imported vegetables, fruit, ornamental plants, car tires, people's shoes. We zap it all, have to."

They came abruptly to the end of the row. Hutt set his glass on the floor and took out a piece of the electronic ganglia from beneath his blousy shirt, which connected him to the outside world, and he attached it to one ear. Without apology, he sat listening to some message being fed to him, then took out another device and flicked a message onto the screen. He punched at it and, when done, went on, "And right next to us is that mess," pointing to the neighboring vineyard. "I don't mind so much having a throwback next door, but I do mind being downwind of all his crap. Whatever lives in that jungle just has to get itself up in the air and over it blows." He was talking about Puddle-jump, his contempt palpable. "His wine's supposed to be 'classic,' 'Bordeaux-like,' 'austere.' I'm surprised Cotton Harrell can get even fifty bucks for that ole prune of a Cab."

He turned and accelerated upslope, toward volcanic boulders coal black in the shadows, blacker still the sun-struck obsidian under the blindingly blue sky. No wonder coastal shell-gathering natives thought the place enchanted. They passed a long, low structure set into the hillside, windowless, plug-ugly. "And that," said Hutt, "is the tail end of the most expensive private water purification system in the valley. May I?"

He poured more wine into their glasses. "Add another million dollars to your tally. First we had to reach out all the way to Saudi Arabia to get decent advice on what to buy for the very best water treatment. And not just because of demands by enviro-Nazis, but because we *wanted* to."

"I'm not following you."

"I had to build this treatment facility to get my permit. The wastewater coming out of the winery has to be as clean as it was when it went in. Well, guess what, it's *cleaner*. Also more or less useless, when it could be dammed up and fed into the irrigation system. Oh, we're green, no doubt about it. We're greener than most. Maybe I'm not as worried about what my messy neighbor calls *habitat*"—he dug crooked fingers into the air, making quotation marks—"or as *sensitive*"—more quotation marks—"to species that never lived here in the first place. But I'm a farmer, I love the environment. I depend on nature, so why would I want to harm it? I love animals, I even love frogs. But you have to take into account market forces, Les. And one side of me says this storage shed full of idle, blackmail water is *fucking ridiculous*."

———

The hole that had opened for Hutt's car opened again, and this time Les too rode in. Wet concrete, towering steel tanks, dense metallic spaghetti, dials, liquid diodes, pressure gauges, gleaming catwalks, everything kid-glove clean. Hutt left the bottle near exhausted on the seat—"There's more where we're going"—and led off with athletic strides, shoulders squared. "Now these tanks are fifty thou apiece. The infrastructure, the latest technocandy, lab, crusher-destemmer, centrifuge, let's just lowball it at twelve mil. Then of course you're going to need a showroom."

Somewhere along the way Les had been cast as a prospective vintner. This must be what Hutt was really good at and enjoyed: selling real estate to people who didn't want it and couldn't afford to buy it.

". . . We'll toss that into the prospectus. Showroom, staff, promotion, marketing. Plus you need an adequate house for entertainment, marketing cred. Let's just say, to get started, that you're gonna need fifty mil. Any idea what the nut is on fifty mil, Les?"

Les didn't, but he wasn't expected to answer. Another call was coming in over Hutt's ear clamp, distracting the man with a vision. Les held his empty glass in a sticky, enpurpled hand, ravenous, as Hutt shoved open the door to the private tasting room and gestured like an impresario toward the end of a slab of exotic wood the size of a small dock. Two places had been set, the result no doubt of one of the cryptic messages murmured into Hutt's ear.

More wineglasses, more bottles, including, in a transparent cooler, a Hutt Family Estates Russian River

Chardonnay. A baguette in what looked like an authentic beaten willow basket, a miniature iceberg sitting in its own accumulating puddle, obviously prepared in advance for just such an impromptu occasion, lifted out of a truck freezer and festooned with freshly boiled crawfish and crab claws. Also a silver chafing dish and an array of cheeses in a muslin cage. A tart of some strange fruit sat at a slight remove from the rest.

"You sit at the head, Les. Now, our forte as you know is red, but there are times when you need a good, crisp white, particularly with shellfish. We also do a dessert wine for estate use only, to feed sugar to those most demanding taste buds at the end of a meal, made from botrytized Sauvignon Blanc grown down by the river. But we'll get to that."

Les watched him pour icy golden wine into their glasses and lavish on him a smile. The guy could turn it on when he wanted. Hutt sipped the wine, evaluating it, and plucked a crab claw from the iceberg while his phone on the slab beside him sent more muted messages. The guy's control is incredible, Les thought, and you can't even manage your own saliva.

Les took a crawfish from the display, staring into dead midnight-blue eyes. He wanted nothing more than to de-tail and devour it, and everything else in sight, but first said, "I guess you heard that Craven-Jones has found a wine he thinks rates a twenty."

"Oh, that's really not very important in terms of the vision, is it? This piece you're working on, nobody's going to be interested in some Cabernet scam next year, or even next month. In the long run people want to read about accomplishment, excellence, don't you agree?"

"I'm not actually working on an article, just investigating."

"For *The Press,* right?"

"Not anymore."

For the first time Les had his host's full attention. "Who for?"

"Oh, a blog."

"What? Which one?" Hutt would have a service that picked up any reference to him in the wide electronic world. "You're not the one who said something about Copernicus being knee-high to champs, are you?"

Les opened his mouth, but nothing came out. Cabernet struck, he thought Hutt wasn't paying attention anyway because he had stood, scrutinizing the middle distance, and placed his uneaten crab claw on white Haviland. Hutt then pivoted, expressionless, looked around the tasting room as if seeing it for the first time, effortlessly erased the present and replaced it with a new version Les could only guess at, and walked out the door.

Les heard his crawfish, tail still intact, bounce off the china. Was he supposed to wait for Hutt to return? The puddle under the iceberg brimmed at the platter's edge, all that tragically uneaten seafood, that undrunk wine, that unsavored cheese and uncut tart. What a waste.

He got up and replaced his napkin, as his mother had taught him to do. No way he was following Hutt, so he headed for the door marked STAFF and found himself in the hallway of the laboratory, where a technician on the other side of plate glass stared straight through him. People around here had trouble seeing what was right in front of them. Les tried the door leading outside, but it was armed, and the last thing he wanted to do was set off an alarm.

Back in the winery, deserted now, he approached the massive industrial hanging door. A portal to one side opened and a figure stepped into the rectangle of blinding light. Not Hutt but a big Mexican pulling on leather gloves. "Excuse me," said Les, but the guy didn't budge, and their shoulders touched. He was older than Les but hard as sacked salt, and firmly planted between him and his little VW a million miles out there, across the shimmering plain.

# 8

HE WAS THE ONLY ANGLO to visit the Doc Shop in a long time. Sara Hutt looked him over: towheaded, blue eyed, shirttails out, big sockless feet in sneakers. He touched the contours of a rib as if unsure what lay under the skin. His admittance form said he was thirty, but he could have passed for less. She smelled wine on his breath while examining him and saw that one hand was purple. Not a good sign.

The usual tasting room dross had cut foreheads from windshield collisions, or twisted ankles from stumbling over stones in winery patios. They usually ended up at Valley Hospital, not at the clinic. "He didn't lay a glove on me," the patient said. "Except for that killer left, a bottom-drawer punch." He touched himself again. "He was aiming for my solar plexus and caught the edge of the rib."

"Costal cartilage," Sara corrected.

"I cracked it in college too. Guess it never really mended."

"Not cracked, bruised. I know it hurts, but try to breathe normally. You can put ice on it when you get home."

She took a blister pack of Percoset from the plastic bin on the counter and placed it on the examination table, watching him button his shirt. "One more question: Where did this happen?"

"Hutt Family Estates. Wine country in the raw," he added, starting to laugh but managing only to wince.

Sara could only stare. "What?"

"I heard you were one of the family, that's why I'm here. A cellar rat came out afterward and told me you might examine me for free."

"Who did this?"

"Big Mexican's all I know."

Paco. It never ends, she thought. First Alyssa trying to force a sale, then Sara's husband going back to New York, sales of Copernicus stagnating, now Paco beating up people on the crush pad. "*Why* did this happen?"

"I was talking to your father. He thought I was still a reporter for *The Press* and I'm not. He must have decided I'm an impostor."

She put down the clipboard. "Who do you write for?"

"A blog, that's all."

"Well, I'm afraid this service isn't free. You're not a patient of the clinic, you're not a farmworker." She paused. "I have to charge you for the X-ray, at least. I'm really sorry this happened to you, Mr. Breeden."

"Don't worry, I'm not going to sue."

Sara walked with him out to the parking lot. Damage

control. "Remember," she said, "only one of those pills every twelve hours, as needed. Is that dent in your fender new?"

"Hit a deer," said Lester Breeden, "up north."

"And is that deer still drunk?"

He considered the possibility. "No, but he's very tired."

# CHAPTER FIVE

*Crush*

# 1

GUESTS TURNING INTO HUTT FAMILY Estates were impressed, as Sara could plainly see. In formal attire, they disembarked from large cars and smaller European jobs, eager for the annual Copernicus harvest party, and she joined the procession going into the winery, under the big unused hay boom, her peach-colored cocktail dress too casual, she knew, but at least she had showed up.

Her stepmother, reigning over the receiving line, turned and beamed upon Sara. Nothing exceptional there—Alyssa Hutt always beamed, a sustained benignity bestowed upon whatever passed before her—but she came forward and gave Sara a hug. Perfect teeth, not too white, ever so slightly varied, lent verisimilitude to one of the finest assemblages of resin and supporting platinum in the valley.

And the set of Alyssa's shoulders, at right angles to the earth, seemed unaffected by gravity, steely foundations under soft skin from which hung, in protuberant conformity, two large breasts perfectly constructed for both cleavage and levitation that she had not possessed when Sara first knew her. Only a suggestion of support where they swept up toward the broad overhang of generous surgically modulated jawline. "*Sara!* I just have to tell you something."

About to impart a secret, coming closer so that Sara caught a hint of breath freshener and glimpsed light reflected from a thin metallic-looking lens inserted behind one pale blue iris. This was the woman Sara had once wanted to be, the teenager's dream of poise and good looks now morphed into a resplendent up-valley matron, another role Sara once aspired to and no longer could abide.

Sara's father stood on the far side of the room, as far from his wife as he could get, turning that low Australopithecine brow of his from guest to guest, his purposefully old-fashioned cutaway coat and elegant tie appropriate to the Bear Republic but not to the present, part of the ongoing period drama that had become Jerome Hutt's valley persona. He recognized Sara with a smile but didn't wave.

Get on with it, she told herself, touch bases. You know most of the people in this room, grew up with many of them, and even like a few. But others had been transformed as Alyssa had, the old personalities—and bonds—shed like chrysalises. Many of those she didn't know were members of the wine press, not part of her world, gathered at the canapé table—and Clyde Craven-Jones, off to one side, as per usual, a catch for any reception. Talk to him, she continued her instructions to herself, share some chatter, find out if there's a chance his mysterious Cabernet is indeed a version of Coperni-cus. But gazing at the platters of hand-massaged, grass-fed beef, the phalanxes of dark bottles, Sara was touched by a sadness deeply rooted in family and departed friends, and she felt like a wallflower at what should have been her own party.

Craven-Jones drained his glass. Ordinarily he would have merely sampled the wine, and almost never did he pick up a fresh glass as he did now. Annoyed by the tightness of his jacket—only Americans could require evening dress at five in the afternoon—he heard an un-welcome sound wetly insinuated into one ear: "*Shlovely.*"

He knew without looking that it was his emissary to the wine writers' rank and file, Larry Carradine.

"Don'chou think so, CJ?"

"You're pissed. Again."

"No, ish a cover."

"For what?"

"*Work*, CJ."

This struck Larry Carradine as inordinately funny. He exposed his Cabernet-stained tongue and emitted the signature shriek of amusement. Thin, sepulchral in an outdated tux, Larry was a dark slash on bright, enam-eled Siena tiles, a living caution to all in his line of work. Wine had more or less replaced food in his diet, and a once-fine palate had gone the way of a physique that now resembled a bunch of dismembered elbows in dark worsted. Larry added, "Caught Zhrome in th'act."

"Caught who in what act?"

"Hutt. Takin' bunches of grapes off the conveyor belt and then puttin'em back on."

"What are you talking about, Larry?"

It came out in a sibilant jumble of words and laughter: after the press tasting, everyone had been led into the winery to witness the culling of the grapes: half a dozen Mexicans, standing next to a conveyor belt, plucking less than perfect bunches from the steady stream being fed into the crusher. Making a show of dropping them into white plastic buckets, the owner of Hutt Family Estates was demonstrating the quality control required to make his showcase Copernicus. This had been duly noted on handheld devices and scribbled into a notebook or two, and then the writers had been ushered into the banquet hall. Except Larry, who had ducked around the tanks in search of the workers' toilet and found those same Mexicans dumping the supposedly culled fruit back into the blend.

"I can't possibly use that allegation without proof," said CJ. "Jerome would sue." Larry dipped into the pocket of his tux and triumphantly extracted a digital camera by the nylon strap, like a dead mouse. "Voilà!"

"All right, send me the images and we'll see." It might be worth a short paragraph in *Craven-Jones on Wine*, attributed to CJ's "correspondent," although he remained skeptical.

Turning from Larry, CJ impulsively took the arm of

Tina Schupe, Jerome Hutt's publicist and a woman
whose looks dominated most gatherings. Requisitely
blond, modish in a blue-black sheath, fetching despite
the drift of old acne scars, Tina was smarter than most
people she dealt with and she looked at him in surprise.
Clyde Craven-Jones wasn't in the habit of approaching
flacks. "Well, hi, CJ."

"Any of that new blend around?" A mischievous ploy,
but CJ was feeling his oats.

"What new blend?"

An unidentified wine arriving at CJ's house in a pashmina shawl had Tina Schupe written all over it, he
thought, but she was too shrewd to take credit outright,
if credit was due. "You must mean our regular Copernicus release," said Tina. "Do you like it?"

"Oh, yes, lovely, lovely. But what I meant was . . ."

"That twenty-point Cabernet you wrote about? Yes, we
should talk about that, but right now Jerome's calling.
Don't budge, I'll be back."

Before CJ could respond, he found himself bracketed
by two vintners, Guy—*Gee*—the de facto Franco-American
emissary to the Bear Republic from Champagne, and
Terry Abruzzini, beefy oldest son of one of the first families of the valley. Terry wore a brocade vest that lent him
a Barnum-and-Bailey touch, entirely appropriate, CJ
thought. "Kind of woody, huh?" Terry asked conspiratorially, as if he and CJ shared an appreciation of subtle
tannins. "I think Jerome pulled a little too much oak out
of those barrels, don't you?"

CJ made it a point never to discuss the wine at hand

in a social setting and so precipitated a discussion of the inevitable American subject, football, without knowing anything about it. (What could a tight end be?) Meanwhile, he watched Tina move on across the room like a ceramic blade through oven-warmed Brie. She leaned close to Hutt, the long-standing intimacy between them impossible to miss. No tougher operator in the valley than Tina Schupe. She drank bourbon instead of wine, without excuse, yet in Hutt's presence she softened, the two of them surrounded by the ne plus ultra of valley society, and whispered something. Hutt looked at CJ across the room and raised his glass, and CJ returned the salute.

"Speak of the devil."

The clutch of wine writers was gravitating toward CJ. Kevin Nomonity of *The Wine Taster* and a constant source of irritation looked at him frostily, his waxed mustache fighting gravity, incommoded by bits of Beluga caviar. The mustache lent Kevin a raffish quality at odds with his litany of fussy wine descriptors that bore little relation to the real taste and feel of wine, idiocies like "flush" and "febrile." CJ vastly preferred Marilee Tavestani, wine critic for the surviving San Francisco newspaper and a logical replacement for Kevin on *The Wine Taster*, when Kevin succumbed to sclerosis.

Sylph thin, Marilee just smiled at CJ and waited expectantly for him to say something quotable, idly driving purple wine up the side of her glass. Anything useful he might utter about his newly discovered, twenty-point orphaned Cabernet would end up under her byline with attribution, or under Kevin's without it. Let them wait. It was early, and yet, as usual, CJ wanted to go home. But across the room Claire was chatting with a Eurotrashy scion apprenticing in a California harvest.

God, what an incestuous world it had become, and what a wonderful one. The existence of hermetic American wine nobility rising in his lifetime, in part on his broad shoulders, was still a source of pride. Twenty years ago there would have been real farmers here, ruddy-faced men not in tuxedos but in lumpy jackets and their friendly wives enjoying a party, companionable and full of advice for newcomers. Today, the burnished complexions all belonged to golfers and mountain scramblers, to wine-besotted inheritors like Terry Abruzzini and hyperdevelopers like Jerome Hutt, all connection to the land tenuous and filtered through immigrants who lived close to the source and did all the work.

Was there someone other than Claire, who enjoyed these gatherings, who could drive him back to his house? No one he could see, certainly. Needing relief from the crowd, CJ turned to the heavy doors at his elbow that led to the caves and the winery and on impulse leaned on an iron handle cast as merry Bacchus. He found himself in the deserted private tasting room, before a long table made of some South American tree, and he pushed through another set of doors and into the winery itself, suddenly engulfed in the smells of wet stone and fermentation, primal and still oddly thrilling after all these years.

He started across the concrete floor toward the

winery exit, stepping over big rubber hoses nuzzling stainless-steel tanks like serpents out of Grimm. Once outside, he could call Claire on his cell phone and escape, but now he was drawn to the towering double-jacketed monoliths silently coursing with glycol that soothed the rage of the microbes. Climate control kept the whole place cool as a mausoleum.

On his right rose the steel superstructure from which the wine's progress could be monitored, impervious to earthquakes. It had been years since CJ had last looked down into the maelstrom of nascent wine. Suddenly he missed the innocence of his early days in the business, wanted to go back and sweep beards of mold from old bottles in Europe, to knock the tops off magnums of bubbly with a cavalry sword and lie hungover on a bench in the Reims railway station, to spit first-growth Medoc onto crushed marble, and to sip Margaret River Chardonnay while watching kangaroos slip eerily through the forest south of Perth.

And, of course, to make love to the impetuous wife of a vintner, canine style, on her tennis court not two miles from where CJ now stood, her crisp white skirt flounced up while she watched through a mounted telescope her husband engaged in a similar pursuit across the property. Things had been much easier in those days, especially at the mere 190 pounds he then weighed.

CJ placed his glass on a tread and a hand on the railing and heaved himself up to the catwalk. An adventure. Take it slow; there was a cane in CJ's immediate future, he knew, but he'd resisted out of vanity. He moved forward and at random chose a handle on hinged steel and, with a grunt, pulled up the trapdoor. Here the smell was strongest: bramble and jam and the acrid plume of alcohol. The hatch slipped from his hand and collided with the tank, bringing a mournful echo from the far end of the winery, and CJ looked down into thousands of gallons of dense red liquid. A scummy blanket floated on the top, the fermentation complete. Calculating quickly, he estimated that the tank's contents were worth a million dollars, more or less, a handsome return for Hutt. Incredible, in fact.

He thought he heard a door close, then nothing. A sanctity in this dimness, humming compressors, softly keening computers measuring temperature in bright, ever-shifting liquid numerals, otherworldly, unspeakably expensive. He felt a mischievous elation: CJ was a journalist, after all. It had been a long time since he had looked deeply into any wine not in a stemmed glass. If Hutt was faking the culling of his harvest, or making a small lot of mystery Cabernet, perhaps he was also manipulating it in these resplendent tanks, but the view down into this one was of darkness.

Bending over, he pushed his face through the wide portal. Clyde Craven-Jones was not above experiencing anew the rawness of the hallowed process, but he was touched by unexpected fear of falling. He pulled away, the stem of his eyeglasses catching on the edge, and they dropped.

"You oaf!"

He could see them in the gloom, hanging from a

baffle blade above the vat of priceless wine. The glasses were almost weightless, thin frames and graduated lenses supposed to lend him an air of authority. Cursing, he lay flat against the smooth tank top and thrust one arm downward. The gap was too great. So he maneuvered his right arm and shoulder into the portal, already hearing Claire's complaints about his soiled jacket, but even with his cheek pressed to cold steel he couldn't quite reach them. No option but to grope his way back to the reception, but his pride—and fear of embarrassment— forced him to try again.

One shoulder all the way into the tank, the rest of him shutting out light, the closeness of the tank's interior oppressing, CJ stretched. He touched the thin edge of one lens but, at that moment, his feet shot upward out of the black dress shoes that hurt his ankles so he had left them loosely tied. "Goddamn it!" he bellowed, the words thrumming off the steel cylinder as he watched the dislodged spectacles sink into primordial ooze.

Head and arm firmly inside now, the other elbow wedged between him and unforgiving metal, America's greatest wine critic was dangerously cantilevered, teetering like a seesaw and lacking strength to right himself. He couldn't fall through—abdomen and buttocks prevented that—but neither could he escape without help. But his cell phone, a hard knot against his hip, was on the wrong side of the hatchway, and to reach it he would have to release his grip on the edge, twist to the left, and work that hand up crabwise along his meandering midrift.

He tried, unavoidably recalling the line, "The probity of a wine critic is inversely related to the size of his waist." What idiot said that? Some people are more disposed to flesh than others. "Everybody"—screaming, surprising himself—*"doesn't fucking jog!"*

He touched the phone at last. Candy bar model, not a flipper, small mercy. Grope the polyester. Where's that Redial button? You last called Claire, all you have to do . . . But his shoulder slipped and he found himself upended, one hand gripping the baffles, the other in new wine still warm and sticky. CJ gasped, his face infinitely heavy, suddenly back in boarding school, under ghostly white goalposts, smelling rank grass as his face is thrust into the earth by beastly rugby players.

Make the air last, he thought, a winery's never empty for long at crush time. They'll come for you. Ignore that fearful heart, abide with dignity; watch the lovely spears of light in that dark pool.

# 2

JEROME AND ALYSSA HUTT STOOD on their broad second-floor gallery with its authentic Queen Anne fretwork and forest of potted begonias and watched the departing guests, smiles in place. She said, "Will you look at that."

A clot of tuxedos and inappropriate dark suits had noisily formed outside the winery—wine critics, always the last to leave, burdened with bottles Tina Schupe had pressed on them. Her work done, Alyssa turned and walked briskly toward the slack profile of the Reverend Buddy Dogeral of the Transformational Church of the Eternal, sitting upright in the drawing room and thumbing through a copy of *Country Property*. Jerome plucked the ringing cell phone from his jacket pocket where he had dropped it because the tuxedo had no belt on which to hang the scabbard, and Tina Schupe said with soft efficiency, "Jer, Claire Craven-Jones can't find CJ. He with you?"

"No."

Jerome preferred it that way, resenting Craven-Jones's influence at all levels but never letting on, of course. Every tasting room in the valley had been altered so CJ could pass easily through; his twenty-point rating system was supreme, outmoded, and an insult. Who wants a seventeen, Copernicus's last ranking? But he added, "I'm coming."

He descended the stairs to the subterranean corridor leading from the domestic to the moneymaking realm of Hutt Family Estates. Fluted sconces set into the walls threw a buttery glow across the floor, and sky shafts revealed at intervals the darkening heavens though glass panels on the surface. He ran a hand through thinning hair and squared his shoulders. His father had spent a lifetime under the exposed carcasses of diesel haulers that dribbled oil onto his pale blue work shirts, his nickname, Barker, stitched onto pockets that always held a pack of Luckies. Barker Hutt had died with a three-foot socket wrench in his hand, much too soon to witness his son's ownership of a high-end wine named for the man who invented the Enlightenment, or almost, anyway.

Climbing the stairs to the Barn, Jerome heard the voices of Tina and Claire Craven-Jones. "Hi, guys." He smiled broadly. "So CJ's missing in action?"

"He won't answer his cell phone." Claire's yellow shift exposed tanned calves cut on a treadmill, small, insistent breasts holding out the silk quite naturally, streaked blond hair above a well-formed neck. "Marilee Tavestani may have run him home, but he usually calls and tells me."

"Since you're here," Jerome said, "you may as well see the new cellar show."

Claire glanced at her watch, and he went on, "It's about stars. Tina, maybe you could tell Alyssa to go ahead with dinner. I'll get there soonest, with Claire if she decides to join us, and CJ when he turns up."

Tina went quickly down the stairs, skirt lilting. Still the best ankles in the valley. Jerome pushed open the door to the cellar and Claire reluctantly followed, poking at her cell phone. He threw the master switch and they were washed in light, before them the regimented treasure of Copernicus, two hundred–plus barrels of costly French oak, midrifts stained a traditional purple, a scene out of the Medoc except that the flickering candles were incandescent bulbs. And up there, at the apex, was a suspended disk of illuminated stained glass conjuring a mole's-eye view of the sky: deep greens and reds, intertwined branches of some mythic tree, an unreal, translucent sky.

Claire asked, "So where are the stars?"

"This way." Down the center aisle to an ornate wooden sled, upholstered and fitted with enough bolsters for half a dozen people. "Don't be shy. You have to be, ah, supine to really enjoy this."

He demonstrated, shoes pointed heavenward, dragging the portable console remote after him. He punched a button and the lights dimmed. "It's evening, see? We've created the twilight effect. Now there's Venus near the horizon, just like you'd see on a clear night in the real sky." He felt Claire lie tentatively beside him. "That's the polestar over there. Here comes Sagittarius. . . ."

"What's this got to do with wine?"

"It was the stars Copernicus used to figure out that the earth's not the center of our solar system. That was entrepreneurial. Now there's Sirius, the dog star. Sirius belonged to Orestheus, a kind of Greek Noah, and gave birth to a stick." Tina had researched all this. "Orestheus buried it." He tried to cover Claire's hand with his own, but she withdrew it. "And guess what happened. It sprouted as a vine, the first ever." And he was out of information.

"I'm worried about CJ."

Jerome moved his hand—ever so lightly—to her thigh. Firm quadriceps, warm through the silk. "Claire, give CJ a break. Marriage is a complicated arrangement. You have to adapt. CJ needs some latitude, everyone does occasionally. You feel that sometimes, I'm sure."

"What I feel right now is Copernicus's high alcohol."

He ignored that, imagining them together, two like-minded people in this spectacular virtual universe, under a hill in this valley, Northern California, U S of A, planet Earth, the Solar System, some galaxy or other—he would have to check that out with Tina—but Claire sighed. Desire? Or exasperation?

"God." She shoved his hand aside and climbed over him, the fading glow of Orion revealing a levitated skirt, a pale thigh, the outline of a thong. In desperation he punched at the console, hitting the wrong button, and

an arcing blaze ignited the face above him, not amo-
rous, stricken. Claire looked down at him as if at a speed
bump and said, "You're a brave man, Jerome."


The meal was ruined for him by that memory. What had
she meant? And his dinner guests weren't sufficiently
intrigued by Jerome's description of his accomplish-
ments, so Jerome left them early and went to bed, alone.

Around midnight his cell rang, and he groggily allowed the caller access. Claire demanded, "Where's CJ?"

"I have no idea."

"If you hear anything, call me immediately. Are you
listening, Jerome?"

Before he could answer, she was gone. Then, much
later, a revolving blue light on the ceiling. Jerome got up,
put on a robe, and went down to find a fresh-faced deputy outside the front door. "Mr. Hutt, there's an APB out
on a Craven-Jones. We're checking his movements.
I understand he was here tonight."

"That's right, hours ago. He's not here now."

The deputy muttered his thanks and left. Jerome
pressed his forehead against antique glass, touched with
foreboding, and watched the car's twin beacons dwindle.


"You better get over here," said Michael Phane, and hung
up before Jerome was quite awake. His head hurt—*not* a
hangover, an alien concept, bad for business; wine pro-
longs life, that's the idea—and he took two painkillers.

Michael apparently had some problem too complicated to explain over the phone, and Jerome dressed for running and went carefully down the stairs in a tank top festooned with chest hair and stepped outside.

The *thwock* of a stroked tennis ball greeted him—the sound of morning in California—and a bright yellow orb rose from the sunken court as if shot from the earth. It fell from sight as two Mexican field hands with red bandannas tied beneath their straw hats emerged from the winery's gaping entrance. Can anyone look more dire than a Mexican? Some invisible glue flowed among these people, who knew things before they were knowable. Jerome wondered what had kept them from hosing down the bins after morning picking, and why there were no groans from the big imported crusher, no rattling conveyor belt dealing with the last of the harvest.

Yellow plastic bins stacked on the concrete pad brimmed with precious Copernicus fruit, suffering in the rising sun. What the hell was going on? He stepped into the cavernous heart of the operation and saw Michael and Paco Cardinal standing together at the foot of the stairway leading up to the catwalk. Michael wore jeans with a crease and a shirt unbuttoned to the sternum, elkhorn belt buckle at odds with this raffish outfit. By contrast, Paco wore his habitual blue work shirt molded to thick shoulders and threadbare if immaculate Carhartts with a pair of calfskin work gloves in one pocket and a sling blade clipped into another. He seemed rooted to the concrete floor, jaw set, the official commander of the bottling line but in fact a free agent, valuable to Jerome in many ways. No one messed with Paco Cardinal.

Jerome asked, "What's up?"

Michael shifted uneasily, and Jerome thought he heard a klaxon. "That a fire truck?"

"First responders," said Paco.

"To what? Somebody hurt?"

Michael said, "You've got to see for yourself, Jer."

He turned and went up the stairs two at a time. Jerome had no choice but to follow. At the top, Michael stepped aside so Hutt could see the length of the catwalk, the big, bright fermenters touched by the glow from skylights impenetrable by ultraviolet rays. Then he noticed what appeared to be a pile of black plastic. "What . . . ?"

"Clyde Craven-Jones." And Michael began to giggle, a desperate sound. "Got to be"—covering his mouth—"dead."

Jerome was aware of his own shoes catching on the metal treads. Up close, some horrible incongruity: upthrust legs in tuxedo trousers, hairless calves like fresh hams, black shoes on the catwalk, all so still. On impulse, Jerome grabbed two handfuls of black satiny material and pulled.

"Jer," Michael whispered, "we tried. He won't budge. I really do think . . ." Eyes rolling, hyperventilating. "I'm losing it."

The report of Jerome's palm against Michael's smooth face echoed like a gunshot. The winemaker fell back against the railing. "Get a grip!" hissed Jerome. "Think. How long's this guy been in there?"

"All night."

"My God! What's in this tank?"

"The last from the Copernicus vineyard."

*"Jesus H. Christ!* Empty it. Now!" And he pushed Michael's willowy form down the catwalk, hearing voices on the winery floor, his heart hammering. Fighting panic, Jerome leaned over the railing to see two men in yellow reflective vests walking shoulder to shoulder, trailing a gurney. The EMTs would have to get past Paco, and Jerome waited until he heard the tank's muted interior pump begin to run before calling out, "It's okay, Paco, let them up."

No time to think. *Terrible accident, boys . . .* The men brought up an oxygen tank and a duffel with a yellow stripe, both impressed by their surroundings. *Take a bottle for your trouble, boys. Take two.* But Jerome said, "Here he is," as if introducing them to the wrong end of Clyde Craven-Jones.

They pushed past and grasped CJ's legs. Jerome had a vision of the wine critic coming apart like some monstrous chicken stewed in a fortune's worth of Cabernet Sauvignon. The men quickly relented and one knelt and pressed a finger to CJ's ankle. He shook his head, adding, "This pooper-dooper settled before rigor."

*Pooper-dooper?* "Gentlemen . . ."

They ignored him, their mounted radios crackling. One of them said, into the ether, "We got a situation here," and the ether spoke back, something about the coroner.

More sirens. Jerome leaned again over the railing and saw not one but two sheriff's cruisers rocking to a halt on the concrete pad, lights going ape shit. What will visitors think of all this? What will the world? Two deputies entered in wheat-colored uniforms and Sam Browne belts, wraparound shades dangling from their ears, and took the stairs as if they owned them, the superstructure shaking. Jerome said, "Officers, I'm Jerome Hutt, the owner. There's been a terrible accident."

They too slid past, looking speculatively at CJ's backside. Maintaining a professional air, they turned to confer with the EMTs, broad backs blocking Jerome's view. One asked over his shoulder, "Who found this man, Mr. Hutt?"

"My winemaker."

"Did you know the deceased, sir?"

"Yes, he was a guest here, Clyde Craven-Jones. We've got to get him out of this tank."

"Sir, I'm going to ask you to stand back."

Jerome hated being called sir almost as much as he hated having young women hold doors for him. "Gentlemen, this is just . . ."

"Mr. Hutt, I'm going to ask you to go down and have those big doors closed. And, sir, please locate the individual who discovered this individual."

# 3

THE DRIVER OF THE FRONT-END loader was hoisting the last bin of grapes as Jerome emerged from the winery. Office staff stood around, unsure what to do, the same with the houseguests on the long porch, with them Alyssa in a new panama with an indigo band, backed by Reverend Dogeral in blue-and-green plaid trousers that reminded Jerome of his overbred, overeducated, missing-in-action, soon-to-be former son-in-law. At a time like this, when he needed real family around him, Alyssa's expression told him that she was annoyed that someone had died and upset her garden tour, after the feverish planting of annuals the day before.

"Who is it?" she asked, and he said, "Craven-Jones."

Her mouth opened, closed. He vaulted onto the porch and went on through the open doors and up the stairs. In his room, he tore off the workout ensemble and stepped into the shower, viciously punching at the temperature control. *Holy fuck, holy fuck, holy holy . . .*

He stepped out and toweled off and walked naked back into the bedroom, finding his oft-invoked publicist standing in front of him. "Sorry, Jer."

He embraced her. "Don't leave, Tina. CJ's not only dead but stuck in a fucking tank."

"I know."

"You've got to get down there. . . ."

The door opened and Alyssa entered, her surprise quickly overcome by an awareness that she had already won this particular argument. "Well, isn't this sweet?"

"Alyssa," said Tina, "please don't."

"Cut the bullshit." Jerome looked around for his underwear. "This is serious." He glimpsed Buddy Dogeral out in the hall, stricken by the sight and unable to look away. "Come on in, Buddy, join the party."

"He wants to help," said Alyssa.

"That's just great. There's a corpse in the winery, Buddy. Why don't you go out there and do whatever it is you do to dead people."

"How dare you?" Alyssa erupted, and joined the reverend in flight.

Tina said, "Jer, why don't you put on some goddamn clothes?"

"You son of a bitch," added Alyssa, over her shoulder.

"Don't you even want to know what happened?" he shouted after her. "Don't you even . . ."

"Jer, two reporters are already onto this," said Tina. "It's just beginning. I'm working on a statement, but meanwhile don't say anything to them except that a freak accident occurred. Remember, CJ was a great

man. That's our line. He came here to further appreciate our wines, had a fall, more or less true, and we're all
shocked and deeply sorrowful. End of story."

"What about the tank? What about a corpse percolat-
ing in our Cabernet all night?"

"Don't let it come up. This is a tragic accident, period.
Keep it vague. In a difficult profession, people of all sorts
take risks to bring to the consumer rare and wonderful
gifts. And shit happens."

Christ, what a woman.

"You can't talk about the particulars," she went on,
"until after the investigation. Wrong word. Until after
the county has completed its paperwork. Meanwhile,
Copernicus is establishing a fellowship program in the
name of CJ, to carry on his great work and to encourage
the appreciation of wine in America. And the coroner's
waiting."


After momentary blindness induced by walking back
into intense morning sunlight, Jerome saw the white
SUV with the title stenciled on the side. A middle-aged
man in what looked like a chef's jacket stood in the
shadow of the winery: colorless hair, glasses clinging to
the tip of his nose, scribbling on a clipboard. Except for
him and Michael Phane, the winery was empty.

Jerome introduced himself, remembering the glow
of the launch the night before, the packed Barn, the
compliments, the beautiful faces like flowers clustered
in his very own human arboretum. The coroner said

pleasantly, "Homicide'll have some questions, Mr. Hutt. How did the deceased get into that tank in the first place?"

"How would I know? Craven-Jones wrote about wine. Maybe he was curious."

"What did he die of?" asked Michael, still ashen, arms folded deliberately across his chest.

"Heart attack probably, maybe suffocation. Was there carbon dioxide in the tank?"

"No way. Fermentation was long over, and there's a fan."

"Pressure on the diaphragm could cause it. Crucifixion death. Was there anything in the tank?"

Michael opened his mouth but didn't speak, transfixed by Jerome's stare. His mouth closed, the hideousness of the morning indelible on Michael's fair face as he said weakly, "No."

"Except pomace," Jerome quickly added. Had there been time to pump all the wine out?

"Pomace?"

"The mass of seeds and skins. It has to be shoveled out after fermentation."

The coroner said, "Well, I think we'd better open up that lower hatch."

"That'll take awhile."

Stalling, he sent Michael after the Mexicans, who had all disappeared. Paco could make them come back, but Jerome had a better idea that would take more time. "Michael," he said, when he returned, "go get a shovel."

———

The portal at the bottom of the tank, when finally opened, revealed a sopping wall of lees smelling powerfully of fruit and alcohol, bleeding what was left of the young Copernicus onto a bright blue tarp. Jerome could not keep himself from mentally calculating the value of even this diminished stream going down the drain.

The coroner said, "Can you get enough of that pomace out for me to get my head inside?"

Michael picked up the shiny new shovel and made a dutiful stab at the vegetative mat, then another, piling up this unlovely residue of quality winemaking. "All this will have to be examined," said the coroner.

Michael kept shoveling, exposing a dank hole.

The coroner reminisced, "I used to take young trainees out when we found drowned bodies"—pleasantly—"called floaters. I'd make those boys stand downwind before I cut into them, and by golly—"

"Could we just get this over with?" asked Hutt.

The coroner put on latex gloves and fished a flashlight out of his kit. He knelt, cleared his throat, and with surprising agility put first the Maglite and then his head through the hatch, rolling his face upward. Pomace darkened his coveralls while the beam made a bright halo about the steel rim.

Long pause, no sound competing with the ceaseless hum of machines. Wriggling free, the man stood and wiped his hands on a rag. "We have a problem. The face is beyond livor, dark blue, in fact. But there's no way to properly evaluate the situation without removing the body. It has to be gotten out of there in any event, and it's lodged."

Jerome waited.

"Think of an hourglass with half the sand gone. Then everything becomes congealed. In this case the sand's the internal organs. The muscles will relax, but the body still can't come down because of the pelvic mass and sizable posterior. And the expanding gut prevents extraction from above, at least by conventional means."

He paused, savoring the dilemma. "Since removal is paramount, the steel up top could be cut. But extreme heat so close to the deceased involves additional problems. Necrosis, for one."

Jerome could hear himself breathing. How had this happened to him?

"Scaffolding could be erected on top of the tank," the coroner continued, "but this is a very large entity being extracted. The longer we wait, the bigger the problem, so to speak. What with more gaseous buildup. I think some kind of mechanical lift will have to be employed outside, for sufficient leverage."

"You mean cut a hole in my roof?"

"It might be preferable, Mr. Hutt, the only alternative being surgery."

# 4

SARA TURNED INTO Hutt Family Estates, unsettled by
Tina Schupe's unconditional summons. The CLOSED
shingle on the lovely signpost surprised her: this was Saturday, biggest selling day of the week. The sheep in the
upper meadow stood still as toys with depleted batteries.

Driving on, she found the concrete pad dominated
by two sheriff's cruisers, empty. A lineman's truck was
parked outside the winery, alongside an ambulance and
the coroner's big SUV. More disturbing, the mobile
transmitting van from a local television station was
screwing its outsized antenna into the hard blue sky,
and a young reporter with brassy hair and a blue blazer
stood in the shade text messaging. Three women from
the front office looked on from the Grove. The death of a
visitor was all Sara knew, a calamity, yes, but what could
require an eighteen-wheel flatbed rolling onto the scene,
snorting and hissing, with an industrial-grade cherry
picker on a telescopic arm?

Paco Cardinal swung up onto the running board and spoke to the driver, and only then did the rig lapse into silence. Sara parked by the house and got out. Not a soul in the limpid pool, no guests in the safety of crazy shadows stenciled by the umbrellas onto violet tiles. No one to enjoy the lavish ranks of flowers or the backdrop of pleached fruit trees screening the Creamery which, in fact, contained the byzantine heating and air-conditioning guts of the main house and dependencies.

She passed under the deep eaves of the loggia and into the hallway, also empty, the sound of voices reaching her from the solarium. "We're not liable in any way." It was her father. "And which is preferable, a nonentity dying upside down in a fermentation tank or the country's foremost wine critic? The latter. I mean, it's gruesome, but think about it: Clyde Craven-Jones liked the wine well enough to risk dying in its proximity."

Sara slumped against the wall, aware of Alyssa's shouts: "That's the stupidest thing I've ever heard. The winery has now killed someone outright instead of gradually, through alcoholism. It's a sign. We need to get rid of this disaster as quickly and beneficially as possible."

How had this happened? She heard Jerome say, "I won't allow that kind of talk. Have you forgotten what we've accomplished here? Has your infatuation with Holy Rolling—"

"Let's try to be civil."

This fruity twang was Buddy Dogeral's, the same used in invocations whenever Alyssa invited him to dinner. *Lord, bless this simple fare*—tournedos of red deer imported from New Zealand, triple-cream cheeses, glazed tart of poached Anjou pears. And now Clyde Craven-Jones killed in the winery and not discovered until this morning. How on earth?

Sara entered the suddenly hushed maelstrom of damage control. Jerome in business suit, Alyssa with her reconstructions outthrust, confronting each other. Sara could see in their stances that neither would win this argument. Alyssa had arrived as a willing young woman taking over a household disrupted by the death of Sara's mother, when Jerome had no idea what to do with a teenage daughter, and money coming in so fast it frightened him, from droughty landscapes to the south transformed into prefabricated suburbs sold before they were finished, his gratitude to Alyssa infinite.

Sitting behind Jerome, in dark business silk, lovely legs crossed and a large manila folder in her lap, was Tina Schupe. She looked tired, and relieved at the sight of Sara, who took a chair at the one end of the divan, and said, "The immediate question is what to do with the reporters. We'll invite them in, give them something to drink, explain our mystification and unhappiness with this. Provide the statement I've already written and refer any questions to the county."

"Jesus," said Jerome, a blanket invocation that brought reverential concern to Buddy Dogeral's alarmingly plastic features. Alyssa turned to Tina. "We had nothing to do with this, and it's none of those people's business, anyway. I don't think we should say anything, wait for it to die down, then have secret meetings with Abruzzini,

VinMonde, anybody else who might be interested in buying us out."

In the beginning, Sara sadly recalled, Alyssa had seemed content to paint watercolors of gladiolas and willingly assume responsibility for the household. If it hadn't been Alyssa, it would have been another in the procession of lovely young women arriving in the valley with vague résumés and a talent for reinventing their pasts. Blondness was a prerequisite, but so was patience. Sara had welcomed her too. Though much older, Alyssa might have been a contemporary. They had talked about clothes and boys and ate whatever they wanted, whenever. Alyssa listened, which mattered most, distracting Sara from the loss of a mother. But at times things passed behind Alyssa's glistening indigo irises that gave Sara the heebie-jeebies.

Jerome shifted effortlessly to decision making. "Tina's right, we obviously have to put the best face on this. What do you think, Sara?"

She wasn't often asked, though she owned a quarter of the winery. "I don't know," she admitted. "*How* did CJ suffocate in a fermentation tank?"

A cacophony of minor, conflicting refinements to this question followed. Finally she said, "Okay. Something happened, we don't know exactly what."

"The sheriff's quarantined the winery until CJ can be gotten out of the tank. Goddamn his three hundred pounds," added her father. "And we're to stay put until we've answered all questions. The detectives will be here soon, so we don't have time to mess around."

"Why don't we just see what the authorities have to say and make sure we don't get out there with anything that could be embarrassing later?"

Tina looked relieved, but Alyssa elbowed her way into this pause too. "Since you're here, Sara, what do you think of selling, considering all that's happened?"

The firm's adviser and financial facilitator, Paul Rothberg, of the white-shoe San Francisco firm Pevin, Blass & Rothberg, had rejiggered the principals in Hutt Family Estates for the sole purpose not of rewarding anyone but of reducing its vulnerability to murky figures in Southern California, who were chasing her father's assets. Sara was just one partner, but before she could even attempt an answer, Jerome said, "Alyssa, stop."

"I won't stop, darling. I own half the winery, remember?"

"You were assigned forty-eight percent, a gift that ought to involve some gratitude. You can't make unilateral decisions."

"I'm sure Sara agrees with me," said Alyssa. "We should at least listen to the offers, it's insane not to, with sales in the toilet and now this disaster." And she having never before decided anything except which furniture, wardrobes, gardens, structures, and collectibles to buy. Including that preposterous metal horse in the herb garden, the sight of which, beyond the glass wall, made Sara want to cry. Daddy, why are you sleeping with the nanny? Where's Mommy in all this? What happened to the notion of getting out of the rat race and going back to the land?

Wine was to make everything clean and wholesome, Sara's mother had told her six months before she died, but Daddy didn't put on a plaid flannel shirt and a pair of lace-up boots; he bought a cravat and leased a Lamborghini. Wine hadn't cleansed anything. Nurturing beautiful landscapes here didn't make up for destroying them elsewhere; wine just whitewashed ignoble transactions the scope of which Sara was just starting to appreciate and made celebrities of many who belonged in jail, another engine of competition for its own sake—tax breaks, adulation—and a way for a developer to get people to ask for his autograph.

"I certainly don't think the winery should be sold now," she said. "It's bound to gain in value when the market rebounds. Even if it doesn't, I want to hold on. The place may not be really historic, but I loved it once and could again. And keeping it's a way to keep my mother's memory alive."

Someone was screaming, outside. The front door was shoved unceremoniously open and other voices—all masculine—joined in. Sara followed Jerome and Tina into the hall. Just beyond the heavy oaken entranceway was Claire Craven-Jones: distorted face, yellow silk party dress from the night before, dilapidated sneakers instead of dress shoes. In one hand she held a BlackBerry. "Jerome, did you know . . . ?"

He said in that disembodied voice used on such occasions, "Claire, we've tried to reach you all morning. We're as shocked as you are, and so sorry."

"You did nothing, Jerome. And he's *dead*!"

Palpating her BlackBerry, she raised it, and Paco took a half step toward her. But instead of striking, she covered her eyes with her fingers, the wet, heavy-throated lamentations genuine and surprising in this slight, isolate figure. As far as Sara was concerned, in that moment Claire proved wrong the nasty rumors about her: that she had screwed young men in the business, taken care of CJ only because she was beholden, remembering names when he didn't, running interference for him everywhere.

Sara eased forward and put a hand on Claire's arm: hot, tense. "You're upset." Remember what the manual said: speak softly, divert. Make the person look at you. "Claire, why don't you come inside for a minute."

"No!"

She withdrew her arm. "You're not going to get away with it, Jerome. Whatever you did."

"You threatening me, Claire?"

Without answering, she turned and went unsteadily down the broad steps and out onto the carefully maintained lawn. Jerome said, "Paco, drive her home if she'll let you."

But she wouldn't. Claire threw open the door of the Prius and slid behind the wheel. She did a vengeful wheelie, the engine sounding anything but environmentally correct, throwing mud and leaving two deep, strikingly dark tread marks that would keep the gardener busy all day.

# 5

SARA HAD NEVER REALIZED how many agencies even a small county needs to clean up human mortality. Everybody from Jerome to the cellar workers was brought into the house and briefly closeted in the solarium with the cops while Sara sat alone down the hall, watching. Also Marty Levinger, hometown lawyer and potter whose dreary ash-glazed crocks sat in various restaurants he patronized, and two members of Pevin, Blass & Rothberg in inevitable dark suits.

At dusk her father and Alyssa emerged from the solarium. "What's been decided?" asked Sara, but neither answered.

Without a word, they went up the stairs together, and Sara, watching from below, saw clearly for the first time the lie of the archetypal farmer competing with the châteaux of the Medoc and the Loire. Jerome had remade the land as it had never been and himself as a principal in a retrocolonial pageant, part vaquero, part royalty. His tailored shirts of pima cotton with the three-button cuffs, trousers without pockets, those sombreros. As a child she had slipped into his walk-in closet and discovered racks of white shirts with button-down collars and a rainbow of thoroughly modern neckties, all for trips to the real world. He had left her to languish in the pageant, and she could hate him for that if she let herself.

Outside, to the west, cameo mountains dug long shadows into the valley floor, and before her spread a bank of calla lilies, luminous with evening. This garden, in existence only a dozen years, had been pushed to vigorous middle age by a benevolent combination of sunshine, unnaturally abundant water, and a deep, cooling ocean just over the distant ridgeline now seemingly on fire. With that illusion came a whiff of smoke, faint but acrid: a grass fire somewhere in the hills and an alarming smell in this season.

Automatic sprinklers coming on with a *whoosh,* the garden filling with little rainbows. Even the palm trees at the far end of the garden looked happy, hairy as orangutans, festooned with splayed fronds that swayed gently, creating the illusion of a world beyond. She watched a scrub jay streak across the dense backdrop of broad-leaf maple and oak, startlingly blue, muted sounds of birdsong competing with the ceaseless murmur of compressors keeping the winery cool as enveloping darkness.

She turned toward her car and almost collided with a dark silhouette in a corona of light. "Paco, you scared the hell out of me."

He waited a beat and then offered a glimpse of those impeccable ivory blocks unadulterated by Coke, Snickers, even his mother's phenomenal flan. "You okay, Doctor? I just heard you're finally getting divorced."

"It's none of your business."

He weighed that. "Anything I can do for you?"

"We already had that conversation, Paco. Say hello to Mia for me," she added, getting into the Honda. "And remind her that your boys have to get their mumps shots."

That should do it, she thought, rolling backward, thinking again of those twenty minutes in the vineyard when she and Paco were seniors at Caterina High, he the son of the vineyard manager, she a posh Pacific Heights exotic. Paco could have pushed it then too, but life had accelerated and the world changed with uncontrollable, frightening speed.

To reach her house she would have to drive back out to the highway and then north to the dirt road that ran along the property line. When she got there, she planned to take off every stitch of clothes and climb into the little redwood hot tub mail-ordered from Seattle, after pouring herself not Cabernet, not Chardonnay, but vodka.

She coasted to a halt at the bottom of the driveway and looked back at the winery. The semi had been backed up to the north side and the copper roof pierced and peeled back like the lid on a tin of anchovies. Newly exposed metal glowed tangerine in the last rays of the sun. The lights on the cherry picker came on, illuminated an oval of roof and a man kneeling next to the ragged hole. A cable with strands of canvas attached descended from the bucket, and he guided it down.

Go home, she thought. Instead, she watched as the man stared into the abyss until finally, without looking up at the operator, he raised a thumb. The cable tightened, the diesel snorted, the cherry picker bobbing as it assumed its load; coiled steel began to slowly spool.

# CHAPTER SIX

*Dropped Fruit*

# 1

THE MEMORIAL SERVICE WAS HELD in the Caterina Episcopal Church, next to the high school, and Les in his corduroy jacket joined Esme in the back row. She wore black from head to foot, including a veil, looking seriously señora-like, her grief remarkable since she had met Clyde Craven-Jones only once. The church was crowded with others apparently as serious, including crimson-faced Terry Abruzzini, brass from VinMonde and a couple of other conglomerates, and Sara Hutt without her father.

The wine writers—Marilee Tavestani, Kevin Nomonity, Lance Stouffer—stared at Les. Notably missing was little Larry Carradine. A florid historian from San Francisco, another Brit, got up and gave the eulogy, in plummy tones speaking of Craven-Jones as "a great and generous man at the intersection of the verities," but without stipulating which.

Claire sat up front, in black, looking exhausted,

apparently alone. Les had tried calling her several times, without success, and now watched as she left the church before the singing was done. He closed the hymnal and put it back in the rack. Esme hadn't even glanced at it and yet she had belted out the stanzas in a very nice mezzo-soprano. "How do you know the words?" he asked.

"I'm Episcopalian, Les. Isn't everybody?" And wiped her nose under the veil with a fine lace handkerchief.


He left her in the parking lot and drove straight to the stone wine mausoleum next to the railroad tracks, climbed the rickety stairs again, and rapped on Larry Carradine's door. He heard an even fainter, sustained, quite miserable, "*Whoooo?*"

"Larry, it's me, Les Breeden." He tapped again, then pushed the door open. Larry sat in the easy chair in an old robe, head resting in one hand, a glass in the other. "Missed you at the service, Larry."

"No photographs!"

Les closed the door behind him and picked his way across that carpet. "I'm telling you," Larry whined, "*no photos*. Claire must have told you about them, but that was then. This is now."

Les hunkered down. "What are you talking about?"

"The shots of culled grapes being put back onto the conveyor belt at Copernicus. And Mexicans putting them back into the blend when nobody's looking. I told CJ, but . . ." He trailed off.

"Where are the photographs?"

"All deleted."

"I don't believe you, Larry. Now listen, this sounds like a good story, but maybe not for *Craven-Jones on Wine*." True enough. "I can find a place for it to appear, though." Also true. "Where it'll do some good, make you proud. It's a scoop."

"And it'll get me stuffed into a wine tank too."

"Nobody stuffed CJ, he fell. And nobody's after you, believe me. If you like we can keep the submission anonymous. I'll bet Jerome Hutt doesn't even know about the photos."

"Got a match, Breeden?"

Les found a damp packet on the mantel and lit Larry up. He fell back in the chair and stared at the ceiling, smoke curling from that angular nose that, people said, could once compete with the master's. Tears ran down Larry's ravaged face and into the neck of his striped pajamas.

"I'm sorry, Larry, you must have been friends for a long time."

"Twenty years. There won't be another like him."

"He'd be proud of you, going with this story. Where's your computer?"

Larry pointed to the tuxedo on the table, the satin lapels scuffed as if the owner had climbed in through the window after the Copernicus party and left the jacket lying there ever since. Les pushed it aside and found the little laptop open, the password scratched into the plastic veneer with the point of a corkscrew.

The computer came alive, and Les passed it to Larry and watched him tease up, with excruciating deliberation, shots of grape clusters going from a conveyor belt into white plastic buckets, then out of the white plastic buckets and back onto the conveyor belt. Nervous men in bandannas laughing at the deception— a lark.

Les leaned over and typed in his own e-mail address. "Okay."

"I'm through with this stuff," said Larry.

"I know you are. Go ahead, shift the burden to me."

"Poor CJ." Larry's cigarette went into the glass, and Les asked patiently, "Any idea why CJ was poking around Copernicus?"

"Not really, the cops already asked. Something to do with that stupid mystery Cabernet, probably. CJ shouldn't have been chasing that story in the first place."

"I agree." And Les reached over and touched Send.


He had just slammed the VW door when his cell phone rang. It was Claire. "Where are you, Lester?"

"Down-valley. I'm sorry about your husband, Claire." Worse than lame. "I tried calling. . . ."

"Thank you, things have been very hectic. And very sad." She paused. "I need a favor."

"Anything."

"Can you go by the district attorney's office and collect CJ's effects. They called yesterday, but I can't bear doing it."

He parked in front of the courthouse and crossed the street to the municipal building shared by city and county. The secretary in the bead-encrusted glasses said, "You're too early for the crime report," not realizing that Les wasn't still on the police beat.

He avoided the slow, steel-punishing elevator and took the stairs to the prosecutor's suite of partitions and walked to the cubicle of William—"never Bill"—Frobisher, an assistant DA. On the wall behind him was a framed color spread from the *Chronicle* about the local production of *Dial "M" for Murder*. Frobisher spent a lot of his spare time trying out for Little Theater roles around the Bay, and wore a silk tie that way outclassed his colleagues'.

"I'm here to pick up Clyde Craven-Jones's stuff," said Les. "His wife sent me."

"I know, she called." Frobisher kicked at one of the cardboard cartons on the floor beside his desk. "Tell the widow there wasn't much left. That tuxedo's history, I'm afraid."

He opened the carton and Les saw rolled suspenders, a little plastic pouch containing cuff links and studs, a pair of black shoes as big as lunch buckets, and a manila envelope. On impulse he asked, "Was there wine in that tank when he died?"

"Don't think so, at least that's what they told the coroner. Nobody really wanted to get into that." Gruesome wine-related deaths were bad for tourism.

"Some people say there was wine in there." Oh, so mischievous. "That the tank was full, in fact."

"What difference would it make?"

"I don't know. But if somebody covered that up, what else might they have lied about?"

Frobisher just looked at him. Reflectively, he took out the envelope and opened it, and extracted an artful arrangement of glass and thinnest steel: CJ's spectacles.

DRIVING UP-VALLEY, LES WENT OVER it all again in his mind. The aftermath of Clyde Craven-Jones's demise was an unholy mess, and that included the future of *Craven-Jones on Wine* and his own employment. They would never know the identity of that mysterious Cabernet because Claire wouldn't want to pursue it, and who could blame her? They would never even hear about the outcome of Wolken's test, either, because Les wasn't about to pay for it. Those five bottles and their crystals, or whatever proofs the mad German might have come up with, were forever lost in the wilds of Lake County.

Claire met him at the front door. She had changed into a smock, and her face was drained of color as she took the box from his hands without looking at it. "Come in, if you like."

They sat, the two of them and the array of wine bottles. He was surprised to find her alone. Devotion to the critic must have been all-consuming, he thought, and lonely. "This is the first issue I've put out by myself," she said, "and it scares me. CJ always wrote the headlines, and checked out label information, and made sure everything was perfect. Changes right up to the end. Doing all that alone is daunting."

They sat in silence.

"And I never thought I'd have to decipher *those*," she went on, indicating a slew of black notebooks on the desk, each held shut with a rubber band and marked with a number on white tape. "The bands were to keep them from flopping open and revealing to alien eyes something he had written. Some of it's indecipherable."

"I talked to some people," Les said, changing the subject. "Hutt, Larry Carradine. Maybe this isn't the best time to talk about it."

"How is Larry?"

"Pretty busted up. He has photos of rejected Copernicus grapes going back onto the conveyor belt when nobody was looking."

"I'm not interested in that. There are bigger issues now with Jerome Hutt."

"Like what?"

"Money. CJ didn't believe in life insurance, and of course a policy on him in his condition would have been very expensive. And although Hutt Family Estates has insurance against accidents, that coverage turns out to be pathetic. And there's no offer of settlement. Now Hutt's refusing to take any responsibility for the winery being unsupervised on the night of the party, so I'm in for a fight. No telling what that's going to cost. We're suing for negligence or wrongful death, and Hutt never, ever settles. Just look what he did to poor Jill."

"Who?"

"Cotton Harrell's ex. She's dead, but it was Jill who put Copernicus on the wine world's radar. Even Clyde liked her and gave Copernicus some exposure in the beginning. Jerome cut Jill off brutally after she got sick, refused to pay what he really owed her. Jerome took that suit all the way to the state supreme court and still hadn't paid when Jill died. That's the thing with him—you can win, but you can't collect."

"Are your subscriptions holding up?"

"No, and that's another thing. They want their money back now that CJ's gone. I'm afraid he's taken *Craven-Jones on Wine* down with him."

Les surveyed the editorial mess covering half Claire's living room and looked down at one page, strikingly free of corrections from that wickedly sharp pencil: "*. . . oodles of briary, berryish fruit. The gobs of ripe red current fairly gallop into the finish. . . .*" He said, "That's a lot of adjectives."

"I used to try to limit those. CJ and I would fight. Now I feel guilty cutting even a word."

"Don't think you want both 'oodles' and 'gobs.'"

"Probably not."

"Especially if the gobs are galloping."

She smiled. Little gap between the front teeth, tiny lines like wings at eyes' edges. "Well," he said, "I guess I'll go. You want me to follow up on anything, just call."

"And the dog's dead. Ran under the the FedEx

truck," and, suddenly crying, she added, "not the driver's fault at all."

Les wanted to comfort her but didn't know how. His ribs still hurt. Watching the light on the telephone console flash on and off, he wondered where this woman's friends were.

She said, "Being a cheerleader and a helpmate's one thing, a major domo another. I can't write and edit, evaluate all this new wine, put in letters from anal dentists and boozy bishops, all the while trying to wrap up CJ's estate. What's left of it. And deal with *that*"—indicating the cellar hole—"and placate an insane Polish printer down in Redwood City. Pay postage that's just gone up again."

"Want some help?"

"I can't afford your day rate, Les. Not now."

"I'll reduce it." By a lot, he thought.

"Doing what exactly?"

"Well," picking up the pencil, "I'd probably start with this." He had read *Craven-Jones on Wine* many times, usually at the bar in Glass Act, laughing at the rococo evocations of smells and tastes, impressed despite himself with the energy and enthusiasm that had gone into it. CJ was a believer, and he had a hell of a palate. Now the words, like ink clots on the printout, seemed careless and excessive, even nonsensical. Something almost sexual in the critic's outpouring, a passionate embrace of each bottle followed by a fount of descriptors left for his wife to clean up.

He assumed an editor's demeanor and made a couple

of marks, taking pleasure in lopping off a Craven-Jones dangling modifier while his wife watched. But Claire seemed to lose interest. She began to shuffle through the letters to the critic, as if he wasn't still there, then fact-checked a parade of figures from a ream of PR releases.

*Rampant oak and violets on the nose* in the description of a Santa Cruz Syrah Les changed to *toasty aromas of violets* and was quite proud of himself. Then a Chablis's *preponderant limestone base fairly dripping with zesty geology* became *a strong mineral component adds pleasant complexity.* Much better. Writing about wine was as much wordplay as expertise, and you could actually learn something about it as you went along. Emboldened, he said, "Claire, you need to create your own voice here. Maybe start with a letter or something up front, about CJ's legacy and how you're going to continue it."

"No."

"People will expect that, otherwise it's going to look like you're ignoring the problem. Admitting defeat. Then nobody will re-up, and you'll be left with a cellar full of product."

She sat uncomfortably in the desk chair, a lovely primate about to be shot into outer space. He felt like a blasphemer. "I'm sorry, it's none of my business," and she didn't contradict him.

The sun was impaling itself on the sawtooth edge of the western range. He asked, "Don't you want some kind of Web site?"

"No, CJ wouldn't even discuss it."

An idea glimmered, receded, reappeared. "I could come back tomorrow," he offered, "if you like, give you a hand with editing. If that goes all right, then we could talk about compensation."

"The rest of today's taken up with the lawyer. Maybe tomorrow, Lester."

# 3

Remember Copernicus? Not the man, the wine, that overhyped, testosteroneissimoed beverage so often in the news? You know about Copernican quality control, right, because you've read Idiot in Chief at *The Wine Taster,* right? And been subjected to the usual unending diarrheal paeans to "flushness," right?

You've heard all about that famous culling process at Copernicus, where less-than-perfect grapes are taken directly from the conveyor belt by trained immigrants before going into the crusher. But Nose has learned that the same supposedly culled fruit goes right back into the crusher later, behind the hype smokescreen, and into the wine.

Such Wizard of Oz creepiness would be funny if it wasn't so despicable, and pathetic. You doubt Nose? Well, check out the attached photos, in all

their unadulterated, pixilated awfulness. And
there's more, but it'll have to wait.
    Meanwhile, sniff, sniff . . .

The blog reminded Sara Hutt of bad pornography and
the shame one felt looking at slathered bodies in a copu-
lative tableau, unable to look away. She turned off the
laptop and there she was, reflected in the black rectangle, her anxious face and dark, knitted brows and eyes
that even in a dead computer screen were her mother's
lapidary pools.

None of the blogs had been favorable to Copernicus
since the accident, but nothing was as bad as *The National Inquirer*'s implication that Craven-Jones had
been sucked into a fermentation tank by killer yeasts.
Other bizarre suggestions in the trade morphed into
jokes that became merciless: *When this vintage of Copernicus is released, expect savory notes of sweaty tuxedo . . .*
Goût de *critic. . . .*

This *Nose* was extraordinarily critical and persistent,
if quite sophomoric. It would contribute to the slide of
the brand at a time when selling high-end wine was difficult enough anyway, and sales of Copernicus in particular slipping. Some kind of reckoning seemed at hand, but
Sara was left to her suspicions because no one at Hutt
Family Estates was willing to talk to her. She had considered hiring her own lawyer to find out what her father
was up to, whether he, Alyssa, and maybe Paco had
reached some clandestine agreement to sell, after all.

All Sara knew for sure was that she hadn't received a quarterly payment in more than a year and that it all made her sleepy. She got up from the table and went out onto the deck where the divan, in sunlight, beckoned. She retrieved the comforter, lay down, stretched out, and closed her eyes. She had been awake half the night, but now the sound of Cotton Harrell's tractor next door—the inefficient electrical whirring that he no doubt wished could be heard everywhere on earth where agriculture prevailed—lulled her, then she was watching people she didn't know grapple in slow motion in an alien landscape, without vines, trees, or houses, under gray featureless mountains.

She woke up to see light pouring directly into Puddlejump's vineyard, her mouth sticky, her mind unrested. The tractor had been put away and its owner sat on his porch, facing west, a book on his lap, but didn't appear to be reading. Men, she thought. You should be able to rent one and keep him in the closet, just take him out for the occasional trip to a restaurant or the theater. Cotton would do nicely, better than most, but he couldn't seem to get over what had happened to him.

Neither could Sara, for that matter. Odd how things turn out. All Cotton needed, she thought—drifting off again—was for someone to go over there and take hold of that rocker and show him how it worked.

When she finally awoke, she made a mug of tea, checked her watch, and, in exasperation, rebooted the computer.

. . . Nose has detected off-odors in the investigation of the untimely death of wine critic Clyde
Craven-Jones and what was in that big steel tank
at the time of his tragic demise. Jerk the cork on a
bottle of rough-and-ready, Dear Reader, because
you're gonna need it. Keep that box of palate
cleansers handy. Now take a swig of . . . this!

THERE'S A CHANCE THE TANK IN QUES-
TION MAY HAVE CONTAINED THOUSANDS
OF GALLONS OF JUST-FERMENTED COPER-
NICUS.

That's a hefty proportion of the current vintage
that won't be bottled for another couple of years;
some of you may be unlucky enough to buy and
drink it. Caveat emptor! The police earlier re-
ported that the tank was empty, but did they really
know? Were investigators too lazy to follow up,
or are they protecting the well-connected owner,
Jerome Hutt, from greater embarrassment and
financial pain? . . .

She saw Cotton, as if summoned by her earlier
thoughts, climbing their common fence. He started
across the top of her property, carrying a wooden case
with a handle, and she knew he was on his way to check
the outflow of water from Copernicus, something of an
obsession with Calamity. Trespassing, but she didn't
care. Cotton's monitoring saved Hutt Family Estates the
trouble of dealing with Fish and Wildlife once a month
because Cotton sent the results of his water analysis

there, an unorthodox monitoring arrangement. What she wanted to know was why Cotton was walking in Copernicus's vineyards the night of the party. She had forgotten about it in the shock and confusion following the death of Clyde Craven-Jones.

. . . Copernicus sales have already been badly affected by this, the most, shall we say, unusual recent development in all of Enotopia. And if this charge proves true—that the critic shared space with a super-Cab—consumers are a lot less likely to get gooey eyed about paying $200 for another overblown fruit bomb.

Another question: why was a respected critic looking into the tank in the first place, besides the fact that it contained wine, before becoming trapped in the hatchway? Was Craven-Jones examining an unusual fermentation process, just one of the ways he sought to bring good info about wines and winemaking to his readers? Neverending research and evaluation were the hallmarks of *Craven-Jones on Wine,* and still are, by the way. . . .

Who was writing this stuff? Suspicious, she looked up Claire Craven-Jones's number and punched it in. The phone rang several times before Claire answered. "It's Sara Hutt. How are you getting along?"

"I'm fine, Sara, thank you." The voice no longer belonged to the woman who left gullies in Jerome's yard.

"Well, if there's anything I can do, I hope you'll call. This may not be the time to bring something else up, Claire, but I feel I have to. There's this new blog kicking our family around pretty hard, and I was wondering if you know who's behind it."

"I don't read blogs."

So much for that. Sara then took a chance. "I know what you think of Jerome, and that you're filing a civil suit against the winery, so we can't talk about that. But Jerome's not the only person with an interest in the place, and I hope everything that's happened won't prejudice you against Copernicus. Against me."

"It won't, and couldn't if I intend to maintain *Craven-Jones on Wine*'s reputation. I've got nothing against you, Sara, I want you to know that. You're tied into something you can't get out of, but your father's responsible, directly or otherwise, for a lot of misery in this valley and elsewhere, and not just mine."

Sara thanked her and got off. *Tied into something you can't get out of* was a fair description of Sara's entire life, but she decided to try. First, wash your hair, then pay the electrical bill, make the appointment to get the car repaired, call Tina Schupe. No, do it now.

Tina's phone rang only once before Sara found herself in the rare company of those whose calls were accepted by Copernicus's ace publicist. "Hi, Sara."

"Tina . . ." She should have prepared for this. "What's up with this blog? Does the writer of *Nose* talk to you?"

"Of course not."

"Know who it is?"

"We think so. Jerome wanted to put a SLAPP on him, to shut him up, but turns out that's hard to do in California. You should check the blog that just went up, by the way. Another pain in the ass at a time when we can't afford to be in the limelight like this."

"What's happening to sales, Tina? And why won't Jerome return my calls?"

"You know I can't talk about all that, Sara. Why does Jerome do anything?"

"I own a quarter of Hutt Family Estates and deserve to know what's going on."

"I know that."

"So why won't you talk to me?"

"I am talking to you. But I'm just a publicist. You have to ask Jerome about the important stuff."

"He owns less of the winery than I do."

"And one hundred percent of the brand."

"He still can't make decisions unilaterally."

"As I understand it, he more or less can. You and Alyssa agreed to that, way back."

How often had Sara kicked herself for that oversight? Tina too must have been barely out of her teens when those decisions were made and things seemed hunky-dory financially, if already a nightmare domestically. So last century. When Tina never dreamed she might become a punchboard in Prada.

Unkind, Sara thought. But she remembered all those times her father had come to her with things to sign, and she gladly complied. Why hadn't she at least read the stuff? Sara said, "I had no idea how far afield my father had gone. I still trusted him."

Tina said nothing.

"I was a fool, and so was everybody else, with the possible exception of Cotton Harrell." Feeling blood rise to her cheeks, Sara added, "Something's got to be done about all this, Tina. I've about had it."

"Haven't we all?"

Sara sat staring into the cold, milky tea, the morning ruined, her hair still dirty. No yogurt, no stroll before work. She touched the keyboard one more time, and up came the luminous, artificial universe with words she still didn't want to read.

. . . and the winery has refused all official comment on precisely what happened that night, natch. Including who knew what when. Was something weird going on in there that Craven-Jones thought should be brought to the public's attention?

If the tank was drained clandestinely after the discovery of the deceased, who ordered it? Who performed the task? Who, if anyone, lied to investigators? The winery's so mum on the subject that scissors will be required for those sutured lips. But did message control slip into illegality? Does silence equal guilt? Are there even bigger issues at stake? Could somebody spend a few months in the county's Big Cellar for false testimony?

Stay logged. Sniff, sniff . . .

## 4

CLAIRE WORE SLACKS and a sleeveless blouse, but no makeup and no jewelry other than a wedding band bright against her tanned skin. Pushing her hair back reflexively, moving her lips almost imperceptibly as she read, she revealed taut little biceps and an underarm that needed shaving. Les, working at the other end of the table now, found her subheads for *Craven-Jones on Wine* as bad in their way as CJ's purple-isms. So understated as to seem schizophrenic when compared to her late husband's impassioned outpouring.

*Central Coast Pinots* couldn't be paired, in his opinion, with the mad rush of flawed red fruit, wilted flowers, and tortured barrel staves filling the next two pages, betraying CJ's well-known prejudice against all New World iterations of the hallowed grapes of Burgundy. So he changed it to *Pinot Purgatory: Will Santa Barbara Ever Get It Right?*

"No." Claire was standing behind him.

"Why not?"

"Too brash."

"You need to punch it up. This is the last issue in your husband's voice. You may have all his notebooks and can go back to his evaluations of past vintages, but no one else is capable of his, ah, exuberance. It seems to me that you could change the tone some, gradually introduce new stuff."

"Who would write it?"

"Oh, there are people."

"I can't just bring in somebody, I'd lose the unique perspective voice of *Craven-Jones on Wine*. And all credibility."

Lost it anyway, he thought, in a stainless-steel tank.

But he fed her more fixes. He had eliminated dozens of adjectives, fussy punctuation, unnecessary paragraphing, and widows galore, drinking shellac-colored coffee, drowsy as the sun angled through the high window, scenting a dewy sensuality that belonged entirely to Claire.

Lunch hour passed before she said, to his dismay, "I don't have a thing in the house but bananas and granola."

He ate some from a bowl with handles like ears, picked up, she said, in Provence. Claire dabbled on with her dark-leaded pencil, he watching her sharp elbows and the way she narrowed her eyes as she concentrated, shadows of doubt passing like clockwork across a perennially bothered forehead. She caught him watching, and they both looked away.

The editing might be tedious, but it was also, paradoxically, sensual. How can a dangling modifier make

you horny? Finally, flushed and irritable, he threw
down his pencil and said, "You should just jettison this
print edition and go online."

Claire stared at him.

"Everybody's doing it. You'd save a bundle on print
and postage, and you could avoid all this"—a nod in the
direction of the unedited reprints festooned with colored tabs—"and fine-tune the product as you went along.
No offense, but it's a no-brainer."

"Who would pay for something anybody could tap
into for free?"

"Those who don't want to be bothered searching, those
who like the idea of having early access to an online 'zine
that's daily tweaked and sent out to an exclusive e-mail
list. Sure, somebody will post it to the Web, but subscribers will get that first crack at it and they can well
afford to pay. And there are the ads."

"Ads?"

"I've checked all this out. If you do it right, wineries,
restaurants, hotels, God knows who will buy them."

"*The Wine Taster* doesn't give itself away free on the
Web. They charge a fortune for that glossy."

"And their wine criticism's unreliable and corrupt.
That magazine's gotten rich pimping for spas, hotels,
and restaurants with phony competitions. You could
do something like that, but with real info. You've got a
primo mailing list and the *Craven-Jones on Wine*'s ar-
chive. Won't take long to reach critical mass, and presto,
you'll be back in the black."

"Presto?"

"You've got to try something, Claire. This Dickensian snail-mailer could be your last issue, before everybody jumps ship. You said as much yourself. I'm just trying to be realistic. You could publish the new online link in this, the last mailed issue, bait the hook with more stuff about the search for CJ's still-to-be identified twenty-point wine. Some of the subscribers will take the online offer; those who won't would have bailed anyway."

"I have no idea how to set up a Web site. The very idea makes me crazy."

"There are as many Web site designers around as empty wine bottles. I can find you one."

He got up and knelt beside her chair. "The guy who's going to print all this is a troll out of the Middle Ages. You don't need him. There was never a better candidate for the net than *Craven-Jones on Wine*. You can have more tastings, more vintage evaluations, a lot less hassle, and maybe even some fun."

"I'd still have to deal with all that wine down there. CJ was indefatigable, but I don't have the energy or the palate. And now I'm supposed to launch some whole new . . . *thing*?"

"I can help with the tastings too. What you need is an anonymous panel that'll establish its own mystique. I have friends who're good at it and can keep a secret. Readers will want to guess who's on the panel, which will add to the buzz." He hadn't realized how badly he wanted this.

"Buzz." She laughed, shaking her head.

"It'll work, I know it will. With some edge."

"What would it be called?"

"Same as now, *Craven-Jones on Wine*. But the address would be cjonwine.blogspot.com. You know, they're your initials too."

"What if such a name's not available?"

"It is, I checked."

Taking out his wallet, he produced the phone number for domain claims he had looked up the night before. "Just call this. Give them the name and pay with a credit card, dead simple." Not the best choice of words.

"That's it?"

"That's it. A hundred big bucks."

"What are you getting me into, Lester Breeden?"

A bleat from the hallway, from the stacked washer-dryer behind folding louvered doors that had been struggling with the extreme grunginess of Les's clothes. He had apologetically arrived with two pillow slips packed with them, like chorizos. Claire had watched him load one and then insisted on setting the dial herself, uneasy with the idea of a man touching anything so complicated.

He got up and before leaving the room handed her a printout of a letter he had written the night before, at his apartment, knowing most of it by heart.

Dear Wine Lover,

You have no idea how thankful I am for your continued support and confidence. For thirteen years Clyde and I were inseparable, working as one. We wanted *Craven-Jones on Wine* to be the ultimate guide for all our partners, and by that we meant you, out there, in thirty-eight countries on five continents in twelve time zones. . . .

When he came back into the living room, Claire said, "How dare you?" But more bemused than angry. "The interesting thing is that some of this I've actually thought. Not in these words exactly, but along the same lines. It's a little weird, coming from somebody I barely know. And some of it's just not me."

"Change it."

"This is an insiders' culture, Lester. CJ wouldn't have done something like this in a million years."

"You're not CJ."

He went back into the hallway and loaded the soggy mass into the dryer, and reloaded the washer using her soap powder instead of his pathetic little vendor-dispensed packet. Claire had apparently decided to trust him with the dryer, and he punched it into motion, both machines rumbling now, the sounds warm, the smell of the soap, the sight of folded towels and a pants stretcher wide enough to serve as a tent frame reminded him of a domesticity he had not experienced since his parents' house. Then he heard Claire talking to a rep for the domain site, somewhere on the Indian Subcontinent. "It's a Visa," she said.

He stripped off his T-shirt, to change quickly into a fresh one, but Claire came abruptly into the hall. "What in the world?" she said, staring at his bruise.

"I had a little trouble at Copernicus."

"Someone struck you?"

"Nothing broken, no big whup."

She deftly touched his side, her fingers cool. In those suddenly flushed cheeks he glimpsed a residual clan ferocity from somewhere much different from California. She said, "*Why*, for God's sake?"

"I asked too many questions."

"That bastard." She withdrew her hand. "Jerome did this, right?"

"No, one of his guys."

Les was undeniably sweating, a further humiliation. But Claire too had half moons under the arms of her green cotton blouse, yellow flecks in her eyes under pale brows flared at the edges. She wet her lips with her tongue. Don't do that.

"Jerome's really asking for it," she said. "I'm so sorry."

She dropped her hand, and for an awkward moment they were both scrutinized by important personages from the world of wine, all cosseted in identical black frames on the walls: Rothschild, Lur-Saluces, Mentzelopoulos, Mondavi, Broadbent, Amarine. Movie, dot-com, and start-up stars, rakes, academicians, savants, clerics, and philanthropists too, but no photo of Jerome Hutt, Les noticed. There was a vacant space where Hutt's image may have hung before Claire shit-canned it.

Embarrassed, their eyes met again, and Les felt his head being drawn irresistibly toward hers, as if both were looped by an invisible constricting bungee. Feebly resisting, he leaned farther. She said, "No."

"I'm sorry."

He turned away and opened the dryer. Moist heat, a jungle in there, fresh smell, visions: sheep at pasture, things growing, bright cotton blooming in the Nile Delta. Thrust a hand into soft, warm, wet darkness. Then her hands were on his back, checking him out: shoulders, latissimus dorsi, waist.

Very slowly he turned. Their lips came together with a tiny bump of enamel, her arms going around his neck, his hands sliding beneath the blouse and up her narrow, muscular backstraps. Then she was shinnying up him, man as climbing wall, and he pulling up her blouse. He took into his mouth a small breast with a dark, engorged nipple and felt for the zipper in the back of her slacks as she went for his buckle.

Claire's zipper stuck, but his Levi's and underwear came down in a piece. She got an unabashed grip on the least intimidated part of him, saying—contradictorily— "We can't," holding on, putting the heel of her other hand on the washer. She tried to boost herself, he assisting, lifting her onto vibrating white-painted metal and stripping off the poplin, then her thong.

Shaking machine, another earthquake, lips to his ear. Whispering, "Spin cycle . . . big whup . . . big whup . . ."

"That was wrong."

"Yes."

"You shouldn't even be here."

"No."

"You can shower before you leave."

The guest bathroom, spiffy towels, rosemary-mint shampoo. Tepid water ran over his body while he tried to hold on to her in his mind. The bungee was still there, on the upswing, tightening again, although he would soon be gone and this sweet respite a memory he could already see trending bitter. He came out toweling and remembered that his clothes were in the hallway.

Claire held the pillow slips while he, wrapped in terry cloth, stuffed. She said, "You left a sock in the dryer," schoolmarmy, back in her ugly smock. He went back into the guest bedroom and put on his Jockey shorts, and she came abruptly in, without knocking. She sat on the bed. He reached for the clean jeans and felt a hand on the soft bump of him. Claire said, "You're bad."

"Yes."

"We're not doing this."

"No."

But she pulled his shorts down and knelt before him, adding, "This is just ridiculous."

They ended up together on the narrow bed, she on top, his hands full of her hips, Claire's arms twisted above her head like a piece of lovely, tortured bonsai. He heard a sound like none other, a sort of melodious exclamation. Were those words? He was acquainted with the panoply of orgasm—howlers, mummers, catatonics—but this was entirely new.

"You can't stay."

"No."

"You're probably hungry."

"Yes."

"I suppose we could order in."

The delivery guy recoiled as Les flung open the front door and plunged both hands into the big padded envelope. Grabbing two fistfuls of paper bag, the slick white cartons with little wire handles emitting a medley of smells: pad thai, chicken with cashews, soggy veggies, something on skewers.

They attacked them at the desk, across from each other as before, he ravenous, she controlled but persistent. The feast moved as if by prearrangement to the floor, kilim as tablecloth, fingers as serving utensils, Claire politely excusing herself and going into the kitchen and returning with a golden, sweating bottle he recognized from the label as a primo anti-Californian: Puligny-Montrachet. She poured two tumblers full, raised one, and said, "Just this once."

"Would you like a shrimp?"

He tried to feed her, and she bit it off down to the tail. He fed her another. She watched him shovel rice into his mouth as demurely as possible with chopsticks.

Suddenly it was dark outside, conversation futile. Les couldn't keep his hands off her, or his lips; she tasted of basil and crispy orange beef. Back in the guest room, she shoved him onto the mattress and pulled off what was left of his clothes, then her own. She stood for a moment with her hands on her hips, breathing deeply, deciding something, then firmly pulled him out into the hallway, back past more notables—Tchelistcheff, Latour, Parker, Masson, Ray—and into the master suite where the bed was vast, the white comforter like surf into which they waded.

Again urging him down, mounting, then under him, back muscles flexed, arching her neck and forcing him to kiss her. He had a view of the valley through tall glass panels as they moved, his hands sliding from her delicate pelvis to her breasts, back again, stunned by pleasure and the spectacle of that shadowy land suffused with pale green light.

He woke up suddenly and lay listening. The only sound was Claire delicately snoring, the comforter over her shoulders and her hip exposed. He got up, fondly kissed her ass, and pulled the comforter over it.

Out in the kitchen, cold floor, ruins of their repast. He poured himself half a glass of Puligny-Montrachet and ran a finger around the dark interior of a paper carton. Peanut sauce. Back in the bedroom, he got her laptop from amid photographs of her family, stolid-looking types in big collars, standing under deciduous trees. Shots of CJ too, in foreign climes, younger, thinner. Also a piece of quartz, a buffalo carved from soapstone, a ceramic lamp from the Mediterranean, a brochure from People for the Ethical Treatment of Animals.

He carried the computer and his glass to the divan in front of the window and powered on. The screen assumed a gibbous glow like that emanating from the dead satellite grown smaller in the western sky. He pulled up a blank page and touched the keyboard. Like one of those hot-air balloons that in a few hours would add bright pricks of pigment to a dawn sky, he levitated, words winging in from elsewhere, unsummoned, unstoppable. Moon to moon.

# 5

MEMBERS OF THE EXPERIMENTAL TASTING panel arrived separately, first Ben, a tentative specter behind the windshield of Les's old pickup, then Esme in her neat little sedan. They barely glanced at each other, Les noticed from the living room, she with something to read until Train's bright Testarossa felt its way up Claire's driveway, careful not to damage its costly undercarriage. As if by prearrangement, all, including Kiki, disembarked together, four doors slamming as one.

They trooped into the house, Esme Southern belle blousy, Kiki in retro Vietcong—crushed cotton, lots of drawstrings—and Train carrying his costly linen well, shoulders touched by the long, never-tended hair. Ben flaunted his ponytail and leathers, but clean socks with the Birkenstocks. "Keep the standards," Claire had insisted: no aftershave, deodorant, perfume, breath mints.

They convened in the cellar—six places set on a white

cloth, flight upon flight of glasses, bottles in brown wrapping paper.

Esme said, "Let's just do it, people," and they did.

After each flight they went around the table, ranking, Claire keeping score. The numbers would be computed later and top slots assigned; results were final. Les collected the notes and would collate the broad lexicon of descriptors and flamboyant put-downs, editing as he went.

"Oodles" was banned outright, as were "plush" and "febrile," and the decision made to phase out "gobs," but gradually. Claire's name was to be affixed to the tastings, and Les hoped, but didn't admit to it, that readers would come to believe that hers was the palate and brains all along, that Claire Craven-Jones was finally coming into her own.

Everyone enjoyed the chance to peruse the lists of archived wines and those arriving daily: second-growth Bordeaux, Côte de Nuits, Champagne, rosé. The old rating system would endure—a standard—but a new, less rigorous approach to headlines might appeal to the younger readers: *Is Contra Costa County Blushing?* . . . *Never Buy a Wine with a Horse on the Label.* . . . Claire put out a spread at the end—baguettes, country pâté, rillettes, Sonoma chèvre, Mendocino arugula, Napa olive oil, SoCal radishes, San Fran tarte au pommes, Willamette hazelnuts, Stumptown coffee. Up and down the coast, across the seas, with a sip of eau de vie or Calvados or sour mash.

Afterward, Les didn't resist the invitation to follow the others to Glass Act. "You go, Lester," said Claire, "I'm bushed."

*"Lester?"*

"Better than Chico," said Esme.

They sat at the bar, Ben on the far side, checkered towel on his shoulder, three glasses of Dunn Cabernet on the old wood. Les said to the two of them, "Why don't you help Claire move some of that wine?"

They coolly appraised each other. Ben said, "Delighted."

"I know somebody in Amarillo who would buy the house just to get the cellar," said Esme.

"She's got lots of bottles she doesn't need." Les had thought about this. "The way to move it would be in small lots, kept secret. No e-mails, no phone calls, no way for the BATF to get involved. Claire could cut her inventory, avoid taxes, and cash in on the closest thing Craven-Jones had to life insurance. So could you, as a service."

"Could we ever." Ben wiped his hands on the towel. "Some of the stuff's incredible. I saw verticals going back to '78. We can rack up."

"No, you can't," said Les. "It's not going to be like that. You can make some money, but you're not going to take advantage of her. And cut the Lester crap."

The door of Glass Act swung open and Kevin No-monity and Marilee Tavestani swept in with the weary smiles and darting eyes of the middling famous. Les felt a slight tightening in the solar plexus as they approached,

Kevin sidling up next to Esme, winking with a lazy lid and hailing the female pourer down the bar, as if Ben wasn't standing right in front of him. Ben raised his palms. "Kevin, would you like a glass of great wine?"

Marilee sat beside Les, one of those thin, shapely legs coiling, a practiced move, eyes on a level with Les's. The wine critic for the *Chronicle* was looking at him this time, and smiling. "You're . . ."

"Les."

"Yes. You wrote about wine for *The Press*. Blogging now." An empty glass had appeared before Marilee, but she waved it off. "Water, no ice. I like everything natural," she explained to Les. "Well, have you read *Nose*? Sure is different."

She winked, but he didn't say anything.

"Doesn't have much gravitas, Les, but it's sure lively. God, how things have changed in this business. And now poor CJ's gone. I already miss him, don't you?"

"I didn't really know him."

"He had a wonderful palate and such stamina. You could have learned a lot from him; I know I did." She drank some room-temperature water. "We're sensualists, Les. It's our job to be stimulated. CJ used to talk about that. 'If you've got the ability,' he'd say, 'flaunt it.' He could smell a broomstick across the street, best nose ever, figuratively and literally."

Her laughter, full of little crescendos, showed bright, even teeth. "*Craven-Jones on Wine* was about as far from this *Nose* blog as wine writing could get." And she coyly pushed her own little snout to one side. She must have figured it out, or heard it from Carradine, or Hutt, or his flack. It didn't really matter. Even if outed, Les was admitting nothing.

"It's a piece of shit."

Kevin Nomonity stood at their elbows, holding his glass of Dunn. He gazed imperiously from one to the other. "I'd like to find the son of a bitch who's writing it."

Les turned to him. "Why's that?"

"For one thing, I'd denounce him, since apparently I can't sue him."

"How do you know it's a guy?"

"Just do, trust me. And it's not Carradine. I talked to that little prick, and he's as offended by the blog as I am. Did you see the entry about one of my colleagues at *The Wine Taster* showing his weenie to a masseuse at Lopalinda Resort? Outrageous."

"Is it true?"

"Who cares? Even if it is true, what's that got to do with wine, its glory, its provenance? Its intimate cultural associations? That blog—like *all* of them—isn't worth the price of turning on your computer."

"Sounds like you do, though, and that you read them."

"I need to know what's out there."

"*Nose* is pretty funny," said Les, pushing it. "Don't you think so, Marilee?"

"Funny?" Nomonity set his glass down. "What's funny about ridiculing your betters?"

"Better at what, Monotony?"

"Nomonity, numb nut. These people are parvenus,

pretenders, pot stirrers. Without the Internet, they wouldn't have a prayer. CJ's turning in his grave."

"He was cremated."

"I know he was cremated! And he'd be appalled by what's happened. He felt an obligation to his readers, as I do. Unlike . . ."

Les stood up. "Look, Moronity, you're being offensive and embarrassing Ms. Tavestani. Why don't you calm down and then extract your head from your ass?"

Even Nomonity's mustache seemed to droop. "How dare you?"

"I'm leaving now," Les said pleasantly. "If you grow some guts in the next minute or two, and want to defend your honor, come on outside." He turned to Marilee, aware that Ben had come around the bar. "Nice chatting."

On the street, his hand was on the door handle when he heard footsteps and wheeled. Marilee cried, "Whoa!" raising both hands. "Showdown at Glass Act!"

One hand alighted on his sleeve. "You have to go?"

"Yep."

"Too bad. Let's talk sometime."

"As in an interview?"

"Maybe." She fished out a business card and slipped it into the pocket of his jeans.


Claire was in the tub when he got back. Les stripped, turned off the light, struck a match to the candle on the windowsill, and got in behind her. He pulled Claire to him, her wet hair in his face.

She asked, "Have you given up the investigation, Lester?"

"No." And he told her, at last, about Wolken and the trip to Lake County. "It's a real long shot. Probably none of those wines will match up, and we'll be back where we started. Might have to admit defeat in this issue, Claire. What happened to the shawl that wine was wrapped in, by the way?"

"It's somewhere in the dresser. Oh, Lester, I feel so bad about CJ," and she fell asleep in his arms.

Nose hears that the columnist for *The Wine Slobberer,* one K. Nonentity, maintained the other night in that finest of wine bars, Glass Act, that mere mortals have no business judging wine. That it should be left to professionals whose hands—and feet—are so deep in industry pockets that they've become quadriplegic.

We already know that Nonentity, after his "blind" tastings, strips the paper bags and makes sure that certain bottles get their expected plaudits. Has Trifecta gotten this favorable treatment? Has Copernicus?

Both wines were in the last tasting Clyde Craven-Jones conducted, of high-end Cabernets from the very valley where he lived. But the winner—hold on to your glasses—the Cabernet that's never identified, may be revealed soon! And for the first time, this strange, fascinating, ground-breaking investigation will be discussed in the pages of *Craven-Jones on Wine,* with exclusive inside commentary, of course, right here in your favorite blog.

Sniff, sniff . . .

# 6

SARA SAW HIM COMING—the lank fluidity, that almost endearing distractedness as Cotton stepped onto the stile and over the fence. He had built the stile more than a year ago; in all that time Sara had not used it once. Not because she thought he would object but because she was a Hutt and her family's freight too much for that frail assemblage of old redwood cut in Cotton's shop and nailed up in less than an hour, after he asked her permission to monitor the water from the winery.

This time Cotton didn't turn up-property but toward her house. She went out onto the deck and said, "Hi, Cotton," noticing his pants leg riding up on one boot, the ragged cuffs on his Levi's jacket. Residual tan, a utility tool in the worn leather case on his hip.

"Hi, Sara," gazing westward, half turning as if he had changed his mind. "I have a favor to ask."

"Okay."

"Can we bring a truckload of washed gravel across

your place, to spread on the bottom of the water storage unit?"

"Why?"

"An experiment, worthwhile. Fish and Wildlife's
all for it. There's a chance something could spawn up
there—salmon, maybe even steelhead—if we mimic the
streambed. And if the inflow and outflow pipes are
pulled and the ground leveled. The stream would move
through the tank naturally without barriers or drop-
offs. It might work as a kind of nursery."

Sara didn't know what to say, uncertainty the only
thing in her life now. Cotton was talking again, as usual,
about fish. "The stream already flows in from the top
when there's sufficient runoff, mixes with the treated
winery water. If there was enough volume in summer,
not for a real flow but something, and since it's already
shaded by the roof, not just fish but mayflies too might
reproduce."

"What will it cost?"

"Nothing. They'll give us the gravel and send over a
soils guy to supervise the grading, which I can do. But
it'll have to be now, at the beginning of the rainy season,
so the truck'll leave some ruts. I think if he came in
along the fence line where the old wagon road was, it won't
be too bad, and I can grade and throw out some grass
seed."

"That's fine, Cotton."

"We'd have to spread the gravel," he went on. "So
there'd be me and Raul and the soils guy up there, stomping around for an afternoon."

"Cotton, you're *always* stomping around up there."

"Your father won't like it."

"My father doesn't own those acres, I do. He doesn't own the water, either. And he has other things on his mind."

"Thanks."

But he didn't turn to go, something else on his mind. He said, "You don't even know, do you, Sara?"

"Know what?"

"About the plan."

"For salmon?"

"No, houses."

They went inside and sat at the kitchen table, where she reflexively poured dark greasy coffee she had no stomach for. And he began to pull leaves off the artichoke of Hutt Enterprises, her father's real estate consortium, not hungrily but relentlessly, almost chagrined at his extensive knowledge of her family's affairs but on a building wave of anger that lifted her as well.

"It started with those lot-line adjustments Jerome paid for years ago," said Cotton. "He dedicated much of the property to the land trust and got some tax deductions. All that black rock and chaparral up there was supposed to remain forever unobstructed, and now, it seems, new houses will soon be there, the lots cut into the mountainside."

"How did this happen?"

"Jerome never actually transferred the parcels to the land trust, as he was supposed to do. Don't know how he got away with it, probably by promising to pay every year and then not paying. Making donations now and then, like a marker, promising to eventually do the right thing while people, including you, it seems, thought it was a done deal and the sites were protected. Now a big real estate play's on rails for those same parcels. The planning commission approved it in executive session, and the supervisors are to vote on it at the next meeting. *The Press* won't touch this story because development's supposedly good for the county, which doesn't leave us with a good option."

*Us.* That was quick, she thought, his assumption that they were suddenly allies. But she felt more resentment of her father than anything else. To the list of Jerome's creditors must be added the Internal Revenue Service, no doubt to be paid off when the sale went through.

"Jerome and his lawyers want to keep the lid on this," Cotton said, "until after the vote. He thinks the deal will help bail out the winery, and county bureaucrats want new taxes and real estate churning. This could also be their way of getting the zoning laws changed to allow more development in the valley, and there are plenty of people who want that. These are bleak economic times."

She imagined cars on the slopes above her property, instead of wild pigs and Santa Ana hummingbirds, the drivers looking down at the spread of Copernicus, and at Puddle-jump's quaint diorama of the lost agrarian past, more scenic contrast for the motoring tourist. "You said something about bailing out the winery. What do you mean, exactly?"

"The place's a fiduciary mess, I'm told. Maybe you

don't know that your father leveraged it to pay litigants in Southern California and here. Sales are way off. Who wants to be moving two-hundred-dollar Cabernet in this market, particularly with a nut as big as Jerome's and all his PR problems, compounded by the death of Clyde Craven-Jones?"

"How can he leverage it when it isn't his?"

"He's empowered to borrow against the property, apparently. He's already done that and probably figured out a way to cut those parcels loose from Hutt Family Estates and get whole again, although I don't know the details."

"What can I do?"

"Object. Your voice would carry a lot of weight, being family. And you'd be the closest downslope sufferer, all that lawn fertilizer coming straight off the mountain, into the creek and over your land. The houses will have to drill deep, depleting wells. The one bright picture in all this is the water he stashed on your property because he didn't want to have to pay for storing it. He stuck you with the responsibility for that, and now there's nothing he can do to get it back."

Cotton's cup was empty, as was hers. This was why her father avoided her and refused to talk shop on the rare occasions they were together. Jerome's alternative to selling the place now was to ruin it, as he had ruined other landscapes, and then sell at the height of speculation over what would no doubt be the sort of exclusive developments he invented. She saw the endgame and it made her sick; Sara had been a fool, so removed that it took a neighbor climbing a fence to bring her back to reality.

"The *Chronicle*'s not interested in another rich vintner's real estate deal," said Cotton. "There are no media alternatives left around here. Some neighbors, and Friends of the Flow, are making calls right now. The only reason you didn't get one is that people assume you're on the other side. There's not much time to get the word out."

"I know of a possibility," she said, thinking of a young man with a bruised rib cage, standing next to his beat-up Volkswagen. "What else can I do, Cotton?"

# CHAPTER SEVEN

---

## *The Adjustment*

# 1

Well, now. Just when Nose thought the Copernicus saga was winding down, another hydra raises its gruesome head—to wit: McMansions!

Jerome Hutt, managing partner of Hutt Family Estates, wants to further dilute his once-formidable reputation by planting not more Cabernet vines but concrete foundations, wells, swimming pools, vast wine cellars, and no doubt towering sculptures, all on slopes above the fabled Copernicus vineyards.

This would take advantage of so-called historic home sites Hutt's minions "discovered" years ago and placed in his personal land bank, apparently for future development of the sort certain to destroy the valley's views to the east, as well as zoning restrictions that have long been the bane of developers like Hutt, who know that more money can be made growing houses than grapes. When

Copernicus's wine sales are headed for terminal tank.

And, on top of this, the district attorney's office is considering reopening its inquiries into the conduct of the winery in the immediate aftermath of the tragic death of noted wine critic Clyde Craven-Jones. Will Copernicus winemaker Michael Phane have to go in for requestioning? Will Hutt himself have to drop by the DA's for a chat?

But Nose digresses. Hutt's new gated community—can't you just see it, "Copernicus Mini-Estates, financing and discounted wine available"?—depends upon approval of a dithering county board of supervisors, since the application was passed by the lickspittle planning department last week—in camera.

How did this happen? According to those involved in the opposition—and by someone who is intimate with the family, so to speak—it happened because Hutt has the winery's legal reins. His lawyers have extensively lobbied for this, promising civic and campaign contributions and short-term jobs and tax receipts.

*The Valley Press*, best suited for the bottom of your birdcage, is in favor of the project and so neglecting to report what's really transpiring in the fabled valley, the resident wine writer, one Lance Toady, terrified of losing his dubious status in the valley's wineocracy.

And wine writers for still breathing newspapers (hello, *Chronicle*!) can't be bothered with lowly real estate transactions when they have glam Cabs to quaff. So the supervisors will approve Hutt's outrage if people don't show up and make their objections known. Should be quite a circus. Will you be there?

Nose will. Sniff, sniff . . .

# 2

SARA PASSED THE MINIMALL and the cut-rate gas station near the county courthouse. She had been here many times and once actually attended a meeting of the supervisors, when Jerome received his permit for the winery and she, in her last year of college, felt the power of a dawning enterprise—*her* enterprise, she had been led to believe. But she felt like a stranger tonight, the ruin of old hopes and aspirations standing taller than this architectural landmark.

She was already half an hour late but parked and went into a bar on Main Street and ordered a vodka martini. Appalled at the price of it, feeling awkward on a stool surrounded by younger people, an attractive, almost middle-aged woman with dark hair and something on her mind looking at herself—again—in an antiqued mirror, this one behind the array of single-malt scotches. How long since you had an impromptu drink like this, Sara? Not since you started a new life in San Francisco, after it had become clear that Jerome's plans for the winery bore no resemblance to those you had once discussed, that he had no intention of someday turning it over to you, his daughter.

Her life beyond the Bay had been busy and expensive. But it was to be all about marriage, and now one side of that arrangement had flown off to Manhattan and the concept fractured. In the meantime, her friends in the valley married and some moved away. Those who stayed kept her at a slight distance now, their intimacies taking on a dilatory quality. This latest turn of the Copernicus screw had starkly revealed the absence of anyone in the hood to help console her, something she found sad, and inexplicable.

Her job at the Doc Shop was supposed to have reconnected her to the valley but instead had cubbyholed her—Sara Hutt, part professional, part servant, roles at subtle odds with the social elite to which she so obviously belonged.

She crossed the square to the county headquarters, its fourth floor ablaze with lights. Take the stairs, avoid the eyes of people standing in the hallway outside the meeting room. These events always had a theatrical quality when issues arose affecting the valley's glamour product, the big moths drawn to the glare, to contend over the future of the money generator—wine and its ancillary activities, all of which boiled down to real estate.

She recognized the president of VinMonde USA; a sprinkling of vintners; two of Jerome's attorneys, Marty Levinger and Anthony, the ranking partner from

Pevin, Blass & Rothberg. They had already made their
presentation, and neither noticed Sara slip in. But Terry
Abruzzini did, and he smiled in a disturbing, ingratiating way.

There was a reporter from *The Press,* and Les
Breeden, looking more civilized than the last time she
saw him. But the one person she wanted to see, her father, unreachable by phone and by proxy now, was not
in the room. Judging by his legal team, Jerome wouldn't
be lacking representation before the supervisors, decked
out in their suits and ties, evincing a collective bonhomie. These politicians clearly gloried in the fact that their
opinions—their votes—were of value, and the woman
among them, also in a suit, was in other ways indistin-
guishable from her male counterparts.

At the lectern, a Hutt Family Estates neighbor was
talking about runoff—"the cumulative effect of downslope
degradation"—and Sara settled into the one empty
molded-plastic chair for a long night. She had barely
slept and felt its absence despite all the caffeine. She had
never been one for all-nighters before college exams,
and the prospect of this hearing had been an awful specter by the bed since daybreak.

Cotton Harrell, broomstick straight in the front row
with other members of the opposition, seemed to be deciding who would speak, and when. He too had missed
Sara's entrance, and she felt relieved, not yet sure she
could stand up before this potent crowd and certainly
not wanting to. She hoped that the need would be over-
ridden by some revelation, some political ploy used by

Cotton and his allies to nullify the proposed development, and they could all go home.

"Sara, how *are* you?"

Standing behind her, bending nimbly at the waist, a silk handkerchief in the pocket of his jacket, flushed cheeks signaling vitality, blue eyes enlivened by his discovery of her, was Anthony P, the Pevin of Pevin, Blass & Rothberg, unprepared for her presence but never overlooking a person or an opportunity in any room. His radar was so sensitive, his instincts so true that he deserved the sums of money attracted to him like iron filings to magnetized iron.

"Hello, Anthony, where's Jerome?"

He leaned closer, smelling faintly of something expensive and masculine. The woman next to Sara shifted uneasily. "Your father couldn't be here so he asked us to drop by." *Drop by.* "Sara, this is a good thing for the property, for everyone. The development won't affect the vineyards, it's to be tasteful beyond belief. People won't even be able to see—"

"Why wasn't this discussed with me?" She realized then that he didn't know and was subtly repositioning.

"Sara, can we talk out in the hall?"

"I don't want to give up my seat."

"Well, everything has happened so quickly. We—"

The woman turned. "Do you mind?"

Pevin lowered upon her a gaze so withering that Sara had no choice but to excuse herself and ease past a dozen pairs of knees. Out in the hall, she turned on him. "Anthony, what the hell is this? Does Jerome actually think I and the rest of the neighbors are going to sit on our hands while this happens? That he doesn't even have to *show up*?"

"Sara, you've got it all wrong." The projection of surprise, the intimation that she had both misunderstood him and hurt his feelings, was classic Anthony. "This little project isn't even going to be seen by half of them. It's the most environmentally correct experiment in residential living in North America, designed to get a top LEED rating."

"I don't care. My question to you was, why hasn't Jerome come to me about this? I own a quarter of the fucking winery."

He winced. "Your father didn't want to burden you."

"He didn't, huh? Well, he doesn't own the land, or the house. He shouldn't make unilateral decisions the way he used to, there's too much at stake now."

"He has power of attorney, Sara. And he does own the brand, which is crucial to the success. . . ."

"What he's doing is wrong and downright pathological. And you know it."

"Jerome's under a lot of stress these days. He's come up with a solution to the liquidity problem, but he's in no shape to deal with the emotional ups and downs of those he loves."

She had to admit it: the guy was beautiful. "This isn't a solution, Anthony. It's a way of putting off the inevitable while Jerome cuts another deal elsewhere. A holding action while he tries to elude his creditors down south. Well, he's not going to get away with it."

"What do you mean? The county's all for this."

"No, the county isn't, just those supervisors you and Marty managed to grease. And all the other developers and promoters who want to turn the valley into some new bonanza."

"Sara, you're upset. Don't mess with this. Your own financial health depends upon its going through. You just have to trust us."

"I wish I could, I really do. That's not the question, anyway, is it? The question's whether Jerome's going to be allowed to milk this property too before he bails. Somebody needs to point that out."

"Sara, he's your *father*." Worried, at last, for her a small, bitter kernel of satisfaction.


Her seat had been taken, so she stood against the wall in the back, listening. The speakers included a predictable few in favor—realtors, the Chamber of Commerce, the tourist bureau, the usual collection of promoters and hospitality jockeys—and a clear majority in opposition. Most of them she knew. They had land within view of her deck, and their complaints were heartfelt but lacked coherence: falling water table, traffic, erosion, habitat loss, stream degradation, night light, every other familiar ecological argument rose and fell before the unstated but clear inclination of the board to get this over and done with.

Then Cotton got up. He introduced himself as a farmer and started to talk. His impassioned plea, boldly exposing him to ridicule from the other side, and his denunciation of the process touched her. Maybe it was a rant, but so what? She and the rest of the room suddenly had an incisive delineation of the inappropriateness of Jerome's latest move. "You owe it not just to the neighbors," said Cotton, "but also to the people who elected you to uphold thirty years of good zoning that has preserved the integrity of this valley and been an example for the rest of California."

Somewhere along the line Cotton had learned the virtues of simple conviction, a rarity. But was it enough with this crowd? She seriously doubted it.

During the pause that followed, the chairman looked around for more petitioners, bright overhead lights penetrating his comb-over to reveal beads of perspiration. This was a bit more testimony than he had counted on, clearly. All of them must be sick of listening to people seeking to influence decisions already made, and secretly contemptuous: the constant push against limits placed on land use had been going on for as long as Sara could remember, and it looked like the developers had finally worn down the preservers.

The chairman said, almost caressing the microphone, "Anyone else?"

Cotton stood up again. She thought he had forgotten to say something, but he turned and stared at Sara. So he had seen her, and she waited for the gesture, the encouraging smile, the command, but got none of it. The decision's yours, he seemed to say, and meanwhile the chairman was feeling for his gavel. "If there are no other speakers . . ."

She pushed off from the wall, and her heart pushed off too. Why didn't you scribble some notes, Sara? Faces turned toward her like memory markers, some going back two decades, expecting what? No lonelier spot than a podium planted with a metal armature at a public hearing where half the people despise you for whatever you're about to say, and the other half are desperately dependent.

The ultimate decision hung noticeably on five very different faces behind the table, all glazed with the anticipation of more work: listen, evaluate or pretend to, the only consideration that mattered finding cover in the company of the others, and broadcast the impression of sympathy, wisdom, fairness, regardless of the truth.

"My name's Sara Hutt," she said, aware of the tremor, "and I'm a part-time nursing assistant at Doc Shop. I'm also a minority owner of Hutt Family Estates."

Water in the little plastic bottle couldn't be sipped without taking off the cap, which required pausing and displaying some physical dexterity before an audience. Drink, replace the bottle. "I am opposed to this development, and I actually live on the property, or adjacent to it, on fewer than five acres, in what was once a little schoolhouse but has been a residence since the nineteen forties. I'll tell you why I'm opposed, but first I want to point out something about these so-called historic home sites being used to justify a radical change in the property's use and, by that change, our long-standing and very valuable zoning laws."

More water, coughs from the audience. She saw her own bloodless hand gripping the podium as she said, "Most of them are historic only in the sense that somebody piled rocks there, back in the day, or dumped trash, or kept livestock in a pen. I know this because I was privy to my father's discussions with consultants when the applications were prepared and a strategy devised for getting historic claims certified that seem to have been, essentially, false."

A scowl crept onto the forehead of the chairman of the board. His futile attempts to dispel it would have been comical if not so disconcerting. More so the pale, moonlike face of Anthony Pevin, attached to a neck that seemed to be growing, a mutant Alice in Wonderland, intent on transmitting his vibe as he stared at her: *Shut up, bitch!*

"Today I went through my file on my own little property and discovered some papers relating to the others, including correspondence between my father and the people hired to locate old house sites. In my opinion this indicates collusion, if that's the right word, or at least proof that the applications should never have been approved in the first place. I would think that if the board now approves this new development, neighbors and others will have grounds for suing the county for failing to enforce its own regulations against construction on agricultural land. I would certainly join such a suit."

More water.

"But I'm opposed to the development primarily because it goes against what our family originally envisioned, and my late mother believed, should be the future of Hutt Family Estates. So you can better understand, I should tell you some of that story, which is long and painful to me," and which, she might have added, once started can't easily be stopped.

# 3

Nose crashed that noisy public meeting in a certain NoCal county where a certain winery—hello, Copernicus!—tried to overturn half a century of law that has prevented wineries there from becoming theme parks and the land around them parking lots.

Now, to understand this stuff you really have to hear it from the horse's mouth, to wit, from a member of one of those families that snaked their way into a once-rigid vintner hierarchy. A family like, say, Jerome Hutt's.

Two decades ago, Hutt, today best known for spectacularly crashing real estate at the other end of the state, began filling the lovely dry air of NoCal with outrageous claims about his winery and filling restaurant wine lists with overpriced fruit bombs. Now he's shilling for a high-end ghetto among the vines, where you can have "your own

personal first-growth château without the bother
of traveling to France," as one promoter puts it.

But Hutt's daughter, Sara, part owner of Hutt
Family Estates, decided she didn't want to spend
the rest of her life on the property line listening to
trash compacters in overpriced custom kitchens
and "charity" concerts on lawns xeriscaped to
look like Santa Fe, so last night she stood up on
her hind legs and told the supervisors how the
Hutts came unglued after her mother's death, and
the vision of an enduring family property bit the
dust.

It was a brave, emotional tour de force and it
had the supervisors' lower jaws bouncing off the
table.

She also pointed out that the justification for
her father's new development is—you guessed
it—phony. That's right: false, cooked up, bling-
bling. Supposedly houses once stood on those
prospective "historic" sites, as required by law for
new structures, but according to Sara Hutt no such
houses ever existed. They were simply dreamed
up by geo- and academoprostitutes and peddled
to the county as legit.

So what happened when the courageous
county supervisors heard of this purported scam?
Well, they examined their consciences, they
screwed up their courage, and they most em-
phatically did . . . nothing! But this inaction meant
the motion had to be "tabled"—hang on, Dear

Readers, ALMOST over—which means the vote was put off to some future date. Which effectively means . . . forever!

Meanwhile, rumors abound, to wit: Copernicus's debt has become unmanageable. Potential buyers are being discreetly vetted; these include VinMonde and the irrepressible Abruzzinis. Can it be that Jerome Hutt sought county approval for his development just to sweeten the pot with a number of high-end house sites amid stylish vineyards that he already planned to sell? Has his daughter's action pulled this finance-enhancing rug out from under that deal?

Sniff, sniff . . .

Sara had recognized most of the voices in her message box, two dozen electronic appreciations, some from people she hadn't thought of in a long time. Cotton's words touched her, in part by their awkwardness and the abrupt way he hung up: "We owe you. That can't have been easy. I never knew, you know, about what was happening when you were a kid, almost a kid. Sara, if you ever . . . Somebody's calling."

Nothing from Anthony Pevin, and nothing from her father. The sharp, insistent pain this caused was surprising, since she had long ago determined that Jerome was another person from the one she had known growing up. Somewhere along the line he had forgotten, among other things, how to apologize. What did you ex-

pect? He's just your father, his strengths unpredictabil-
ity and suspicion, winners in the maelstrom of corporate
maneuvering, pushed to the point of paranoia. Trust no
one, including what's left of your family, scope out what
the adversary will do before the adversary knows, act in
a way that's incomprehensible until long after the score,
if ever.

*Get over it.*

But she couldn't. If her testimony was seen by him as
a form of betrayal, his silences had been doubly so for
her, for a very long time. Now added to the death of the
agrarian dream were these proposed boutique châteaux,
and then, apparently, a decision to sell outright. Or had
it been the other way around, as the blog suggested, the
decision to sell made and then the development scheme
devised as a feint? *Jerome Hutt's not selling, he's saved
himself with bricks, mortar, and a million-dollar view?
As per usual. So offer him more money. . . .*

Selling McMansions wouldn't cancel out Jerome's
debts; neither would selling Copernicus outright, but it
sure would sop up a lot of red ink.

Why hadn't she been told by someone? Even Paco
must have gone along, Sara the only problem. She could
almost hear Jerome and Alyssa, temporarily reunited in
disinvestment: *Sara's difficult, just present her with a
fait accompli.* But the fact that Jerome hadn't warned
Sara of impending failure rankled and was inexcusable,
far worse than handing off the place to one of the valley's big boys who were amassing property for a time
when bedroom communities could spring up where

vines had been. Oh, yes, vineyards are nice, but by comparison, land on the edge of San Francisco Bay makes profits from glossy blue-black grapes look ridiculous.

Could *Nose* be right? Had she sacrificed top dollar in any sale by torpedoing the development option? Had she hurt her own prospect of getting anything from a sale, after Jerome's debts were deducted? She tried calling him again, again got the switching sounds and the strange, disembodied voice: "The party you are calling is not available. . . ."

She called Tina Schupe, but her message box was full too. For a long while Sara sat looking up the mountain. She had slept maybe an hour the night before, but with resolution she slipped on her shoes and a pullover and walked out to the car.

The quarter-mile drive to the entrance to Hutt Family Estates felt like it took forever. The house looked unchanged, the landscaping impeccable, the ruts left by Claire Craven-Jones's Prius at peace under well-watered grass. But the front door was locked, and Sara's key, she found, useless. She went around and tried the kitchen, also secure, a deserted theater of stainless steel and dangling copper pots visible through the panes.

Wading into the forest of new calla lily stems at the back of the house, she cupped her hands to the transparent wall: the big living room seemed unchanged, but something was missing. Ah, the Basquiat that had hung behind the divan. And the Frank Lloyd Wright weed vase had vanished from the vortex of glass and Precambrian slate.

Sara knew instinctively that the house was empty of human beings, probably offered *as is* after the things of real value had been extracted. Retaining the less costly furnishings heightened the house's appeal in the eyes of a large commercial entity that would be acquiring it, one that didn't want to worry about accoutrements and could just move in and assume the good taste as its own. She had removed her own effects long ago and was surprised to find herself caring about the other stuff, tallying all the things she might have missed, some left from distant, happier times. Sara had to remind herself that this notion of home as an adjunct of selling had been building since her mother's death, and the transition was now complete.

In angled morning light, she could discern the seam of the winery roof and the patch where CJ had been extracted, the bizarre beginning of an end in process for decades but unforeseen. The big portal to the cellars remained closed; ordinarily Jerome's Lamborghini would be inside, but surely that elegant transport had gone the way of the weed vase. Employees' cars, clustered in the Grove, were fewer than usual, and no Lexus belonging to Tina. Sara knew better than to seek knowledge in those offices, or here, for that matter, winery and house an inseparable unit in the service not of life but of product.

Driving home, confronted with cloud banks to the

west that in spring hang above the great conifer wall, Sara felt like crying. Tears wouldn't come, just the pathetic little sounds that accompany them, the figurative well dry and no incentive to dig another. She turned into her unpaved, rutted driveway and noticed, as if for the first time, the rows of Cabernet vines extending from the Copernicus vineyard onto her land. Two dozen of them, at least, arrogant, well-tended extensions of the mother of the storied wine, trespassing with impunity.

There had been talk in the beginning of Copernicus leasing this planted frontier strip from her, with token annual payments; none had been made, but she had never cared. Her contribution to the greater good. Nothing made her feel like a bigger chump than the sight of all that expensive trellising and bright metal cordons tight as concertina wire.

Without getting out of the car, she made the decision—and felt the lift of imaginary wings as they began to beat. Thumbing up her electronic address book, she punched in Cotton's number. He was no doubt outside doing something, so she left her urgent message: "It's Sara. I have a job for you, if you'll take it. It's not going to be easy, but I really hope you will."

# 4

SHE NEVER HEARD THE PUTT-PUTT of Cotton's electric/solar-enhanced tractor because there had been no putt-putt, just a hiss audible at close range, an entirely unreassuring sound when you're used to the authoritative throb of a real engine. He had fitted it with a blade that rode perilously close to the ground, snagging the occasional weed, and he sat solemnly in the bucket seat under a baseball cap, in a Pendleton shirt gone in cuffs and collar, his expression somewhere between dubiousness and elation. Sara had never been so glad to see anyone.

"Would have been here sooner," he said, "but I had to go out to the highway."

"You should have just come through the fence."

He looked at her in surprise. "You all right?"

"Yes." But Sara felt herself blush.

"And you're sure you want to do this?"

"Quite. I've marked the property line, as you can see." After striding out with a roll of ribbon she had bought for wrapping Christmas presents. Big, tight, yellow bows sat on the top trellises of twenty-two rows of vines, indicating the edge of her few acres and the beginning of Copernicus's sprawl. The line ran down from the edge of the wastewater settling pond almost to her deck, none of the rows extending more than a few feet onto her property. Still, in total, that was a hundred-plus individual vines, mothers of Copernicus, and she knew too well how much money had been lavished on them and on the proselytizing of them. She could only guess at the volume of nutrients and chemicals that had inundated their roots.

Without another word, Cotton moved on the closest row. The blade dropped, the odd little machine seethed and stalled against a post, a kind of dry-land bollard anchoring the row, then the post moved and toppled and the blade cut deeply into the earth, the first vine coming up quickly, nakedly. Sara could plainly see those roots now. Instead of going deep, they formed a weak, hairy mass the size of a medicine ball seeming to shake off dirt in its distress.

The second vine too gave up without a fight, and the third. Cotton pushed past the yellow ribbons, leaving snarls of vines, plastic irrigation pipe, trellising, and wire dumped unceremoniously three feet inside the Copernicus vineyard. A load of demolished lyres, she thought, in an interstate pileup.

The Copernicus vineyard manager's pickup swooped past, then hightailed it for the winery. Before Cotton was done with row four, the manager was back, trailed by Paco Cardinal's big blue pickup. It rocked to a halt in the dust, and Paco came out as if ejected. Sara hadn't seen him move that fast since he left the Caterina High football field, broad shoulders now rolling with a deceptive languor as he slipped on leather gloves.

Cotton glanced in his direction but didn't acknowledge him or the peril he presented. No hauling back on the throttle for Calamity Harrell, no raised hands, just a kind of bemused attention to the angle of the blade and the requisite juice required to get at another vine, as if between Cotton and the two-hundred-pound bundle of aggrieved, muscular energy hurtling toward him existed a shield.

Sara got there first. *"Paco! Stop!"*

He did, looking past her in murderous confusion as the tractor finally wheezed to a halt.

"Get out of the way, Sara," said Paco.

"I'm not getting out of the way, this is my property. And I want you off it."

"He can't do this."

"Yes, he can. He's working for me."

"Sara, what the hell's wrong with you? I mean, look at this mess."

"I'm putting in my own vineyard, and I want these gone." The words had come out of nowhere. Her own vineyard? "I don't want to have to deal with some big corporation after you, Alyssa, and Jerome have cut and run."

That got to him. "I had no choice," Paco said.

"There's always a choice. And you could have told me, even if they wouldn't."

"Don't do this, Sara. We can put this stuff back." He

sounded almost pathetic, looking at prostrate vines trussed with steel and black plastic ganglia. "You can make a deal with whoever."

"I don't want a deal, I want out. Now back off."

He did, and leaned against the fender of his truck, arms crossed. The vineyard manager approached him, and Paco said something that had the effect of a physical blow. Meanwhile the tractor wheezed and another vine came up, fainted, and rolled with the rest toward the line of yellow ribbons.

Cotton glanced at Sara in passing, the same expression as before, when she had told him what she wanted him to do, except that now he was smiling. If he had worried about her coming unwrapped, that seemed to have passed. Sara hadn't felt this good in a long, long time.


A small crowd of Copernicus workers had gathered by the time the tractor ran out of power. Neighbors came tentatively up Sara's road, among them Jerry Vacaros, whom she hadn't seen in a decade. He leaned against his fender, the mirror image of Paco Cardinal on the other side except that Jerry was half Paco's size and twice his age. His clean chinos and plaid shirt announced that his working days were over. Wizened by the sun so that he looked as much Navajo as Mexican, his bitter opposition to the Copernicus winery permit still vivid in Sara's mind.

Cotton came down off the hybrid looking chagrined but trying not to. He told Sara, "I didn't hook it up to the power source until too late. And the trip out to the highway took some juice." Looking around, as always, as if salvation was imminent. Maybe someday, she thought. The Copernicus vineyard hands simpered, but not Paco. Jerry Vacaros ambled over and said something to Cotton, and together they ambled back to Jerry's pickup. After a brief palaver they shook hands.

Jerry drove off, and Cotton stood there. No biggie, his stance said. Sara wasn't going to ask what passed between the two men, or how Cotton's amusing little two-treaded Luddite alternative vehicle would be rejuvenated. Instead she slid down the post supporting her deck and sat in the grass, the sun warm on her face, and watched Cotton Harrell watch the road, the set of his narrow hips, the barely restrained fidgeting that said a lot about his eagerness to get this job done, whatever the consequences.

Sara smiled despite herself, feeling some of the weight of the deed borne by Cotton's squared, bony shoulders. The little crowd had grown silent, witnesses at an interrupted disaster. A station wagon came up Sara's drive and a vaguely familiar figure got out and looked awkwardly at the damage: Lance What's-his-name from *The Valley Press*. Had Jerome's scheme finally interested his rancid employer in land use? Or was it just the promise of more familial sparks in a dry season?

Lance didn't see her and Sara had no intention of talking to him, anyway. I'm not here, she thought, and found that comforting.

Jerry Vacaros returned with a two-wheel trailer in tow, on it mounted a much-used little Bobcat bulldozer.

He left his pickup door ajar and climbed onto the dozer, fired it up, and backed off the flatbed, ejaculating smoke in angry snorts. Cotton came over as if to say, *What have we here?* Kick a tire, all the time in the world. They talked, their faces in shadow, their smiles sudden white slashes under the bills of their caps, Cotton's misshapen and discolored, Jerry's a pristine tribute from the Caterina Elks Lodge.

Cotton mounted the Bobcat. More oily smoke, Jerry showing him just how to use the lift lever, then stepping back so Cotton could noisily engage what was left of his quarries. No pause before collision of blade and hapless vine—*Thank you, Mr. Diesel!*—he watching the depth of the cut, taking it slow, Jerry watching Paco, in the old man's unwavering gaze a measure of satisfaction he didn't try to disguise.


Cotton was on the next-to-last row when the white Channel 7 van showed up and squatted far down her road. Sara decided to go inside. She got the shakes in a minor way and had to sit, out of sight of the door, squeezing her thighs together. When she looked up again, the van was gone, and everyone on the Copernicus side too, except for Paco. Then the dozer fell silent, and Paco headed back to the winery. It was done.

Aware of footsteps on the deck, Sara went to the door. Cotton, hat shoved back, dust from eyebrows to boots. He repeated, "You okay, Sara?"

"Yes."

"Expecting someone?"

"Not really. Thank you, Cotton. You have no idea."

"I'll be back tomorrow for the tractor, if it can wait."

"Sure."

"Were you serious about putting in new vines?"

"I think so."

"You'll need a year of cover crop," he said. "I could put that in for you now, and when the soil's healed some, we could talk about planting." He looked around. "What you did today took a lot of guts, Sara. I admire you, so do other people, not all of them here today. I hope you know that."

"Thanks, Cotton."

He went down the steps and up the stile and off through the riot of Puddle-jump's old clover. Would her place look like that someday? Would she forget to change her shirt and be content with dysfunctional gadgets and a world of work? She wanted to thank him effusively, but couldn't, and was exasperated with herself for not at least trying.

She made tea and put on some music, turned it off. Shadows lengthened across her exposed ground, the piles of vines and wire truly dreadful looking, and she yearned for darkness to finally erase them.

Her cell phone throbbed repeatedly with light and clarion calls, none of the numbers to her liking, and she didn't take the calls. Night fell as it does even in early winter, abruptly, which meant minestrone from a can, her eyes on the road. She couldn't see the highway, but the headlights would come cutting upslope and she

would know the car instantly, although it might be a
rental, a black Lexus, say, and Jerome would get out and
there would be no sombrero now, no fine linen shirt, just
a jacket and tie and maybe a trench coat, the bygone
uniform. The two of them, father and daughter, would
have it out, once and for all, and she could say to his face
the things she had wanted to say for so long, her breath
rising in clouds through air at last grown cold.

But he didn't come. Gradually the cell phone subsided,
and she lay on the couch and closed her eyes but couldn't
sleep. Most definitely not okay, the barrier between it
and you as palpable as an iron gate with a cruelly efficient lock. She could almost hear the clash of it, the slide
of the bolt.

More time passed, but she refused to look at the clock
or take a pill. Not disapproval, fear of something larger,
and when she got up again there were no lights anywhere except in Cotton Harrell's kitchen. Sara slipped
on clogs and her old wax jacket and went outside.

Walking quickly, she climbed the fence and made her
way through thick vegetation, toward that light. Once
there, she didn't hesitate, clogs loud on the porch boards;
Cotton opened the door in sweater and jeans and stared
at her. "Well," he said finally. It wasn't a question.

She said, "I can't."

"You mean you can't plant new vines?"

"No, I just can't . . ."

A very long pause.

"Put in a cover crop?"

She shook her head.

"Ah . . . go to sleep?"

"That."

He took her elbow and eased her inside. Sara registered rugs, books, prints, a lamp with a tasseled shade. Couch stacked with old files. He led her past it and into the hall, where he pushed open a door. More books, plus a bed supporting piles of carefully folded Levi's, khakis, shirts, undershorts: the bachelor's recumbent closet.

He said, "Don't move."

He went in and stacked it all up; when he passed by again she couldn't see his face for all the clothes. In another room, Cotton dumped them and came back. He turned down the bed. "Bathroom's right across the hall," he said, gently pushing her, closing the door.

She took off the jacket and clogs. A knock and the door opened again, enough for a hand to be inserted and in it a clean, threadbare white shirt. She took it and the door closed.

Too big, she thought, stripping. She put it on anyway and buttoned it up and slid under the covers. A medicinal but not unpleasant smell. She took the sachet from beneath the pillow, tied with pale blue ribbon. How long has that been there? Since the days of Jill? And how did you, Sara, get this far from the beach before that tsunami of oblivion now making landfall? Just enough time to recall the vision she had on her very own porch, of people struggling in a dreamscape under mountains worn down by time, and then she slept.

## 5

More off-odors emanating from that winery in NoCal that Nose can't seem to stay away from. As in prospective bankruptcy for Copernicus. The proprietor, Jerome Hutt, holed up in the house, not answering the door, claiming the place as his residence so the property couldn't be seized for nonpayment of debt. Yes, the former vintner extraordinaire and current scofflaw, who if rumor's true is soon to be majorly out o' there.

Imagine this creator of manipulated Cabernet rattling around in a postmodern, beaucoup-million-dollar charade of a farmstead, waiting for a new deal to pop. Then riding the cork all the way back to SoCal, to blend in with the rest of the boom-bust, bottom-feeding fugitives hiding out with their leathery spouses and Chihuly chandeliers.

Apparently an unlikely marriage of colossi—in this case, VinMonde and Abruzzini—is being hastily arranged to take over Hutt Family Estates, the corporations' chubby arms entwined to cash in on Hutt's disaster. Nose hears that the amount the partnership's paying for this prime real estate— sans the discredited Copernicus brand, by the way—is barely enough to cover Hutt Family Estates' financial obligations. If so, co-owners like daughter Sara Hutt get zip and creditors are settling for pennies on the dollar.

How strange, all this, coming directly from the death of critic Clyde Craven-Jones in the winery, a tragic event that has never . . .

Les angled the computer screen so only he could read the post, then turned his attention to the plate of charcuterie—hard salami, radishes, Dijon, sourdough rounds. Claire was watching. "Lester, there's something I need to discuss with you."

He put down the container of sea salt with the gorgeous label—puffy white clouds, windswept dunes, dipping terns—and waited.

"I'm dropping the suit against Hutt," she said. "I talked to the lawyer again yesterday, and he advises settling for whatever I can get from the insurer. Moving on. The money's not much, but it's something. And I'm seriously thinking of taking your advice. If *Craven-Jones on Wine* went electronic, my accountant says, it would at least be revenue neutral for the moment and might be profitable eventually."

Outside, two birds—not hawks, vultures—hung in a

gray sky. The rainy season was upon them, and so, apparently, was more work.

"It's our readers I worry about," she went on. "We have a very serious audience, one that, in the end, is very cautious. Connoisseurship depends upon maintaining wealth—now let me explain, Lester—which provides access to rarity. Like in art. Wine's no exception, so our readers are, for the most part, in their unique way, conservative."

"Reactionary."

"I knew you'd say that. Reactionary where technology's involved, maybe. They distrust it and like holding on to something real. Like paper, so . . ."

He ruminatively bit into the marbled disk of salami.

". . . if we do this other version, I'd like to know, Lester, that I can count on you to take some real responsibility. To sign on and, ah, I don't know how else to put this, grow up a little bit. Spend less time hanging around . . ."

"Glass Act." He dragged a radish reflectively through the sea salt. Maybe she had a point. "Okay. I can help jolly the subscribers onto the Web site, but we're going to need some serious technical help. And you're going to have to grow up too, Claire, in the sense of accepting the mantle. You're the voice of *Craven-Jones on Wine* now, you've got to jump on it."

She got up, walked over, and leaned to kiss him. It felt like the endgame, the process having gone on since he first came here, nothing to do but plunge back into assembling the mock-up of the last print edition for the printer waiting down in Redwood City. Included would be a version of Claire's letter that Les had written for her, with Les's name on the new masthead as managing editor, and an official announcement that a Web address would forever be the best reference for true wine aficionados—conservative, liberal, anarchic, whatever—*the enophilic lodestar in the vast heaven of buying, imbibing, and enjoying the fruit of the eternal vine,* as Les intended to say in *Nose* when the proper time came.

The landline jangled, and Claire answered. "Just a moment," she said, offering Les the phone. "I think it's that Wolken character."

"Hello, Rudolf."

"Yes," said Wolken, his accent heightened by bad transmission. "The tests are complete. I have documentation. And an informed opinion now as to which wine matches the unknown one."

"You do?"

"There's no proof, I warnt you of this. Only a collection of anecdotal data, a statistical what you call nonstarter. One test was only partially successful, the crystals, because the blotting paper was excessively damp." He broke up. ". . . the generator stolen, and so no electricity for a time. And there are similarities in either alcohol or volatile acidity in several samples, but only one matched alcohol and VA precisely. Furthermore . . . please wait."

Les heard thin, feminine laughter followed by Wolken's half-muffled command—*"You must stay from the window if you insist upon taking off . . . My*

*God . . ."*—and remembered a young woman running away from Wolken while he fired a shotgun over her head. Apparently their relationship had improved.

"As I suggested earlier," Wolken said, "the fungal test was the most rewarding. Mineral uptake strongly suggests to me that the test wine is the same as . . ."

"Which?"

*"What are you doing . . . ?"*

"Rudolf, you okay?"

"Yes, sorry, as I was saying, in my opinion, and as close as can be determined, there is a match, and it will, I think, surprise."

"So who made the wine?"

"I will tell you, of course, and provide the documentation, pictures of crystals, other things I can send. But only after you send to me a cashier's check for eighteen hundred and thirty-six dollars . . . *Arrggghhh . . .*"

The line went dead.

"What's going on?" asked Claire.

"I don't know how else to put this, but I think Herr Wolken's getting a blow job."

He explained on the way to the bank. Claire drew a cashier's check, and they overnighted it to Lake County. When the packet arrived, together they tore it open and dumped the contents on the table. As promised, Wolken had sent a chart, photos of wine crystals on blotting paper taken with a cell phone, and a schematic ranking of the wines according to alcohol, volatile acidity, and some other stuff, much of it irrelevant.

At the bottom of the pile was a letter from the scientist absolving himself of legal responsibility and closing with the name of the unknown wine.

"Can't be," Claire said.

"No way," said Les.

# 6

MORNINGS WERE BEST, but in the beginning strange and a little scary: a mug of coffee seemingly growing on the bedside table, which Sara didn't touch, and waking up again to find it transformed into a beaker of tea. Some of which she drank, and went to the bathroom, aware of someone else in the house and assuming it was Cotton. Bathroom smelling of pine oil—a hiking hostel somewhere in the Sierra?—and blinding light beyond the curtains, her senses dominated not by sight or smell but by sound: a succession of strings stressed at times to the breaking point and at others seamlessly bound up in a gorgeous mathematical equation beyond her ken.

Bach, she assumed, but which? And why the periodic interruptions, the faint scratching, the resumption of music similar but never, it seemed, quite the same? She went back to sleep and woke up to the strings again, imbued now with a kind of shielding power: an impervious curtain of composition, an aural prophylactic between her and whatever lay out there.

A slice of quiche appeared, a bit of yellow squash resting on top like an appraising eye, and a peach. Then more sleep, and then—alarming—an absence of Bach. Birds scoring imperfect Victorian panes, striking at something beyond the window, before the gathering darkness ruined their chances. Sara padding out into the hallway, finding a note taped to the wall: *Gone to FOF meeting, back 9ish. Food in fridge, tub works.*

Was that a hint? She ran steaming water into the old footed eyesore and went into the living room. On the turntable was stacked black vinyl, which explained the scratching; open on the floor a heavy cardboard sleeve for *The Art of the Fugue.* Johann Sebastian, by a bunch of musicians in formal wear from the '50s, looking tense. She ate a bowl of cold ginger-carrot soup while reading the liner notes, remembered nothing of them, got into the bathtub, then back into bed, exhausted by it all.

She woke up crying. The gray light of dawn, birdsong, then kitchen sounds. She feigned sleep when he brought some books—T. S. Eliot's poems, the *Tao Te Ching*—and tea, drank some when he was gone, went back to sleep. Awoke to more Bach, more tears, the beaker gone, untouched toast remaining. *Sometimes it's preferable not to intrude on another's mood.* Or so said the nursing manual. What about intruding on your own mood?

Just let it flow without too much analysis. Use the pillow, sleep.

Then she awakened to Cotton's tap and tried to return

his smile when he put his head into the room. He wore a straw hat and looked adorable, if comical, carrying the beaker. "Morning, Sara. I've asked Dr. Gomez to drop by," and he was gone.

Nervy, she thought. This meant another of Cotton's old shirts, an attempt to alter the disaster of face and hair before she propped herself on the pillows. Bach's strings, and then Gomez's soft, guttural greeting blended in a considerate late morning rouse, as if the two of them had conspired, composer with unnatural energy and doctor with a leather bag and a jacket with elbow patches who happened also to be her boss. "Hi, Sara," smiling as he entered, without invitation. "Sorry you're not well."

"I'm sorry Cotton felt like he had to call you. It's nothing, really."

"We'll see."

He pulled the chair up and examined her with the directness of a dedicated clinician used to unobliging patients. *Tongue . . . breathe. Turn over . . . cough.* Lymph node probe, ear peek, tummy nudge, temperature poke, eye exam. "Head's congested," he said, "but that's because you've been crying a lot. Take the week off from work. In fact, take as much time as you like. We're overstaffed at the clinic right now and some people could use the extra hours."

Tears again, so exasperating. "I don't know what's wrong with me, and I'm supposed to."

"You've had a loss."

"It has to be more than that, Dr. Gomez."

He patted her hand, a tough little man who had seen it all. "There's nothing wrong with you or your diagnostic abilities. You're in the middle of something, and it's been so long you don't remember what it feels like."

"What are you talking about?" She couldn't believe it: the man was laughing.

"You're in love, Sara."


The rain came down in earnest, water everywhere, in the mountains, when she could see them, on the windows when noon looked like dusk, beading, streaming. On Cotton's bathroom walls too, when she let the tap water get too hot, on her sweaty upper lip, wetness all, the sound of dripping constant, day and night, outside and in.

It seemed she spent much of that week in the bathtub, noticing that it was, in fact, a very nice historic one. Pewter faucets, ornate soap dish, sloping sides more suitable for rest than scrubbing, elegantly curled lip, and, at her elbow, casement windows framing a view often wreathed in the rising steam.

She heard his footsteps in the hall in the evening. Deferential to a fault, this lovely man. "Cotton," she called softly and heard him pause to listen, felt his indecision through thin plaster infused with horsehair as a binder in the old days. Unlike sheetrock, this wall was imperfect, wavy, beautiful. "Oh, Cotton, come on. *Please.* I can't stand it any longer."

# 7

"IT'S A HELL of a story."

Les could see the layout plainly in his mind: CJ's in-spired notes on the tasting and an account of the long search for the identity of the mystery Cab. "I'll interview Rudolf and then write a sidebar about how it was done, with graphs and the photos and stuff, wine crystal patterns, all great visuals. Later, we can stage the tasting all over again, this time with Puddle-jump and our new panel. Let them—us—see what we think. Readers will eat it up, Marilee Tavestani will be all over it, even Kevin Nomonity'll have to get in on the act."

"Lester . . ."

"Good publicity, and more. We might be ushering in a new thing, you know: *New Wines Passed Under Reclusive Scientist's Nose.* Or *Experts Versus the Sage of Lake County.* Hot stuff, Claire."

"But we'd need some kind of confirmation from the winner," she said.

"I'll ask him. He'd be a fool to deny it, and he's no fool. Also honest."

"Yes, and unpredictable."

Les drove thoughtfully up the valley, folded pashmina in a large manila envelope on the seat beside him. It didn't bear too much thinking about, but the valley had begun to feel like home, and his work, such as it was, almost like a profession. Sightseers in their bulbous rented convertibles held up traffic even at the outset of winter, and, far to the west, forested slopes sucked light from the still powerful sun.

He passed Hutt Family Estates, or what was left of it, no longer the center of its own universe, big bright sedans parked outside the main house disgorging a gaggle of well-dressed pilgrims. Were these the new corporate owners, looking happily if confusedly displaced as people seem to be when they've bought something overpriced?

The neat rows of vines gave way to not-so-neat rows. He peered upslope at the isolated, overgrown anomaly of Puddle-jump Vineyards. Cotton Harrell watched from his rocker on the porch as Les shuddered the VW to a halt and got out, envelope in hand. "May I come up?" he called.

"Sure."

Les did, and sat down, trying to decide how to begin, restive under this man's gaze. From inside the house came the lilt of stringed instruments, a classical concert of some kind, amplified beyond what Les considered comfortable.

Harrell said, "I want to thank you for covering the supervisors' meeting the other night. It was a help. I got a call from the *Chronicle* as a result, and *The Bee*."

"You're welcome."

Harrell set aside his book. "How can I help you?"

An admission would do nicely, Les thought. This guy might not play at all. "I have something here," he said, tearing open the envelope. He put his hand inside, the shawl soft and cool to the touch, and pulled it out, the rosy geometric design in the weave bright even under the eaves of the porch. Les shook out the shawl, leaned forward, and draped it over the unprotesting vintner's knees.

"What's this?"

Harrell stared at the fabric, hands in the air, almost afraid to touch it. Inside the house, violins and cellos peaked, subsided, began again; at that moment Les glimpsed someone crossing the living room. The shade was partially drawn so he couldn't see the face, but it was obviously a woman, a pretty one in a baggy man's shirt, moving quickly. For a moment he thought he had recognized her, thinking: can't be. And then she was gone.

"A shawl," said Les, "made of the hair of an endangered Asian goat or something. I think you wrapped your Cabernet bottle up in it for luck, before you delivered it in the middle of the night to the home of Clyde Craven-Jones, hoping he would put it in his tasting. You did, didn't you?"

Harrell didn't answer. Instead, he raised the pashmina and pressed his face into it and held it there for a moment. When he removed the shawl his eyes were intensely bright. "Smells good," Harrell said and held it out to Les.

"Keep it. It's yours anyway. I'm right, aren't I, that the shawl belonged to Jill and the unidentified Cab was yours?"

"So what?"

Wolken had brought it off; Les felt a lot more than eighteen hundred dollars' worth of relief. "For one thing," he said, able to suppress a smile, "we can write about it. That was Craven-Jones's last, historic tasting, and he thought your wine deserved a twenty. Tell me something, why didn't you put your name on the bottle and submit it in the usual way?"

"Because Craven-Jones already had his opinion of me and of Puddle-jump's wines. It wasn't great. I don't think he even bothered to taste my recent vintages when I submitted them the usual way, and that made me mad. Neither he nor Claire would have ever put it into a tasting with those other high-enders. I decided to do something unorthodox, but the fact that Puddle-jump ended up in that tasting was pure luck. A fluke."

"And it won."

"Yes, that was personally satisfying."

"But you knew before today. So why didn't you step up when the word went out?"

"I considered it, but then Craven-Jones got killed. It seemed in bad taste and suddenly not very important."

Les shook his head: *personally satisfying; not very important.* Cotton Harrell, American primitive. "Well," he said, "I—we—thought you ought to officially know you won," and got up to leave.

"Thanks for dropping this off." Harrell waved the pashmina in the thin air of winter. "And what exactly are you going to do with all this information, if you don't mind my asking?"

"Oh, nothing much," said Les. "Just make you famous."


It took them a week to close the issue, Les reminded, after a long hiatus, of what it's like to have a boss. Then he and Claire stood on the stoop and handed the editorial packet to the FedEx driver, still sheepish from having run over Missy, and when he was gone both raised their hands and slapped palms.

"Done!"

The driver had brought with him an ornate envelope, and Claire opened it. *Please join us for the launch of AVM, the valley's new, premier brand, one hundred percent Cabernet Sauvignon from vineyards formerly part of Hutt Family Estates, including Copernicus, now the proud possession of two recognized producers of world-class wine, VinMonde Ltd. and Abruzzini & Sons, a unique collaboration.*

Claire said, "They don't want to wait for more rumors to spread about the health and viability of the acquisition. Get it launched, they're thinking. Wipe the slate."

"There had been a tug-of-war over which of the two companies would get mentioned first in the press release." Les had heard all about it from Ben. "Just as there was over the name and placement of the initials. VinMonde got two letters, and that rubbed Terry Abruzzini the wrong way, so he insisted on having the "A" come first. His argument was that AVM would put their Cabernet first on shelves arranged alphabetically."

"Are there any such shelves?"

"I guess. Now they're celebrating—presto!—AVM."

"Jerome's gone," said Claire, "and the ink on the contracts barely dry. Well, I suppose you'll have to represent *Craven-Jones on Wine* at the party, Lester. By that time this issue will be out, and people will be talking about our Web site."

"Why don't we go together?"

"I've done this stuff too often, I'm afraid. Part of your job now, Lester. You'll need a tuxedo."

She crooked a finger, leading him down the hall and into the spare bedroom. How long since they had made love on those bolsters, against Victorian filigree? Not very. Claire passed it by and went to the door in the corner, what he had assumed was just a closet. Now he saw a long, narrow wardrobe packed with a man's clothes, redolent of fresh cedar.

"CJ had this built," she said. "He grew out of really nice things as time passed and couldn't bear to discard them."

The smell reminded Les of mornings in the high Sierra: mist, campfire, evergreens. Claire was taking from a wooden hanger a wool jacket with a fine houndstooth weave, in autumnal browns and muted heather. "This closet was one of CJ's delights, like a time capsule now.

This was made in Savile Row, as were the suits. We went there once when we were in London, and they remembered him and pulled out his measurements from the time he was young. CJ loved that sort of thing. Here, try it on."

"Claire . . ."

"Oh, go ahead. It's just a jacket, hasn't been worn, I'll bet, for twenty years. Way before my time."

It fit, more or less. Les quickly took it off. "Why does it have flaps in the back?" he asked.

"They're not flaps, those are English vents. Stylish, and always will be."

She reached down a dark pinstripe and displayed it, silk lining and all. "This is from a few years later. You're not big enough for it. Yet. And there are the tuxes. Let's see, this one goes way back. I'll bet it'll fit, with a couple of stitches. And look, CJ even saved his handmade shirts."

Claire poked around in the box he had brought back from the district attorney's office, shaking her head. "These studs and cuff links were gifts to his great-uncle from the earl of Northumberland. Thank God the coroner returned them. Think of it: a candy bar phone, silver studs, and cuff links set with amethysts, dress shoes, suspenders. Are these things the sum of a man?"

He began to compose an answer, but she added, "Lots of lovely linen in here too," and took down a dark blue blazer with gold buttons. She slipped it over his arms and shoulders. "Perfect up top, a bit loose in the tummy. We'll have it taken in, or"—running a hand down the front of him—"I'll just have to fatten you up, Lester Breeden."

# 8

So in a tuxedo once owned by someone else, steering that same man's car, Les drove to AVM, né Hutt Family Estates, on the appointed day. The beautifully crafted wooden sign that once bore Jerome Hutt's name and rococo marketing message was now emblazoned with three simple initials, nothing more, in red Gothic script. The sheep were gone from the meadow, he noticed, parking in the Grove among SUVs and elegant sedans left far enough from the eucalyptuses to avoid their sloughing bark. Those big trees, girdled with yellow tape, were to go the way of the sheep.

Guests filed in through the hospitality center and Les joined them. He received a name tag and entered for only the second time, catching a glimpse of a stranger in the mirror: jet-black lapels, blue eyes, blond hair, the new Les Breeden. A smiling young woman in bright colors, with great hair, murmured his name to a woman in black, with great hair, who took this information to the line of men in frilly shirts grasping people's hands.

Terry Abruzzini turned to Les. *"Heeeey!"* A big, soft arm enveloped Les. The valley's foremost scion's face was planted between broad lapels. He said conspiratorially, "You're going to love this wine, man," massaging Les's shoulder and proffering a stemmed glass.

Les took it. "Thanks. I don't think we've actually met. . . ." But already he was being passed to another frilly shirt. This one sawed with Les's hand, his intensity unsettling. "Mr. Breee-den, I am Maurice de . . ." something, a bigwig from Paris, winged in for the party with his charming Gallic accent. "We at VinMonde are excited about this new partnership and so happy you could join us. We have long desired a truly, ah, fitting property for our company, you know, an American jewel in our crown of great estates, our new home in the emerging world of American wine. . . ."

"Now, Maurice, cut the crap," said Terry Abruzzini, laughing loudly. "We've been making the stuff here for a century and a half. We don't need a bunch of cheese-eating surrender monkeys"—more laughter at his own joke, slapping Maurice's rigid shoulder—"telling us how. Right, LB?"

Les had never been called that and took a moment to figure it out. He had also never seen anyone so visibly offended recover so well, the Frenchman again beaming his smile on Les, as incandescent as Abruzzini's was maniacal, urging Les into the reception proper. Mostly strangers, a few familiar faces—Lance of *The*

*Press,* Larry Carradine, apparently not through with the wine business, ruddy as an activated incendiary device, and Kevin Nomonity of *The Wine Taster*—all feeding from a stalagmite of ice draped with seafood. The new owners must have found it in the freezer and brought it out: spoils of war.

"LB." An older woman he didn't know passed, followed by a man he didn't know. "Hi, LB. I read you." Les wanted to ask what he thought of his new column, but he was gone too, replaced by a sturdy figure in what appeared to be a leather tux.

"Ben! I didn't expect you."

"The AVM net's wide," he said, his ponytail held by a turquoise-and-silver clasp, gripping Les's elbow. "Esme brought me. And what think you of this wine, my friend?"

"It's familiar."

"Should be, it's Copernicus. Hutt sold the brand after all, along with the winery. He's got a new label, I hear, Galileo, somewhere down south. He's buying Central Valley shiners and hyping them."

"Shiners?"

"Bottles without labels—junky Zinfandel or Petite Syrah mixed with Cabernet. He's going to put his new labels on them and make money in the short run. A fifty-buck fuck. Then he'll unload it on some other SoCal developer right before the new brand tanks."

"Les, darlin'."

Esme, plumply fitted into black tulle, kissed him wetly as she slipped a hand through Ben's arm. Was she finally overcoming hypoactive sexual desire disorder? She and Ben certainly seemed happy about something. Les had given them a wee heads-up on Puddle-jump before the piece about the mystery wine broke on Claire's new Web site. Both had bought some of Cotton Harrell's signature vintage before the price went off the charts. More spoils of war. What have you done? he asked himself, remembering. *This wine tolls on the nose with all the power and precision of Christopher Wren's gem, the Church of St. Mary-le-Bow. . . . The finish is a soothing convergence of light and shadow in a distant clearing. . . .*

Ben had him firmly by the back of the neck. "Where'd you get those cuff links?"

"From the earl of Northumberland, where else?" He was already feeling the effects of the overripe Copernicus/AVM. He took another slug and said, "LB wants a shrimp."

But he was blocked by another woman in black; this one, the skinny yin to Esme's curvy yang, sexy ectomorphic antiphon to mere endomorphic eroticism, was Marilee Tavestani, appraising him with her professional sensualist's eye, showing lots of teeth. "You've been here before, I hear," she said. "So show me around, Mr. Breeden."

But it was Marilee ushering him, hand on his arm, pausing so the waiter could refill their glasses. She urged him toward the door leading to the private tasting room and the winery and amphitheater beyond. People were watching, but any fate was better than more frilly shirts and great hair, although two of those trailed Les and Marilee like fruit flies. "Would you like a tour?" asked one of the young women, and Marilee said, "Not really, just nosing around," laughing at her own joke, pushing open the big door with the Bacchus latch.

He recognized the table at which he last saw Hutt, could almost smell the briny promise of uneaten craw-fish, taste golden, oaky Chardonnay. It seemed a very long time ago. Marilee stood outside the amphitheater that had been converted to a planetarium by AVM to which schoolchildren were invited up from the city, try-ing to make up her mind about something. "Let's see what Abruzzini and VinMonde are up to," she said and shoved on into the cavernous winery.

The last of the day's light barely infiltrated slits in the massive steel curtain at the far end. Marilee sauntered across the floor, stopped, and cocked a bony hip. "Hey, nosy, come on!"

Playful, drawing out the smile, she gestured, but he was struck by the smell of grape decomposition linger-ing in the scrubbed concrete. Tons of doomed fruit had given forth new life: sweet, ethereal, older than time, sugar and microbes locked in combat, the microbes win-ning. Soar, he thought, but the descent can be calami-tous. Somewhere up there in the gloom a fat man expired, as gone tonight as evaporating $CO_2$, so much celestial gas chipping away at the ozone layer.

Marilee called gaily, "Oh, the smell of fermentation is *suuuch* a turn-on!"

Les braced himself in the doorframe, watching that

angular, antic silhouette, thinking: this far, but no farther.

. . . and so, as the Copernicus melodrama comes
to an end, so do, ironically—cruelly?—the peram-
bulations of a sincere if weary Nose. The unadulterated truth has had its time in the sun and, like
all things, must move to a more shaded spot in
this uncertain world. In short, Dear Reader, Nose
has decided to hang it up.

However, having had a glimpse of how things
work in the nether regions of the transmogrified
grape, you should be better able to deal. Having
seen things as they are, you can better avoid the
snares of the unrepentant egotarians and corpo-
rapers. Nose hopes your knowledge of wine has
been expanded as well, as Nose's has, and your
enthusiasm enhanced along with your skepticism.

The field's still played upon, wide open, largely
unrefereed. Now it's your turn. Transgressors will
always be there for the tracking, and you can read
the spoor and unearth critters in holes as well as
anyone. Just do it!

Nose may well return someday because—
remember!—Nose knows. One fine evening you
may pour something into a glass, hit the power
button, kick back, and . . .

Sniff, sniff . . .

# 9

SARA AND COTTON each carried a pail. They had to stop and rest twice between the barn and what they were calling the nursery. Cotton's pickup would have made it much easier, but the water would have spilled and the salmon fry panicked, and he had talked a lot about good early imprinting and trauma and residual effects, and whether or not the young fish would take to the new stream and return next year. So they schlepped the buckets the whole way, the tiny fish like slivers of silver against the galvanized bucket bottoms.

Shoulder to shoulder, Sara and Cotton looked down into the long metal culvert with the top cut away, broad enough to avoid scouring in times of heavy runoff, deep enough to accommodate gravel and bigger rocks. Treated winery water, pure now, dribbled in from the man-made marsh at the top, and a broader fan flowed out the other end and into the natural streambed that snaked down through Cotton's property, passed under the highway, and joined with the river. From there the little guys would swim to the sea and, so the theory went, one fine day remember this place and return.

Cotton said, "You first."

Sara knelt and tipped her pail into the tank, where the slivers frantically sought cover. Then Cotton did the same. He had caught the fish that afternoon, and his hair, though dry, was still plastered to his head. She ran her fingers through it absently, and when she looked again all the fish had disappeared.

"I hope they make it," he said, "and that they'll come back."

"I'm sure they will, Cotton."

He moved behind her, both of them facing west, and encircled her with his arms. The sun was gone, and in the air a faint odor of burning from the far hills, despite the damp. Someone burning vine cuttings in the aftermath of the rain.

The old fence separating their two properties was gone, and with it Cotton's stile, as if posts and wire had pulled themselves loose and marched over and reset themselves on the line between Sara's few acres and AVM's hundred. Except that AVM's was a much nicer fence, all the debris from the jerked vines long since vanished and with it all institutional memory of discord.

The cover crop Cotton had put in seemed to be taking. Sara's house looked like an afterthought in the middle of it. Puddle-jump's vines stood expectantly at the edge of the property and would soon be marching across

Sara's ground too; they would knit the holdings together, and in a year the seam wouldn't show at all.

From up here, at the nursery, she could see the roofline of what had been Hutt Family Estates' winery, the as-yet-unoxidized seams in the new copper roofing agleam. She said, "Cotton, there's something I've been meaning to ask you."

"What's that?"

"The night of that party at Copernicus, when the accident occurred, I came home and saw you walking over from that direction. Where'd you been?"

"At your winery."

"Doing what? Jerome certainly didn't invite you."

"No, he didn't. I was checking things out. I often went there, to tell you the truth, to see what Jerome was up to. Obsessive, I know, and I never found a thing."

"Did you see Craven-Jones that night?"

"Yes, I did. He came in from the party but he didn't see me. I think he was poking around too. There was nobody else in there, and I thought about approaching him. But he was climbing stairs to the catwalk, and I slipped out."

The entire valley was in shadow now, the temperature falling. Cotton went on, "Something about that's bothered me ever since. CJ got himself stuck in that tank, but I can't stop wondering what I would have done had I seen it. There was no love lost between us, and I might not have helped him."

"You would have."

"You're an optimist."

"And lucky for you, Cotton Harrell."

It was Sara who had risen from bed when he came in so urgently that morning saying, "Get up, I need you," Sara who had urged him to consent to interviews after the story of Puddle-jump's success broke, Sara who convinced him to sell futures in his next vintage and take full advantage of that bonanza, Sara who pitched in and made herself part of it all.

The water in the tank had grown inky. Cotton took a thin flashlight from his pocket and switched it on; there was a silent explosion of silver shards beneath the reflecting surface. Sara said, "Shooting stars," and he said, "Spermatozoa."

Lights came on in the lee of the far ridge, before the chill drove them home. The valley had lost its distinctiveness and become, in a few minutes, just another wrinkle in a vast, slumberous world.

# EPILOGUE

---

*Covenant*

TWO YEARS AFTER the passing of Clyde Craven-Jones, almost to the day, AVM released the vintage of Copernicus intimately, and grotesquely, associated with that critic's demise. Ben bought only one bottle for Glass Act, thinking that the timing of the release was an insensitive corporate decision that would cause a backlash, but few remarked on the coincidence of the release, and those who did didn't seem to care. The half life of the memory of a dead journalist was notoriously short, but that of a dead wine writer was even shorter.

No one asked to taste it, so on the last day of the existence of Glass Act, Ben put the bottle on the bar at 11:00 A.M. and pulled the cork at 11:30. He lined up five tulip-shaped glasses, then propped himself on big, hairy forearms to wait.

Sunlight angling through the window this fine autumn day fell across a floor devoid of furniture, illuminating the grunge that had collected over the years behind the settees before they were hauled off. The horned heads too were gone, leaving ovoid shadows where they had hung. The holey mule deer and the antelope he had given away, but the buffalo had brought $200 from a blustery middle-aged vintner new to the business, enhancing the Wild West motif of his new tasting room.

The shelves behind Ben were empty, the hardest part. No tasting treasures, no cred. The library ladder and its brass track had also found a buyer, but for the most part no one was interested in leftover, half-consumed, oxidized wines, no matter how good their provenance, or in the used accoutrements of what was—he had to admit it—a low-end wine bar about to come under the wrecker's ball. But Ben had refused to sell or to give away the name.

At precisely noon he poured the Copernicus, apportioning it equally among the glasses. As if summoned by the distinctive fragrance of Cabernet Sauvignon, Esme came in, spiked heels drumming on the floorboards. "Hi, darlin'," she said, reaching out, and they held hands across the bar until Train and Kiki arrived.

That couple lacked the old insouciance, Ben thought. They had broken up, gotten back together, married, divorced. How can two people sandwich so much into only two years? Train looked a little worse for wear, his hair shorter, the car he had left at the curb no longer what Ben called his "Testostarossa." And Kiki's crumpled khaki look was history, as was the broad-brimmed safari hat.

Esme asked, "He coming?"

"Don't know."

Ben had left a message, all he could do. Without everybody together one last time, Glass Act could not properly pass along its karma to the IHOP about to replace it, but for the first time ever there was no outstanding Breeden bar bill. Ben couldn't remember the last time he had been in. "He has responsibilities," he added, and Esme made a faint snorting sound.

Then, out of the sunlight and into this fading if unique nimbus, wearing a well-cut, well-broken-in Harris tweed, heavier than the last time Ben had seen him and his hair beginning to thin in front, stepped Les, aka Chico, Nose, LB, Lester. "Speak of the devil," said Esme, who turned and hugged him.

So did Kiki. The men shook his hand, and there was a confused scattering of pleasantries all around, released like party balloons, soon deflated. So Ben raised his glass, remembering that it could not be washed later because the water had already been shut off, and said, "To Glass Act."

"Hear, hear . . ."

They all tasted, then looked stricken. Ben had prepared himself for this moment by banishing all thoughts of death, dying, putrefaction, anything to do with the man who had been suspended in, or over, the wine for so many hours, long ago. Now his guests all gazed at one another, lips sealed, eyes wide: to swallow, or not to swallow?

They swallowed. More swirling, sniffing, even tasting, air sucked noisily over teeth but no wine jets colliding with the sides of the spit bucket because that battered old thing had gone out with the trash too. They were doing what they were supposed to do, a source of some satisfaction to Ben, who had chosen this profession instead of that of winemaker, or wine seller for a megadistributor, or introducer of expensive bottles into dining experiences in some fine restaurant, because all he had ever wanted to do was pour the stuff for friends, talk about it, get under the skin of it without being owned by it or anyone.

This Cabernet, however, was half gone before he remembered he had nothing to follow it with. And they, the most famous closet tasting panel anywhere, hadn't really discussed what they were drinking. This lapse of standards bothered Ben, and he said, "Well, so what do we think?"

As if suddenly aware that this was indeed the end of something, everyone began to talk at once: *jammy* . . . *oaky* . . . *alcoholic as hail* . . . The criticism heartfelt, as always, contradictory, mostly useless. Finally they just raised exhausted glasses and agreed to agree that, despite its many flaws, this was a lovely, lovely wine.

# Acknowledgments

I WANT TO THANK Joy Azmitia for finding a good home for *Nose* at Thomas Dunne Books, Jesseca Salky for continuing to represent it so well, and my editor, Katie Gilligan, for invaluable suggestions and guidance during the novel's development. I also want to thank all those who read it in various iterations, including my brother, Frank Conaway, my nephew, Dan Conaway, my wife, Penny, John Lang, and other dear friends whose ranks include some who live closer to the subject than I and shall remain anonymous. I owe them all a debt, as I do to the unique landscape of so-called wine country wine country, subject to all the impacts of human desire and ambition but an inspiration in its own right.

I hope readers will remember that this is a work of the imagination even though the terrain bears strong resemblance to specific places in Northern California. There is no valley of the Caterina River and no town of that name; there's no Copernicus and no Puddle-jump, no Glass Act, no Jerome Hutt, and no Clyde Craven-Jones; they are all mere antic shadows in the novelist's mind.